RISING

-Book One of the Adept Cycle-

by

Shanan Winters

RISING

Book One of the Adept Cycle

ISBN 978-0-9969982-0-8 (paperback)
ISBN 978-0-9969982-1-5 (ebook)

Cover art, cover design and typesetting by Courtney Herz, Ravensong Digital Publishing. Editing by Victoria Hay, Ph.D., The Copyeditor's Desk, Inc.

The title, *Dungeons & Dragons*, as referenced in this book is a registered trademark of Wizards of the Coast LLC, a subsidiary of Hasboro, Inc.

This is a work of fiction. Names, characters, businesses, places, events and incidents are either the products of the author's imagination or used in a fictitious manner. Any resemblance to actual persons, living or dead, or actual events is purely coincidental.

No werewolves were harmed in the writing of this book. However, many darlings were mercilessly killed during the editing process.

Visit http://adeptcycle.com to sign up for contests and learn about upcoming releases!

First printing December 2015.
Printed in the United States of America.

To see more books from Ravensong Digital Publishing authors visit
http://www. ravensongdigitalpublishing.com.

Acknowledgements

How is it that I can write a novel, yet when I sit down to do the acknowledgements my mind goes into full-on shutdown? Probably because there are too many amazing people who have helped bring this book to life. I apologize in advance; this round of acknowledgements is long because it is the first. Know that if you don't see your name here, and you have been a part of my life, you've probably played some role in the creation of this novel. It is, after all, influenced and shaped by all of my life experiences.

I've wanted to be a novelist for as long as I remember. I don't recall the act of learning to read, but I know I had a bookshelf in my room that was so tall I needed a chair and my tiptoes to reach the books on the top shelf. My first thanks go to the writers who've inspired me from the time of my earliest memories; to my mom, who made sure I always had shelves full of books; and to my siblings, Renee, Keith and Janet, for their countless hours of reading to me as a child.

I have to mention my cousin Max in here. Without his crazy imagination, I'd never have believed in werewolves. He also introduced me to *Dungeons & Dragons*. Thank you, Max, for opening me up to entirely new worlds of fantasy.

There is also a special place in my heart for all those friends who I've gamed with over the years... too many to name! But especially to my former DMs (Lawrence, Terra, Mark, Brian) who created vivid worlds in which to explore endless possibilities. There are many ways to shape and craft a story and I grew up steeped in lore spun by some of the best storytellers imaginable.

Before launching into the team of outstanding professionals who helped with the writing and publishing process, I have to call out two very special teachers from my college years: Pam Herring, for pushing me to my first publication, and Jimmy Chesire, for believing in me when I needed it the most. I also want to add a shout out to Michele, who encouraged me to enter a writing contest at precisely the right moment in my life. You all validated my belief that I am, in fact, an author at heart. It might have taken a while for the lesson to sink in, but I heard you. You made all the difference.

Okay, now we get down to brass tacks.

I want to thank my beta readers – Ken, Hillary, Michele, Abby, Jason – beta readers are pure magic wrapped in gold. My book is stronger, better, and makes a hell of a lot more sense because of you. Thank you for taking time out of your lives for li'l ol' me. I'm humbled by your generosity and your honesty.

To my editor – Victoria Hay, Ph.D. at The Copyeditor's Desk, Inc. – you snapped me out of some very bad habits (see what I did there?) The end product is vastly improved because you are amazing at what you do. Thank you!

To my cover designer/typesetter/publisher/late-night-web-chatter, Courtney Herz at Ravensong Digital Publishing – what would I ever do without you? You have become a sister to me, and I'm forever grateful we met. Your artistic touches pushed this book over the edge to make it extraordinary.

To my critique group and my publishing and book promotion meetup group – it's amazing being surrounded by such supportive and encouraging compadres. Thank you for the lessons, the opportunity to teach what I know, and the copious amounts of laughter and friendship. It's nice to know I'm not alone in this dream!

To my children – my daughter, for being a constant source of inspiration. And my son, for his sincere belief that I'm going to become a famous millionaire by next year. Thank you for being patient with me to the extent of your young abilities, for all the times you let me write, and for the times you pulled me away and made me play. I'm thankful for your spunk, your spirit, and your unique and fun personalities. You're going to do amazing things! I'm so happy I get to share this life's journey with you.

And right here, holding up this list in due fashion - Ken Smith - my best friend and the love of my life. Thank you for your encouragement, for listening to me rant, and for letting me ruin the story for you when I excitedly gushed out all those spoilers. This one is for you!

For Ken - You are my Mahoney; I'm your block of wood. Thank you for believing in me and bringing me to life.

Chapter 1

The heavy scent of pine and wet autumn leaves stirred memories I'd suppressed for fifteen years. The unearthed body, dotted with evidence markers and splayed out like a science experiment, added an array of offensive odors that didn't help my nervous stomach. I was used to gruesome crime scenes. It was for other reasons entirely that I'd tried to avoid returning to the Pacific Northwest to the point of nearly losing my job.

"Special Agent St. James," I said, taking the hand of one of the detectives milling around the scene.

"Detective Rick Schild." He met my eyes and gave a firm handshake. He stood my height, and a ring of mouse-brown hair circled his balding head. That and his ruddy cheeks added to his overall appearance of roundness. A slightly plump belly resting at his belt line indicated that this was probably more action than his unit typically saw.

"I'm sorry we have to move in on your investigation," I said, taking in the scene with my customary stoicism. Horse flies and cops swarmed the body in equal numbers. "We typically don't get involved in murders, but I guess you guys found someone we care about."

"The more eyes on this one, the better," Schild shook his head as if he was trying to rid himself of the horror before him. He lifted the crime scene tape and I stepped underneath.

"Don't get a lot of these around here?"

"No, the Key Peninsula is a farily quiet area. We spend most of our time bagging speeders; occasional drug op; broke up a drunken teenage party a few weeks ago."

He chuckled. "This is the first murder I've encountered on the force here. Don't remember any from when I grew up here, either."

Wet leaves squished underfoot. A chill ran the length of my spine. No matter how many homicides I'd investigated, the first sight of a badly mangled body is never easy to process.

"The victim was found in a shallow grave by the landowner's kid and dog," Schild continued, wringing his hands. "Poor kid's going to need years of therapy."

A petite woman in jeans and a plaid, flannel shirt stooped next to the body, scraping at a long gash on the victim's forearm with a scalpel. There were similar wounds raked in parallel patterns of threes or fours across the man's chest, legs and arms. His relatively unmarked face made identification pretty easy. I had seen that face, smiling and full of life, on a campaign sign on the drive in: Senator William F. Mansfield.

"Do you know what the senator was doing out here?" I asked, turning to face Schild. "The Key Peninsula is a pretty isolated area, isn't it?"

"He made an appearance at the Halloween masquerade at the Civic Center a couple weeks ago. Right before the election. Campaign push, I guess. Reelection, and all that. We don't get many celebrity guests out this way. It was a pretty big deal. Most of the KP showed up. Lots of suspects." Schild's voice trailed off at the thought.

"Well, we can work together." I smiled for a second before my lips set back into a grim, thin line. "I'll be handling your public relations, too."

"I heard you were coming in from remote?"

"Yes," I said, scanning the surroundings. The dense, pine forest closed in around the scene, giving the clearing the feel of a small room. Salal and blackberry bushes snarled under the trees, broken here and there by trails only the youngest of deer could squeeze through. Stark white alders, their last leaves of gold and brown clinging to mostly bare branches, stood out against to the pine groves that seemed to suggest twilight even at noon. Memories long suppressed threatened to come to the surface. I swallowed hard. "I'm from the San Francisco field office, but my uncle used to live out here. We used to visit a couple times a year."

"Here? On the KP?"

I nodded.

"Don't we have bureau up here?" Schild asked.

"Seattle, yeah. I'll be working with them. They're sending out a profiler. Haven't been to the office yet."

"Too bad you couldn't just come relive some good memories." He nodded toward the body.

My mind spun at the involuntary recall of running, my heart hammering in my chest, with my cousin outdistancing me, despite his lack of athletic ability. Adrenaline and fear crept up my spine, and I shoved it down hard. It was a stupid prank. Had to have been.

"Where about did your uncle live?" Schild asked, filling my silence.

I forced a smile. "His house was about three miles from here. He's long since moved, though. Down to Oregon."

"Small world, huh?"

"Yeah, never thought I'd have to come out here again." I shifted uneasily at the accusatory look Schild flashed, and quickly added, "It is beautiful, though."

The forensic analyst stood, zipping shut an evidence bag, and faced us. The nappy, auburn bun atop her head frayed like old rope. Freckled cheeks crowned her full lips, and her emerald green eyes reflected hues of the forest floor. The badge clipped to her shirt read Jan Stevens.

"There's hair in his wounds," Stevens said in a high voice, holding up the bag for inspection as if it was a prize. "Particles of skin, too, I think. The hair's not his. It's longer and darker. Hopefully we'll get a DNA match and make this an easy case."

"That would be great," Schild's voice sounded hopeful for the first time since I arrived.

"That could help with suspects," I agreed, "but it could also be his wife's hair. Or his pet's. Let's just start with what we know, and start pulling in suspects. Take video from the Halloween party. Put out a public notice asking for pictures, video, and volunteer witness accounts. Set up an anonymous hotline. We need to narrow this down. We can't start with a suspect base of..." I looked at Schild.

"Roughly fifteen thousand."

I heaved a sigh, "Yeah, we need to narrow this down."

A car door shut behind us, and I turned to see a familiar black government cruiser. The driver was tall with thick, dark hair. He wore jeans and a standard-issue FBI jacket. Sunglasses covered his eyes, even though it was overcast and threatening to rain. He walked with long, confident strides toward us.

He pulled off his glasses and extended a hand to Schild. I felt like a ton of bricks slammed me in the chest. My heart raced. It was Danny. My mind's eye saw him drawing his bow, loosing the arrow, and striking whatever it was that was chasing me. I gulped down the memory; I had to get a grip.

"How's it going, Rick?" he asked, taking Schild's outstretched hand. The two exchanged broad smiles.

"Good to see you, Danny!" Schild grabbed Danny's hand and clapped him on the back.

"And you would be Special Agent Kessa St. James from San Francisco, yes?" He turned toward me. The twinkle in his ice-blue eyes told me he remembered exactly who I was.

"Seattle field?" I asked dumbly.

"Agent Danny Harmon, at your service." He smiled, performing a half-curtsy, half-bow. "Let's get a look at our late senator."

He squatted down next to the body and pulled a purple latex glove from his jacket pocket with a flourish. Holding his hand high, he wiggled his fingers as he snapped the glove in place. The effect was like bad TV comedy, and I immediately thought *prostate exam*. Fifteen years later, and he was still as dramatic as ever.

I moved around the body to stoop down opposite Harmon. Getting in close is never fun. Iron mixed with salt mixed with feces assaulted my nasal passages. Harmon's mouth set in a hard frown.

"You sure this wasn't an animal attack?" He looked up, directly at me.

"I don't think so," said forensic analyst Stevens from behind him. "Maybe a rake or a garden trowel?"

"The patterns aren't consistent. Some wounds are three gashes; some are four." He pointed to various lacerations on the body, poking a gloved finger into a spot on the victim's sternum. "And they're jagged like they could be claw marks."

"There are no bite marks," Stevens continued. "If it was a coyote or bear..."

"Or a wolf," Harmon interrupted, flashing me a searching look. I suddenly took great interest in the wounds covering the victim's left hand.

"Or a wolf," she continued, "there would be bite marks, too."

"A wolf wouldn't bury its victim," Schild added dryly.

"True," Harmon conceded with half a nod. He continued toying at the wound on the sternum.

"What's so interesting there?" I asked.

"This one is much deeper. Like a puncture before the claw mark. I think this is probably the one that did him. Bled out through the aortic. I'm going to hazard a guess that cause of death was exsanguination." He flashed a sideways smile back at Stevens, "Though you should probably still perform your autopsy."

"That would have to puncture the solar plexus," Stevens countered.

"It would, and I think you'll find that it did. I think this claw mark…"

"Or rake mark," Stevens interjected.

Harmon traced a finger across the senator's chest, cocking his head to the side, "…is covering a puncture wound of some sort."

"If so," I said, pulling a glove on my own hand, "then we definitely don't have an animal attack." Harmon shot me a questioning glance, and I added, "Animals don't use piercing implements, as a general rule."

Schild chuckled, "That would be something, though. The bear did it in the woods with the samurai sword." He shook his head and wandered away from the body to where a pair of investigators emerged from the woods. Stevens followed behind him, holding up her bag of bloody hair.

"You know what this is," Harmon said in a low voice, pulling off his jacket. He wore a short-sleeved, black polo shirt, seemingly unaffected by the cold November air.

I just looked at him. His eyes still held the piercing quality they had when we were kids. His black hair clung to his temple, only the last time I'd seen him, it was plastered on his face from the rain. Now he had it expertly gelled to one side and cropped short in the back. He had filled out over the years; lean, muscular arms indicated a lot of training. Straight teeth replaced a smile full of braces.

"You can't be serious, Harmon." I scoffed, studying the puncture wound.

"Call me Danny, please."

I ignored him. "But you're right about this puncture. It's deep, and he definitely bled out. Which means he was also cleaned up. It also explains the missing shirt. Probably removed because it was blood-soaked. Might even identify the murder weapon. Maybe we'll be lucky and it'll turn up."

"You still good in a fight?" Harmon asked. I met his eyes. He smiled with his entire body.

"Look, if you think it's funny to bring up some stupid prank played by my cousin on a murder scene, I'll have your badge."

"You still have fight in you, that's for sure," he said, his smile turning down into a flash of a frown, before resuming an expression of puppy-dog playfulness.

"This is a serious case, Harmon." I indicated the senator. "We don't get pulled in on these cases—*I* don't get pulled in—unless there's some serious shit going down. And *this* is *serious*." I punctuated my words with fingers pointed at the victim before us.

"Serious," he said, forcing the smile from his lips, "Yes."

I couldn't tell if he was messing with me, or if he was actually trying to be professional. I guessed the former.

A moment of tense silence crept on between us. I finally broke it. "We should interview the family of the boy who found the body."

"Yes, we should." Harmon held eye contact with me until I felt discomfort creep across my skin.

"Something on your mind?" I asked, with more challenge in my voice than was intended.

He looked at me, his face a question mark, "You know this could have been us, right? As kids, we were this close..." he held his thumb and forefinger an inch apart, right in front of my face, "—to winding up just like the senator."

"Harmon, that's ridiculous," I scoffed, pinching my brow. "If there is some crazed, lunatic wolf-man running around, why is this the first attack—ever—out here?" He started to answer, but I held up my hand. "No, on second thought," I said, "don't answer that."

He darted glances around the scene and lowered his voice to nearly a whisper. "Like I said before, you *know* what this is."

"Harmon..."

He cut me off with a wave of a hand. "I know. You don't want to believe me. You don't want to remember. You think it was a kid's game and a well-played prank. Let me convince you otherwise."

I stood up, and he rose with me, locked onto my eyes all the way.

"I'm going to go interview the family," I said, crossing my arms. "You can come with me, but keep your local legends to yourself. I have a murder to solve."

Schild tapped me on the shoulder, and I spun on my heel, startled. "Find anything?" I asked after catching my breath.

"Nothing of use. But we're getting a dog team out here to search." He handed me a card. "Here's my cell; give me a call if you find anything, and I'll do the same."

"We'll be in touch, detective," Harmon said, handing him a card of his own before I could produce mine. I shot him a glare. He pretended not to notice.

Chapter 2

The slightest whisper of rain dampened the air as I opened the car door, and I marveled at the Pacific Northwest weather. Nowhere else can it rain without actually raining, and still manage to flatten the hair and the spirit all at once. My rental car was very un-FBI-like; a white Toyota that a dealer might describe as "cozy." I fiddled with the seat, trying to give myself enough leg room, and readjusted the mirrors for probably the tenth time before starting the engine. A notepad sat in the passenger seat containing names and addresses pertinent to the investigation: Meg and Justin Rushing. Theirs was the house I was about to go find.

At the top of the page, Daniel Harmon's name was scrawled in my blocky print. I shook my head. Who would have thought that Agent Harmon was my cousin's friend from years prior? He had tried to talk me into riding with him—*so we can discuss the case*—I was positive that his line of discussion was not a track I would take in an investigation such as this.

I hadn't relished the thought of taking this assignment. When the orders hit my desk, I immediately thought up a thousand convenient excuses to get out of it. I'd promised my fifteen-year-old self I'd never return to the area, even if it was just stupid kid's games that led to my avoidance. I'd even gone so far as to suggest that Seattle Field needed to gain experience in handling the press and that by making them do it alone, they'd become skillful in this critical aspect of high-profile investigation. I thought it was brilliant. My director's exact response was, "If you don't get on a plane today, I'll put you up for review."

"I should have told them my dog died, except I'm pretty sure Crase knows I don't have one," I muttered to myself as the car tires crunched down the gravel driveway toward our key witness—a ten-year-old boy.

Interviewing children was not my favorite part of the job. Sometimes you turned up gold, but more often than not you got partial truths interspersed with scenes from the latest animated movie. And the entire exercise was a constant reminder that some poor kid was caught in the middle of something so heinous that it warranted Bureau homicide support.

The driveway ended at a circular parking area. Harmon's car was already there; he stood on the porch, ringing the bell. I slammed the car into park a little harder than was necessary and grabbed my notebook and a pen. By the time the front door opened, I was half-way up the porch steps.

The woman who opened the door looked to be in her early thirties, lithe and tall, with lightly-graying brown hair and small, wire glasses. She wore black yoga pants and a soft-looking sweater of gray wool. Her face was a mix of anxiety and worry, but she still managed to burst into a huge smile when she saw Harmon on her front stoop.

"Danny!" She threw herself at him like he was her long-lost lover, just home from the war. "Oh, Danny. I'm so thankful you're on this case. Please, come in."

"Thanks, Meg," Danny said, returning the hug in earnest. He let go and motioned toward me. "This is Special Agent Kessa St. James from the San Francisco office. She is serving as our media relations expert and is assisting in the homicide investigation."

"I thought you were homicide, hon'," she said to Harmon.

"I am," Harmon said, nodding toward me. "We're partners on this investigation."

"I'm part of the bureau's high-profile crime task force," I said, extending a hand in greeting. She took it limply, but cordially, and flashed me a tight smile. Her expression reflected the same pain I had seen in so many victim's faces over the years. Confusion and concern coupled with a hopeful sort of interest.

"Please, come in." She stood aside allowing us entry into the old farm house.

Tattered rugs covered a painted wood floor at random intervals down a long hallway with doors on both the left and right. The crystal doorknobs seemed too low and too small, but they somehow fit the house perfectly. Oak paneling adorned the bottom portion of the walls, with an intricate chair rail setting off whitewashed plaster above. Portraits hung beside each doorway like labels. The hall ended at an open living room/kitchen combo decorated with antique furnishings. A table of dark, rough wood sat between two twill couches that faced one another. An old, boxy television sat in the far corner. The glass slider on the back wall led to a square cement patio that was dwarfed by an expanse of meadow beyond. Pictures and statues of chickens in all colors, shapes and sizes decorated walls and every available surface. A wicker basket overflowing with books and magazines sat to one side of the couch closest to us.

I took a seat on the far sofa, and Harmon sat next to me. The cushion threatened to give way underneath me. Whatever springs had once supported the couch had long since worn to the point of uselessness. I sat with my back straight, perched toward the front of the cushion so the frame could offer enough support to allow sitting, rather than slouching.

Harmon took the opportunity to sink back into the failing cushion, one leg crossed over the other, which he extended to prop up on the coffee table. He rested his head on hands clasped behind his neck. I rolled my eyes at him, and he shrugged in response.

Meg Rushing sat across from us, her knees pulled tight together and feet tucked up against the sofa. She wrung her sweater sleeves in her hands, glanced from Harmon to me, and back again.

"Mrs. Rushing," I said, "please know that neither you nor your family are considered suspects in this case. But we do need to ask you a few questions."

"Please, call me Meg," she said. "Are you going to be interviewing Zach?"

"Zach is your son, correct?" I asked.

Harmon darted upright, "Of course Zach is her son." He reached across the table and took Meg's hands in his own. "Meg, we're not here to scare you. And we'll get that body off of your property by the end of today, I promise. But yeah, we're going to have to ask Zach a few questions. How old is he now?"

I couldn't help myself. I had to ask. "Obviously you two know each other? Where from?"

"Remember," Harmon waggled a finger toward the back door and smiled at Meg, all Cheshire cat. "I grew up out there. Well... not out *there* specifically. But on the Peninsula. Meg and I went to school together."

I opened my mouth and immediately shut it, looking for words to express my professional concern without sounding condescending. Failing miserably, I settled for holding it for later. It was a necessary discussion, but not at that moment, and certainly not in front of a potential person of interest.

"So, where is Zach?" I asked instead.

"He's with his grandparents right now. They live in the Harbor. He needed to get away. He-..."

"Can we get their information?" I asked.

Harmon glared in my direction. "We can come back later, Meg," He said, still nurturing her hands between his. "You just let us know when will work for you. I'm sure Zach is pretty shaken."

With those words, the dam burst, and Meg broke down with a heave of her chest. Racking sobs overtook her body. Harmon hopped the table to sit by her side, cradled her in the crook of his arm, and stroked her hair gently while she cried. I studied my shoes intently, silently wishing anew that I'd found a reason not to be on this case.

When her breathing slowed, and the tears stopped. She pulled off her glasses and wiped at her face with the back of a sweater-covered wrist. "I'm so sorry," she said, "it's just, we don't have things like this happen."

"I understand," I replied, allowing a practiced and professional modicum of sympathy to accent my words. "We will also need to talk to your husband. Is he home?"

"He's working today," she looked away, out the back door as she answered.

I pulled out my notepad. "Where does he work?"

"You're not going to go to his job site, are you?" She asked, her voice quick and sharp, and her brown eyes widening.

"We'll leave Justin alone until he's done with his day," Harmon said, giving her shoulder a squeeze.

Heat rose inside me, and I nearly lost my temper with him. I took a deep breath and continued, "Meg, I need his place of business, just for the investigation. We can set up a time when you'll all be available to talk. No need to interrupt him at work."

Meg's shoulders visibly relaxed, "Ok. Well, Danny knows he works for J & L Lumber. He's out on site today. Will be every day until Thursday."

"So we can come back Thursday?" It was a question and statement wrapped in one.

"He works a second job," she said, her lips forming a thin line. I could tell the conversation was going nowhere.

"How about this," I said, standing up and straightening my jacket, "you tell me what day and time we can come back, and we'll see you then."

She looked down at her knees and played with an unraveling yarn on her sleeve.

"Friday. After school. 4:30."

"Wonderful," I made note of the date and time, "then we will see you on Friday. Until then, please don't talk to the press. That's three days—an eternity in a case like this, and they're sure to start poking around and asking questions." I fished one of my cards out of my pocket and shoved it at her. "If the press contacts you at all, you call me."

Meg nodded slowly and took my card before returning her attention to Harmon.

"Harmon, let's go."

He stood up and turned toward Meg, his hand lingering over hers. Sadness crept over his eyes, and he blinked hard. "It'll be okay, Meg. I promise."

I turned on my heel and stalked out of the house, vaguely aware that they were following me. He was hugging her tight in a lingering embrace as I sped away, tires spitting gravel. A call to Seattle was in order; this wasn't going to work. Harmon had too much emotional involvement in this investigation. He was compromising my ability to gather facts and interfering with witnesses on an emotional—possibly even intimate—level. I punched the number for Seattle Field into my phone as I made the turn onto highway 302.

Chapter 3

The phone rang before I could finish dialing. I clicked "Send" and idly wondered why it didn't say "Answer" to incoming calls.

"St. James."

"Kessa, this is Danny. We need to talk."

My knuckles went white on the steering wheel at the sound of his voice. Through clenched teeth I said, "It's St. James, Harmon. And we don't need to talk. I need to have words with your director."

"Don't do that, Kes—St. James. You need me on this."

"Like hell I need you on this! I need a professional. This is going to be a media circus as soon as it gets out. I need facts. I need answers, and I need them now. Your wild speculations and doe-eyed ogling of witnesses is not going to get us anywhere on this case."

"Look, I'm sorry about that. Meg and I go way back."

"Yes, that much was very apparent."

"Meet me for dinner. The Shoreline. It's down on the water at the end of the harbor."

"I know where The Shoreline is, Harmon. And I'm not meeting you there."

I heard him inhale sharply, and then slowly let out the breath. I could picture him running one hand over his hair.

He started again, slowly, "Kessa, I'm really sorry."

"Sorry for?" I let the word *for* trail off. He didn't answer, so I continued. "Are you sorry for schmoozing a witness? Or maybe for insinuating that your stupid, fifteen-year-old prank has something to do with the death of a senator? Or how about your stupid hoax in general? I'm sorry I'm even here!"

I stopped talking when I realized my voice was getting louder with each sentence.

Silence.

"I'm sorry you don't understand what's going on. I just want the chance to talk. I need you to hear me out."

Not trusting my words, I clicked "End Call" and tossed the phone into the passenger seat.

The road curved through a thick forest of pine. I rolled down the driver-side window. The rain had let up, and the sudden blast of damp, cool air chilled the flush from my cheeks and helped me clear my head. I had to get answers. I flipped a quick U-turn in a driveway and headed back toward the crime scene. Without Harmon there, I might see something I'd missed earlier out of sheer irritation.

The coroner's van was just leaving as I pulled in. Crime tape still outlined the clearing, but I knew the body would be gone. The local police had likewise cleared out. I looked down at the dash clock. 5:04. Single FBI agents really didn't keep track of time like the rest of the world. I'd never had anyone to go home to, so I never stopped working.

It was darker than I thought possible for so early in the day. Hundred-foot-tall trees skewed the sunset by a good half an hour, and the hush of twilight crept over the clearing. I'd only have maybe fifteen minutes to poke around until it was too dark. I grabbed a flashlight out of my field bag and clicked it on to scan the mess of a crime scene. Footprints everywhere. One of the forensics team had left his coat draped over a tree branch. A half-empty water bottle lay forgotten inside the perimeter. I *tsk*-ed at the lack of care and attempted to cover the same ground I had walked earlier.

The site where the body had been lying was easy enough to find. Blood-soaked earth compressed in a torso-shaped pattern. Two divots where his heels had dug into the soft ground. Similarly, the turned gravesite was still fresh, with small mounds ringing a two-foot deep, six-foot long indentation. It was no wonder the Rushing kid's dog had been able to dig up the senator so effortlessly.

Movement in the woods caught my eye, and I turned to see low branches rustling in an otherwise still crop of pines.

"Who's there? Come out." I said with practiced assertion. They teach you this stuff in the academy, and it comes in handy. You can't sound weak, or you become the next victim.

I walked over to the stand of trees and shined my flashlight through the undergrowth that dotted the forest floor. There was enough room to move about in this area; whoever was in there could be hiding anywhere in the darkening forest.

"I know you're there, so come out," I repeated, not taking my eyes from the bushes.

I turned to the sound of rustling to my left. My right hand fell instinctively to the Glock on my hip. I froze and scanned the edge of the woods.

A brown cottontail rabbit hopped out of the bushes, caught sight of me, and changed its mind about crossing the clearing. It darted back under the cover of the tree line. I exhaled in relief, laughed at my hair-trigger nerves, and was tackled from behind.

The hit came hard and high, but I reacted on instinct with the type of muscle memory response that only happens after years of extensive training. I pulled my arms in and tucked my chin, exposing my shoulder. Most assailants expect the typical arms-forward reaction that usually results in a sprained or broken wrist. Instead, I hit the ground in a shoulder roll and let the momentum bring me up on my side, still gripping my mag light. I landed a foot directly in my assailant's gut and continued the motion to propel myself upright. My heart hammered against my chest as I flipped my flashlight around to brandish it as a weapon. I widened my stance, prepared for a fight.

The attacker stumbled backward and tripped, landing flat on his back. His black hoodie covered most of his face. He wore black jeans and work boots. Construction gloved hands gripped at his abdomen, and he let out a throaty moan. I pulled my gun, spread my feet into a solid stance, and shouted, "On your stomach! Hands on your head!"

He rolled onto his side and sprang to his feet.

"Don't move!" I yelled, feeling adrenaline course through me as I released the safety on my Glock.

He stood hunched, his arms dangling awkwardly to the sides as if he was holding a giant, invisible ball. From deep within his hoodie came a low and rumbling growl, animal and fierce. He took two steps forward.

I squeezed the trigger. The shot hit him directly in the chest.

He staggered backwards but didn't drop. The distinct smell of wet dog carried off the man before me. He brought a hand to his chest and ran a gloved finger over the spot where the entry wound should have been.

"Get down! Now!" The quaver in my voice betrayed the confusion and panic that rose within me. I shoved my mag light under my gun to steady my hand.

He bolted into the woods. I trailed him with three more shots before he disappeared behind the tree line. There was no way I could have missed.

As I ran for the car, I shoved the gun back in its holster and pulled my cell phone from my pocket.

Harmon picked up after half a ring. "Kessa?"

"Shut up and listen to me!" I stammered into the phone, my heart pounding.

"Are you okay?"

"No!" I shouted. My hands shook so hard the phone slipped from my fingers. I scooped it off my lap and clicked it to speaker. "I was just attacked at the crime scene. I shot the perp. He didn't drop. Must have had Kevlar. We need a unit out here!"

"Why were you there without backup?" His voice rose in both pitch and volume.

"To find answers!" I shouted at the phone. "Poke around. Find some information. Maybe see something we missed earlier."

"You want to meet up?"

I swallowed and gathered my thoughts. Harmon wasn't my ideal partner, but at the moment, he was my only Bureau contact. "Yes. After I call in my report and get a unit out here."

Silence.

"You saw it, didn't you?"

"I got attacked," I countered.

"You were attacked by *it*."

"I can't believe you're still going on about this."

"You shot it, and it didn't drop. It ran off. You fired some more, didn't you? And all the shots missed?"

"How the hell did you know that, Harmon?" I asked.

"Because you would have called Schild first if it was a normal perp. And you haven't reported to your director. You called me first. Kessa, you know what attacked you."

I leaned back against the driver's seat and exhaled long and slow. "Look, you know this area better than anyone. You know these people. I need you to fill me in. Shoreline. Thirty minutes. Be there."

I clicked *End*.

I fished Schild's card out of my pocket and turned it over in my hands. I had no idea who the attacker was, but the fact that he didn't drop when shot worried me for the safety of the local force. There was no way they were equipped to handle someone with armor. I knew well enough that suspects wearing Kevlar typically carried armor-piercing rounds as well.

With half of Schild's number dialed on my phone, the vision of Danny Harmon from my teenage years popped into my mind. *How could a federal agent make it as far as Harmon had while still believing in local legends and supernatural creatures?* The scent of my attacker came back to me, and the way he stood. It was exactly as it had been all those years before. I hugged myself in the chill of the darkness that had settled over the car.

I flicked Schild's card onto the passenger seat, set the phone down, and put the car in drive. I needed answers, and I doubted Harmon had them, but he was the only hope I had.

Chapter 4

The Shoreline stood at the back end of Gig Harbor, built on pylons that extended the structure out over the water. The building was two stories high, with three mini-levels on each floor, so that every table had a pleasing view out of the wall-to-wall windows. Below the restaurant, boat docks extended in neat rows, with mooring to either side. Lights twinkled on masts, and dark shapes against nighttime waters portrayed hundreds of sleeping vessels, waiting for their next excursion out into the channels of the Puget Sound. Harmon had gotten there before me and had been seated at a window table off in a corner and away from other diners. He was carrying on a conversation with the waiter, his arms and hands doing half of the talking.

"Speak of the devil," He said, folding his arms and leaning back in his chair.

The waiter pulled out my chair and I seated myself across from Harmon. Having my back to the entrance set off paranoid alarm bells in my head, but I squelched the noise. Harmon was a cop, too. All of us dislike having our backs to the door, and he'd gotten there first.

"Mike, this is Kessa. She's my partner."

I took the waiter's hand and glared at Harmon.

"Ok, *St. James* is my *temporary* partner for a case we're working. Real hush-hush. Can't give details." He winked at me.

"Nice to meet you, ma'am. Would you like something to drink? A glass of wine or a cocktail, perhaps?"

The waiter looked to be in his twenties, with close-cropped blonde hair and a day's worth of stubble. He'd look more at home in jeans and flannel with a skateboard in his hand than he did in his waiter's tuxedo. At least he had some manners. More than I could say for Harmon.

"I'll just have water," I said, smiling as Mike wandered off through the tables. I turned my attention to Harmon, still cross-armed and relaxed. "Do you know everyone in this town?" I asked.

"Well, I did grow up here. It's not that big. Everyone pretty much knows everyone." He leaned forward and half-whispered, "I *knew* that lady right back there behind us."

I felt my cheeks flush and redirected the conversation. "That's not good. Not with a case like this. The locals are going to talk, and the media will get wind of what's going on. We're going to be running interference instead of solving the case."

"We can solve this case right now if you'll just hear me out."

I held up a hand. "Let me guess: werewolves?"

His eyes seemed to darken a shade at the word.

"Whoa," I said, pushing myself back from the table, "you look nearly serious."

His smirk returned immediately, "And you just made a sarcastic joke! I think we're making progress."

"Hardly," I said, taking the water glass from Mike, who appeared out of nowhere. Good waiters do that. They slip in and out, and suddenly, you have food and drinks, and you hardly know where it came from. Maybe he was better off in that waiter's tuxedo after all.

"Thanks, man," Harmon said, taking a swallow of a nearly black beer. He wiped the foam from his upper lip. "You sure you don't want one?"

"I could have your badge for drinking that while we're working."

"I'm off the clock." He smiled over the rim of his glass.

"Well, I'm not," I said, pushing my chair away from the table.

Harmon motioned for me to stay seated, and then steepled his index fingers under his chin. He closed his eyes for a moment, then opened them and looked at me with eyes and jaw hard-set and serious. "I know you don't want to do this. Here. With me." His voice was quiet. Calm. "You probably don't even want to be here. I know you remember what happened when we were kids, and I'm sure you've rationalized it all away by now. This case; me; your attacker; we're all just bad memories come back to life."

I started to protest, but he ducked his head and held up a finger. One second. I waved him on.

"But we're here. And we do have a job to do, you're right." His voice got so quiet I had to lean across the table to hear him. "We have a dead senator, some very frightened locals, not to mention a crazed lunatic with personal SWAT gear running around dodging bullets."

"Finally," I said, sitting back.

"Finally, what?"

"Finally, you sound like a qualified agent. I figured you had it in there somewhere, or you wouldn't have the badge and field jacket."

"Don't let the moment of clarity fool you." His expression reclaimed his customary playfulness, but only for a moment. "Tell me exactly what happened out there tonight."

"Well, after we left the Rushing's—after you finished *whatever* that was with Meg—I went back to the crime scene."

"I told you, Meg and I go way back."

I pursed my lips before continuing, "The coroner was just leaving, and the scene had been mostly picked up, except the tape. By the way, the police here have no idea what to do with a murder scene. There are tracks everywhere, and they left trash out there."

"So you went back to critique the unit, got it." His impish grin made me want to smack him.

"There was someone in the bushes, rustling around. It was getting dark; I shined my light in there and scared out one of the local critters. When I was distracted, the guy jumped me. I fought him off, and he wouldn't drop. I put one in his chest and followed him with three more. I don't think I broke skin, though."

I stopped my description of events when Mike reappeared. We ordered, and he hurried off.

"So, that's *all* that happened?"

"Yes. That's all that happened."

"Oh, come on Kess. That can't be all. Where's your forensics? What did you see? Hear?" He leaned in. "*Smell?*"

"It's St. James. Not Kessa, and especially not *Kess*." I blanched at the shortened version of my name. I'd always hated it. "Ok, perp was roughly six feet, medium to large build; arms seemed on the long side. Wearing a hoodie, and maybe a mask underneath. It was dark, but I couldn't make out facial features at all. He had work gloves on his hands. Sturdy boots. Smelled like he just came from washing his horse or dog or something. Wet hair smell."

Harmon clapped his hands together. "See! There."

"There, what?" I felt my brow scrunch.

"There you have what you need. The wet dog smell. You know exactly what this is."

"And we're back at square one." I closed my eyes and rubbed my temples. "Ok, I have to ask. How did you guys pull that off back then? It was a pretty elaborate trick."

Harmon shook his head and placed a hand over mine. I pulled my hand back. "Kessa, I promise you. It wasn't a trick. You have to hear me out. You're in this, and we need to solve it. I've been trying to solve this one since I was nine years old. I need your help."

I wanted to scream at him. I was tempted to grab my phone and call for his badge. Yet, his expression had softened. His shoulders tensed, and his eyes pleaded. "Ok, you have ten minutes. After that, I'm calling Seattle Field, and we're going to have a little talk. About your fitness for duty."

He held his hands up in surrender, "Fair enough. But give me that ten minutes. No interrupting."

"Fair enough," I agreed.

Harmon sat upright and straightened his shirt. Then he leaned forward, resting one forearm on the table. For half a second, I was tempted to tell him he was... the most interesting man in the world. I stifled a giggle.

"What?" he asked.

"Nothing. Go on," I said, faking a cough into my napkin.

"Fifteen years ago, the day we all snuck out to the old Harmon house—my grandparent's home before my grandfather died—was the last time, but not the first, that I saw what I believe killed my grandfather."

I shook my head, "Wait. You're telling me that your name isn't just coincidental with the name of that abandoned property next to my uncle's old place?"

"Look around." I did, and he scoffed. "Not physically, metaphorically. We're in the middle of nowhere. If you share the same last name, you probably share a woodpile or two. Yes, that was my grandparents' home. My parents both died when I was very young. Car wreck on the 302. Snow season."

"I'm sorry," I said, trying not to make it sound like an automatic response. His eyes met mine, and his expression changed quickly from sorrow to hardened intensity.

"It was a long time ago. I grew up with my grandmother. We lived just down the road from their old house on an adjacent tract. I was told that my grandfather died in a logging accident many years before. When he passed, my grandmother couldn't stomach the idea of staying in their home, so she just left. Left everything there, just like it was. Replaced all her furniture. She even bought all new clothes, new silverware. Everything. She never went back."

Harmon's expression shifted; he looked past me with a polite smile. I quickly glanced behind to see Mike coming with plates of food: Salmon, wild rice and asparagus for both of us.

"Anything else?" Mike asked after setting my plate, then Harmon's.

Harmon interrupted my "no thank you" with, "Yes, we'll both have a glass of the house white." I tried to protest, but he turned to me, "You'll want it. Trust me."

"It's local, and it does go excellent with the salmon," Mike agreed.

We waited in silence, sampling our meals until Mike fetched our drinks. Harmon slowly chewed his salmon and took a generous swig of his wine to wash it down before he continued. I picked at my food while he talked.

"So my grandmother told me, 'Never go to the house. Just don't go there. Ever.' So of course, I went. Often. For years."

I raised an eyebrow over a forkful of asparagus.

"What do you expect? I was a nine-year-old boy! It's in our nature to do what our elders tell us not to. So I went to the house—or at least I tried to. You remember that barrier? The one you couldn't get through after you crossed the threshold of the yard?"

I frowned over my water glass. An involuntary shudder ran up the length of my spine. Unfortunately, Harmon noticed.

"Yes, you *do* remember, don't you?"

"What I remember is that you..."

"You said I could have ten minutes, *sans* argument."

I relented and waved him on.

"That barrier worked the other way when I first started visiting the grove. It kept people out, not in. I think it was meant to be a prison for whatever was in there. I saw the beast for the first time on my second trip, testing the barrier. It would scream out in pain when it touched the force field. But something was getting through. I still don't know what or how, but the beast was able to get hold of certain elements that allowed it to tip the scales. You remember how there was a cauldron on the fire?"

The memory hit me, and I saw the pot hanging on a long arm over a smoldering pile of smoldering tinder. I'd run back to the house after Harmon had wounded the wolf-like creature that had been chasing me. He'd told me to toss the cauldron, so I used the fire poker to hoist the pot and throw it against the wall.

Pulling myself from the memory, I nodded, and absently reached for the glass of wine. I had taken a sip before I'd realized what I was doing, and I set it farther away from myself.

Harmon sighed. "It's really alright, Kess; you can have a glass of wine with dinner. I said we're not on the clock. Otherwise, I wouldn't be able to tell you this very non-FBI-sanctioned story, right?" He pinched the bridge of his nose and shook his head. "Let loose a little.

"Anyway, a few weeks before your visit, I was watching the beast from a tree-stand I'd erected a good distance back from the house. That was the day I saw it walk directly across the barrier. It stopped in the trees, turned, and, as best as it could, smiled. I could see the row of sharp canines in his contorted, half-human, half-wolf face from across the field. That was when it looked directly at me. I thought for sure I was dead, but instead, it dropped to all fours and took off into the woods.

"I recruited your cousin, Mark, that week. He knew I'd been keeping a secret in the woods, and he was thrilled that I was finally letting him in on it. I realized at that point, whatever was in that house—behind that barrier—must have been what had killed my grandfather. Somehow, someone—maybe even my grandmother—trapped it there. I started doing some research and determined it must be some sort of werewolf. That day, when you were there, I shot it with a silver-plated arrow, and I learned that silver did indeed have an effect on the creature.

"Only problem was after I shot it, it disappeared. I heard rumors that the house got demolished about a year later. I've spent the better part of my adult life trying to figure out where the beast might have gone, and what it was. Now I'm thinking it's back."

I eyed him in scrutiny. "That's it?" I asked.

"Well, that's not all there is to it, no. That's the short, short version."

"While it would make a most excellent campfire story, I haven't heard much that's dissuading me from that whole 'fitness for duty' review. And none of this gets us closer to our killer."

A simultaneous ring on both of our phones pulled us from an intense stare-down.

"Harmon," he said into his cell.

"St. James," I answered, ducking to one side and covering my other ear so I wouldn't hear both our conversations.

"St. James, this is Crase. There's another vic. Same M.O. Same area. I'm texting you the address. We need you out there, now. Media's picked it up, and locals are spilling rumors."

"Shit. On it, sir." I hung up.

Harmon had paled a few shades. His hands shook as he fumbled his cellphone back into his pocket. I could see the strain in his throat like he was biting back tears.

"You look like you just saw a ghost," I said. "Was that Seattle Field? Did they tell you..."

"Kess," he inhaled sharp, and his voice trembled, "the new victim is my grandmother."

I picked up my glass of wine and finished it off.

Chapter 5

Walls of pine trees stood as sentinels on either side of the 302, blocking from view the habitats of people and forest creatures alike. The full moon ducked in and out of patchy cloudbanks, and wisps of fog licked up from the roadway, flashing around us like ghosts. Palpable blackness swallowed all visibility beyond the glow of the headlights. Harmon sat in silent contemplation; his head leaned against the passenger side window. He hadn't spoken a word since we left the Shoreline. Sadness had crept around his eyes and found a permanent home in his furrowed brow.

His grief had become a discomforting void in the space between us. It had been less than an hour since I'd been irritated by him and wanted him to straighten up. But driving in silence down that lonely highway toward an impossible crime scene, I wanted for the time only hours before when I was annoyed by his jokes. I thought if we could only go back and start over, maybe I'd listen to his fantastic stories. Maybe if I'd relented at the start, we'd have been out there, interviewing his grandmother. The very idea was ludicrous, but it seemed to be a much better alternative to the reality before us.

I didn't want to imagine how he was feeling, but still my mind took me there again and again.

A flash of moonlight filtered through the clouds and washed over the car. I looked at Harmon without turning my head. His eyes were closed. If not for the emotions visibly vying for escape, I'd have thought he was sleeping.

"She was a good woman," He said, his eyes still shut. "A good woman."

"I'm sure she was." I searched for better words, but none came.

I'd dealt with the family of homicide victims for most of my career. I was the one that got sent in to deal with the mother of the missing child. I got to help the grieving husband come to terms with the horror he faced. I knew how to handle these situations. Trained by the best. A communications undergrad, psychology master's and a few years of homicide under my belt. At that moment, my training failed me.

When I leave a typical crime scene, the affected family is left behind to pick up the pieces. This time, the ancillary victim was sitting next to me, and knowing Harmon even in my limited capacity, he was going to want to help solve the case. I wondered whether he could separate personal emotion from the investigation, and for yet another reason questioned his fitness for duty.

We passed my uncle's old property, and nostalgia draped me like a shroud. I longed for the simple days of playing *Dungeons & Dragons* by flashlight, deep into the hours of the night. Solving mysteries and fighting bad guys on paper. When we went to sleep, everyone who had died would come back to life with a magic potion. When we played again the next day, our avatars would live again to fight the fiends and slay the dragons.

A few years in the Bureau had delivered me to a harsh reality. I went into the FBI with the same delusion that every law-enforcement hopeful entertained: I was in it to save the world. There were good guys and bad guys. I'd help the former by catching the latter. I'd slay the dragons. Every case taught me that nothing is so black and white.

"Why you?" Harmon asked, still leaning against the window.

"What do you mean?"

"We have homicide in Seattle." His voice took a sharp edge. Accusatory. "Why did you get sent here?"

"Because of the senator," I replied, as I turned the car onto Harmon's grandmother's driveway. "I'm both a psychological and a public relations specialist; I deal with the press. I've dealt with plenty of high-profile homicides, the families, and the public. I can help out with the case."

The car rolled down the long, straight drive toward the house. An ambulance and two police cruisers sat askew in the driveway, lights churning, flashing red and blue across the dashboard. Harmon swiped at his face, evicting the silent tears that had been masked in the darkness.

"Yeah, but *you*." He sat upright and turned toward me. "It's an interesting coincidence, don't you think? Out of all the agents in the bureau. Out of all the people in the world. Here we are, you and I, back where we started years ago, fighting the same battle all over again. Now...." He swallowed hard, "Now the stakes are raised. Kessa, this isn't coincidence. It can't be. You're wrapped into this somehow."

I stared at him, open-mouthed and unable to express what came to mind. I'd explained to him my involvement the only way I knew how. I could have told him that I didn't want to be there. I might have said I'd always secretly felt like there was some truth behind what I'd dismissed as his prank.

I shrugged off a sense of uneasiness that fought for control of my good senses. Years of homicide had taught me to shove the discomfort down, lock it away. *Not feeling* had become a comfortable habit and a way of life. I ignored the tiny hairs that stood at attention, beckoning me to dig deeper into the idea that there might be some reality wrapped up in Harmon's crazy notions.

"Are you going to be alright in there?" I asked, nodding toward the trim little white bungalow that glowed against the impinging darkness.

"No," He said, "I'm not. But I do have a game face, and I'll get it on by the time we get inside. This has been personal for a long time, and it just became more so."

He started to open the door, and I grabbed his sleeve. He frowned at me.

"Harmon," I said, measuring my tone, "let the facts speak for themselves. You know you can't go in there with preconceived notions of what happened. You can't solve a case on speculation."

Harmon yanked his arm free from my hold and pushed the door open. He slammed it shut and stalked off toward the house. I jogged to catch up, thought of offering more words of wisdom and decided against it. Police milled about the front entry; we flashed our badges and stepped into the tiny foyer.

The inside of the home was the complete antithesis to the darkness outside. White plaster walls sprung from the light yellow wool carpet. Cheery wall sconces radiated pinpoints of light through faceted glass. A clear crystal vase sat on the entry table, bursting with fresh dahlias in crimson, orange, and gold. Cinnamon and vanilla wafted on the air, reminiscent of snickerdoodles complemented by a hot cup of tea. To the left of the entryway, the snug living room held a plush, cream- and tan-striped sofa, a paisley wing chair, and a lemon-yellow, circular fringed rug. Family photos adorned every wall. Harmon's five-year-old face smiled chubby-cheeked through the glass, flanked by a woman who would rival Audrey Hepburn in both beauty and class. Her eyes matched his in azure hue but radiated a crystal clarity. She stood tall, shoulders back. Confidence wrapped with intelligence. Strength embedded in steadfastness. The rock of the family.

Stevens, the spunky Tacoma forensics analyst, emerged from the doorway at the end of the hall. Her eyes widened at the sight of us, and she hurried toward Harmon.

She squeezed his shoulder gently. "Danny, don't go in there."

"I have to, Jan. It's my job."

"I can call in another agent," I offered.

He held up a balled fist and slogged down the hall, his shoulders slumped forward. Stevens and I exchanged nervous glances and followed.

The salt-and-iron smell of fresh blood wrestled with my full belly as we rounded the corner into the room. I took an involuntary step backward. An older version of the beautiful woman from the hallway photos stared at the ceiling, her mouth contorted, slacked open sideways, indicative of a painful death. Her body lay sprawled across the double bed. Blood pooled on the hand-knitted afghan, spreading through the fibers, changing them from yellow and white to dark maroon. Gashes across her arms, legs, and torso seeped and oozed, and the puncture in her chest plainly displayed the cause of her death.

Harmon stood stock still, hands on his hips, jaw set like stone. He looked up and down his grandmother's body, appearing emotionless and detached like it was any other murder investigation. He approached the body and pulled on a glove.

"Same M.O.," he said, prodding at the chest wound. "Same deep puncture."

"This one is slightly different," Stevens approached the body on the opposite side of the bed from Harmon. "If you look here," she pointed toward the neck, "there's an abrasion on either side. Maybe a chain or necklace was pulled from her by force?"

"Her locket," Harmon said, lightly lifting his grandmother's hair and stooping down to inspect the neck wound. "She always wore a locket. It had my grandfather's picture inside. At least I think it did. I tried to open it once when she'd left it on her bedside table. Earned myself a swat on the butt for touching things that weren't mine." He lowered his head and breathed heavily, then looked back to the thin, red line on his grandmother's neck.

"The killer must have taken it," I said.

"Nothing was missing from the senator," Stevens added.

"Anything else missing?" I asked.

"We're hoping Harmon can help us answer that question," Detective Schild said from behind us in the hallway. I turned to see him standing in the door, careful not to lean on the frame. "We have some preliminaries back from initial forensics. Two sets of tracks outside that didn't match the victim. A couple fingerprints we still need to run."

"Wait," Harmon said, holding up a finger, "when was she found? And how?"

"Called in," Schild said. "Anonymous tip. We didn't get a trace. Number was a cell, but we think it came off a burner phone, anyway."

"But *when*?" His eyes narrowed, mouth turned down with a scowl, as he stalked toward Schild.

"They called Gig Harbor right after you both left for the Rushing house. Stevens and I left the first scene and came straight here."

Harmon rushed Schild, grabbed his shirt in fistfuls and shoved him back against the wall. Schild's toes barely brushed the ground. "And you didn't fucking call me?" The vein in Harmon's neck swelled, and his face flushed red.

I grabbed Harmon's right arm and twisted it hard behind his back while lowering my center of gravity. He dropped Schild, who stumbled sideways, catching himself on the doorframe. He took half a step toward a fuming Harmon, but Stevens stepped in between the two men.

"Rick, come with me. Outside. Let's go see if precinct has a match on those prints."

"Harmon," I lowered my voice and spoke slowly. "Breathe. Harmon..."

He pulled against me, but I had his hand and elbow locked against the joints. Any amount of struggling just made it hurt worse. He gave up after a moment.

"Sorry. I'm sorry. I..."

"It's fine; we get it." I said, letting him go.

He breathing became quick and shallow. "I have to get out of here."

"Let's get you home," I said. "We'll come back in the morning."

We rode in silence across the bridge and into Tacoma. Harmon directed me to his house—a small duplex unit near Point Defiance—using a series of grunts and gestures. I got out of the car, and he looked at me from the corner of his eye. "You coming in?"

"I figured I'd at least get you inside," I said, feeling my cheeks flush. "I just want to make sure you're settled before I go."

"With the reception you gave me earlier, I figured you for the 'not caring' type."

I shrugged, "If you can make it on your own, go ahead. Just thought I'd be nice and help out a fellow agent."

He burst into a full belly laugh, "Yeah. Whatever. I'm just going to go in and drink myself into oblivion. It won't be pretty, and it definitely won't follow the Bureau-psychology-approved coping guidelines, so I'm betting you don't want to stick around to watch."

"Harmon," I said, but stopped short.

Silence.

"Yes?" he finally asked.

"Just be safe."

"It's not me I'm worried about." He eyed me up and down.

"What's that supposed to mean?"

He laughed again, ending in a heavy sigh. "Kessa, you're here for a reason. I know you are. Do you really think all of this," he turned in a circle, arms thrown open, "is all just some big, amazing, happy coincidence? For a girl with a master's degree, you're not that bright."

"Excuse me?" I asked, hand aggressively at my hip. "Enlighten me, ô wise one."

"We stopped it years ago. We *wounded* it. Me with my arrow to its shoulder, and you with your disruption of—whatever that cauldron was brewing—at my grandparent's house. What we did fifteen years ago put a serious dent in its plans. Now it's brought you here from San Francisco, and it's made sure I'm going to stick around on this case. It's made this professional for you, and personal for me. It knows us, I think, better than we know ourselves."

"Harmon, you're profiling a fantasy," I said, feeling the vein in my temple throb.

"Maybe I am, Kess. But right now, it's all I've got." His shoulders slumped. "Well, that and a bottle of whiskey."

The sky suddenly opened up. Fat, cold raindrops pelted us. He ran for the door. "You coming in? Or taking off?"

I glanced at the car and back to Harmon as he opened his front door. He was right about one thing—I did know a thing or two about coping skills, and I knew a bottle wasn't the best plan.

I clicked the lock on the key fob, ran for the house, and ducked inside.

Chapter 6

"You surprise me, Agent St. James," Harmon said, slipping his shoes off by the door. The front room was living area, dining and kitchen all combined. A door-width square of scuffed linoleum stood as the entryway for the unit.

"Well, sometimes I surprise myself." I followed suit with my shoes. "Just don't want you to do something stupid."

"Oh, you mean like return to a crime scene alone?" he asked with an edge of challenge in his voice. He took my coat, which he unceremoniously tossed onto the small card table that sat to the left of the door.

"Touché." I stood in the doorway, surveying the decor. That action only took a brief moment. A lone sofa that looked to be twenty years old, and might have been bright yellow once-upon-a-time, sat faded and sagging across from the front door. Movie posters hung in thin black frames on the wall above. The breakfast bar above the galley kitchen counter was littered with notes and unopened mail. The massive, flat-screen TV with full surround system across from the couch probably cost more than everything else in the entire apartment combined, three times over.

"You really don't have to hang out," Harmon pulled a green bottle from the top of the refrigerator and jiggled it at me. "Want one?" I shook my head no, and he waved me off with a sneer. "If you want to stick around, be my guest. Make yourself at home. Cop a squat. I'm not a very good host. But don't try and stop me."

He poured himself a shot, downed it and slammed the glass on the counter top, hands spread to either side as if to support all his weight. He closed his eyes, shook his head and whistled. "God, that's good."

I took a seat on the couch, tentatively perched at the edge of the cushion, feet pulled in together. Wringing my hands in my lap, I asked, "You want to talk?"

"I'm a big boy, Kess." He paused to take another shot, then crossed the living room, bottle in hand, and sat beside me. "But since you're here, we can talk about the case." He took a swig directly from the bottle.

"I don't know. Maybe you should back off this one, Harmon. Call in backup. It's too personal for you now."

"Exactly why I'm staying on. I need to show you something."

He shoved the bottle into my hand and disappeared into a back room. Moments later, he emerged with a box overflowing with pictures, notes and newspaper clippings, which he set between us before reclaiming his seat. After taking the bottle for another long pull, he shoved the box toward me. "Just go through it. Take a look."

I sat on the couch with the box on my lap and picked up the item on top. A stack of pictures was clipped with a binder-pin to a news article. A faded, black-and-white snapshot of the old Harmon house displayed the home in good repair, with flowers blooming along the stone path that led to the front door. I unbound the clip and pulled off the attached news article: *Disappearance of Local Man Leaves Family Broken, Wondering.*

"Is this about your grandfather?" I asked, skimming the article. Harmon nodded silently and sat on the couch beside me. His eyes had taken on a watery appearance, and he hunched forward, propping himself up with elbows on knees.

"It says here that he just disappeared. Did they ever figure out what happened? Find him, or..."

"No, they never found a body," He said harshly. "What they did find was claw marks in the door frame." He grabbed the stack of photos and flipped through them, shoving one in front of me while leaning on me for support. His breath was too close and thick with alcohol. I pushed him off me and took the picture for inspection. The close-up of the door showed visible scratches across the frame and surrounding siding near the doorknob.

"The article doesn't mention these marks," I said, taking the stack of photos and shuffling through each one. Gouges appeared on the bed and down the hallway at various intervals. "So what do you think happened?"

"It got him. Just like it got the senator." He clasped his hands behind his neck and rocked himself gently, "and Grams," he added, just above a whisper.

I dipped myself down to catch him eye to eye, "Tell me about her, Harmon."

He sat upright, "Only if you stop calling me Harmon. My name is Danny. At least while we're off duty."

I conceded, "Ok, Danny, tell me about her."

"Virginia Harmon. Ginny. She was a firecracker. Raised in a time when smoking and drinking and speaking your mind was a man's game. But Ginny O'Leary, as she was before she married my grandfather, couldn't be held down." A wistful smile overtook him, and he beamed with pride. "She put up with me. I was a right pain in the ass." He raised the bottle toward his lips.

"You? No way!" I mocked, pulling the bottle from his hands before he could take another drink. I held my breath and took a small sip, ignoring the burn of my least-favorite alcohol.

"Whoa! Special Agent St. James goes off the clock!" He nudged me, shoulder to shoulder. The twinkle in his eye said he was enjoying our teasing game a little too much.

I scooted to the other end of the couch and thumped the box between us. "Anything else in here? Something that might lead us to our killer?"

He dug in the box until he came out with a photo of a locket. Intricate Celtic knot work adorned a circle of silver that hung from a linked chain. A pattern of three dog-like creatures with backswept ears, long snouts, and interwoven legs leaped around a spiral in the center. Jagged points of fur accented the bodies, legs, and chins of each animal. The fangs of each held the tail of the next. A flourish of knotwork edged the outer circumference of the locket.

"It's exquisite," I said, turning the photo over, hoping for a date or other piece of useful information, "but I'm not sure how this is supposed to help."

"I took this picture one day while she was in the shower. She never took this locket off except if it might get wet. It was pure silver, and she kept it spotless." His words slurred together, and he slouched forward and tapped the picture. "That's what our perp took from her neck. Ripped it off her dead body and took off with it." He yanked the bottle from my hand and chugged. "Right after he pierced her heart and shredded her body."

Harmon stood and heaved the bottle across the room. It smashed against the wall, spraying glass and liquor across the carpet. He pushed off the couch left the room, slamming the bedroom door behind him. I could hear him stifling sobs, still trying to hold it in. Leaving him to his solitude, I busied myself by picking glass out of the carpet, which turned out to be a thankless and nearly impossible task once the large shards were cleaned up. Giving up, I returned to the box and shuffled through pages of newsprint, copies of microfiche, and heaps of photographs.

"Werewolves: Fact or Fiction," I mumbled, reading titles aloud. "To Catch a Wolf. Werewolf Anatomy. Convincing the Nonbeliever." I let groaned and leaned back against the couch, reading the last one I'd picked up.

According to legend, the werewolf is a creature of the night, able to use its power only by the light of the full moon. But research shows that this is not true. The lycanthrope is able to change at will, once he comes into his power through his first human kill. He may appear human before the moon, or in wolf form in broad daylight. It is impossible to distinguish who might be afflicted with the lycanthropic curse when the victim is seen in his human form.

"Convenient," I said, tossing the paper back into the box. "Conveniently loony." I crept across the room and pulled my phone from my jacket pocket. I tapped on the table and watched his bedroom door, contemplating. Harmon needed help, and I knew he wouldn't take it from me. I dialed the contact number I'd been supplied for the Seattle director.

"Agent Chester," the voice on the other end barked.

I paused, my heart sinking to my feet. I could hear Harmon clattering around in his bedroom.

"Hello?" Chester's voice queried.

"Sorry Agent Chester," I spoke just above a whisper, "this is Agent Kessa St. James from San Francisco. I'm with Agent Harmon."

"Is he holding up?" Chester's voice immediately softened, radiated with concern.

"Yes. Well, no. That's what I need to talk to you about. He's…"

"His grandmother, yes. We know. St. James, your director said you're excellent at handling volatile cases in the field. Are you able to take care of this?"

"Well," I started, "I can look after him, but I don't think he should stay on this one. I don't believe he's of sound mind. I'd like to recommend administrative leave. Grievance, at least. But honestly, I think a psych workup is in order."

"Negative," Chester said.

"Excuse me? Don't you want to know why?"

"St. James, you're going to have to follow his lead. He's the best man we have for this case. We're a white collar crime shop up here. He's the best profiler we have. Plus, he knows that area better than anyone else in the Bureau. He's a little quirky, but he's sharp. Stick with him. You do what you do, and entertain the press when they show up. He'll do what he does, and you'll have this case solved in less than a day."

"But sir..."

"That's all, Agent."

The line went dead. I stood there, holding the phone, wondering what the hell had just happened. I was recommending a psych review and got shut down. I started dialing my director's number but stopped at the sound of Harmon's voice.

"They trust me," Harmon leaned against the bedroom doorframe, wearing an army green t-shirt, plaid boxers, and black dress socks. His bloodshot eyes sat in a face of stone. "You should, too." He flicked his head toward the bedroom, "Want to join me?"

I grabbed my coat, slipped on my shoes and left him there in his underwear without another word. I ran for the car through pouring rain. The engine roared to life, and I sped back through Tacoma and across the bridge to find the Breakwater Bed & Breakfast. I had a date with a minibar. Harmon was not invited.

I'm certain the FBI had never run a case out of the Key Peninsula before. The small, family-owned cabin where I was booked was little more than a room with a bed. From the smell, it was fairly close to the waterfront. "Red tide," the owner had said. "It happens."

Not in San Francisco, it doesn't.

With my service weapon and belt tucked safely into the bedside table, I sank into the armchair and clicked on the tiny TV to the ever-scrolling news channel. The cabin was conspicuously devoid of any form of minibar, but the owner was kind enough to hand me a bottle of Sam Adams from her personal stash. Her name was Shari. She was a short, chubby woman with peach-glow skin and a cheery smile. The type of person you would look forward to visiting during the holidays.

I muted the TV and relished the silence. Headlines ticked across the bottom of the screen, and I only half-registered what they said. It would all repeat in ten minutes anyway. I took a long, slow sip of my beer, leaned back and closed my eyes. A moment of peace.

Interrupted.

A single rap on the door had me on my feet, hand flying for the weapon that wasn't on my hip. I looked through the window to see a tall, slender woman with shoulder-length brown hair looking around nervously. Without unbinding the chain lock, I opened the door as far as it would allow and asked, "Can I help you?"

"Hi." She juggled a notepad from her right hand to her left and stuck a hand in the door in greeting, "Kessa? Ms. St. James?"

I ignored her hand. "Do I know you?"

"No, but I was hoping we could talk. I might have some information you want." She looked everywhere but at me. "Would you mind if I came in? Or maybe we could go somewhere to talk?"

"I don't think so, Miss..."

"Martina Eccles. I'm from the P.I.?"

"Is that a question, or a statement?" I asked, holding the door open with my foot and crossing my arms.

"You're Bureau, right? Here about the senator's murder?"

I pushed the door to close it, but she wedged her foot inside. "Ms. St. James, I'm not here to ask questions. I have answers. I can help."

"If you don't remove your foot," I kept my voice level, "I will call the police, and then you can give your answers to them."

She pulled her foot back, and the door slammed shut. I collapsed on the bed and turned my attention back to the TV just in time to catch the ticker flash the message I'd dreaded across the bottom of the screen:

Breaking: Senator William F. Mansfield reported missing in the Gig Harbor, WA, area. Local police are teaming with FBI. Credible lead states that a body has been found, but no suspects have been identified. Stay tuned for updates.

"God dammit," I swore, clicking the TV off.

I leaned back in the chair, and my eyes drifted shut. Exhaustion enveloped my body, and my mind began to drift, first replaying the events of the day, then reliving glimpses of the past. One by one, scenes flashed like clips from movie reels, and in the background I saw my younger self, watching. Waiting. Seeing if I'd admit that back then, I'd believed my cousin and Danny when they prattled on about werewolves and creatures from other realms. My present and younger selves played an ethereal tug-of-war in my half-dream state, and suddenly the memory I'd repressed all day crashed into the foreground, demanding attention.

Thoughts of my father filled me with an equal mix of guilt and grief. He'd been a police chief in Astoria, Oregon. As far as cities go in which to be a cop, Astoria was among the safest. He'd made sure the town drunks got home safe and that the neighborhood spats ended amicably. We'd never anticipated that one of the locals would take his life in a routine stop.

I was seventeen years old when he died. After we had gotten the call, I'd waited until my mother had cried herself to sleep, and I'd snuck down to the bar in our billiards room. She'd been drinking an amber liquid from a crystal decanter. I'd not known that it was thirty-year-old Scotch, or that it was worth a lot of money. I'd just known that she'd poured through half the decanter before passing out. I'd decided I'd finish it off. My mother thought I'd stayed in bed for the next two days because of Dad. In a way, she was right, but I'd also had a mighty hangover.

My anger toward Harmon gave way to sympathy. I knew full-well the extent of that grief. A shocked mind makes irrational decisions, and I knew it wasn't right to condemn him. I reached for my phone but stopped myself. It would do no good to call him in the state I knew he'd be in, so I left it for the morning.

Another day, another chance to start again. Those were my father's words-to-live-by, and I'd heard them often. His gentle voice, a ghost of my past, rocked me to sleep.

As I slept, another voice spoke my name, slow and steady, calling to me as if it drifted with the tide.

I awoke to bright daylight streaming through the thin curtains.

Chapter 7

Harmon didn't answer his phone.

I called again as I crossed the Purdy sand spit, where early risers dug clams along the rocky shoreline.

I called as I sped down Highways 16, passing the few exits that led to the quaint fishing village of Gig Harbor hidden behind tall pines.

The line went unanswered as I drove through the toll booth and onto the Tacoma Narrows Bridge. The water, some 70 feet below, glittered like diamonds scattered across a blue-black velvet cloth. Rows of houses vying for a view of the channel dotted the hillsides jutting up from narrow beaches.

I pulled up to the curb at an angle, jumped out of the car, and rapped on Harmon's front door. Right before I started to knock a second time the handle jiggled and the door swung open. The apartment smelled of stale booze and vomit mixed with overtones of fresh-brewed coffee. Harmon, however, looked surprisingly chipper compared to the night before. Showered, smelling like spring rain, and dressed in black slacks and a blue polo shirt that mirrored the color of his eyes. I noticed the thickness of his eyelashes.

"Morning, sunshine!" He said, motioning me inside. "Ready to take me in? Have me evaluated? Or you just going to stand there staring at me?"

"Harmon, I..."

"Don't worry; I would have called me in, too." He waved me off and walked into the house. I followed and shut the door. "Coffee?"

He really didn't give me a choice, handing me a steaming mug. He'd obviously listened to my messages and he knew when I'd show up. I took a sip, my eyes going wide. "How'd you know I take mine with sugar?"

He tapped his head, "I'm smart. And I do my research."

"Well, that's reassuring. In a creepy stalker kind of way." I laughed and took another sip. I'd not gotten to enjoy a cup before leaving, having feared for Harmon's wellbeing; I had just gotten dressed and left. My eyes closed instinctively as heady steam enveloped my senses. Setting the cup down, I met his eyes and measured his composure. If he wasn't emotionally stable, he certainly was pulling off a good ruse. "How are you? Really?"

"Kessa, don't worry. Yesterday was rough; I'm not going to lie. And last night, I said some things…" He ran a hand through his hair and looked away from me.

"Forgiven," I said, feeling heat rise in my cheeks.

He smiled a crooked and somewhat nervous grin that seemed forced, "It still hurts, but I know she won't be there today. I want to solve this, Kess. I need to."

"I know," I said, crossing back to where his box of memorabilia still sat on the couch. I rummaged through, just to give myself something to do other than staring at him. My hands brushed something hard under all the paperwork, and I came up with a small, leather-bound book with a ribbed spine and trimmed with silver embellishments at the corners. The cover bore an embossing of the same Celtic triple-wolf pattern that adorned the late Ginny Harmon's missing locket.

"What's this?" I asked, holding up the journal.

"That belonged to my grandmother. There's a bunch of drawings and writing inside, but I can't read it. It was in the attic. She didn't know, but I took it years ago."

I opened the book and flipped through the heavy linen pages. Etchings of plants, animals, and various implements accompanied something that was obviously script, but nothing I could read. The illustrations themselves seemed alien. Ferns with mushrooms growing from the stalks. Trees with purple bark. Flowers with tiny faces.

"Your grandmother had quite an imagination," I said, thumbing through the pages until I reached blank parchment.

I went to shut the book, but movement caught my eye.

Maybe the page wasn't blank. I wondered how I could have missed such an obvious drawing.

Fire in a hearth at the old Harmon house, with a cauldron swinging from a thick, iron arm. Searing heat.

I pushed back from the book. It didn't make sense; how could I possibly have felt the heat from the scene. Then text swirled into view.

Spiraling letters in shimmering green over a field of silver drew me into the page, hypnotizing me, beckoning me to stay. Read. But I couldn't make out the words—just the shapes of the letters.

Let me show you. A gentle, feminine voice sounded in my mind.

I became one with the scene. The smell of decay from the crumbling house overwhelmed my heightened sense of smell. My ears twitched at the sound of an intruder. I looked at my arms and legs, covered with fur, and ran a hand over my face, now bearing a snout and fangs.

No! I can't be seen! Not like this!

The scene swirled before me, and I saw my younger self hoist the cauldron with a fire tool, toss it at the wall, and sprint out the door, seeking safety beyond the brittle grass and dead leaves. Pain radiated across my left shoulder. They had brought down the barrier, and I lay wounded. I looked up from my blood-soaked shoulder to see Danny Harmon, his hair plastered to his face by the rain, holding his bow out on an extended arm. The arrow in my shoulder dug itself deeper, and I loosed a long, frustrated howl.

I felt the world shift and spin once more. I left the vision and was once again holding the book in my hands.

The script took readable form.

That which I have feared most has come to pass. The beasts of the other realms are rising, and he has suffered a fate worse than death.

"Kessa!" Harmon grabbed the book out of my hands and tossed it away, a heat pulsed up my spine and down my arms. The book landed on the couch, face down.

"What the—what happened?" I hugged myself, rubbing the back of my arm and pulling at my shoulder. "It feels like something stung me."

"Well, I've never seen it do that before," Harmon pointed at the book, and I turned to see a faint silver glow dissipate to nothing.

"Was it?"

"Glowing? Yes. It was getting stronger and brighter. But you were staring at a blank page."

I shook my head, "I'm not sure I can even explain it. There was nothing. Nothing at all. Then images started to appear. Then it hurt. Like I'd been shot."

He took me by the shoulders, stooping to meet my eyes at level. Deep pools of blue reflecting compassion and concern. "Kessa, tell me exactly what you saw."

"I saw us. I saw that day, Harmon. It felt so real." I collapsed back into the couch. "But I wasn't me. I was..." I shook my head. "No, that's not possible."

"Stay with me, Kess. Keep talking." He sunk to the couch with me and gently cupped his hands over mine. "What were you?"

"It. I was that thing that chased us. That you shot." I shook my head, my thoughts clearing. "Dammit, Harmon, what the hell is happening? Things like that don't... This can't be... This isn't *real*!"

I tried to pull my hands away, but he clamped down to keep me still. My stomach leapt. An exhilaration took root deep in my belly and began spreading up my spine. I clamped down on the feeling and resigned myself to facts and logic. There had to be some reasonable explanation that I was just missing.

Harmon's face was question marks and concern. "I know you don't want to believe any of this, but if you don't at least entertain a few ideas, I think we're both in serious trouble. This isn't about the senator. This isn't about my grandmother. This is about us. More to the point, I'm starting to think that this is really about you."

I yanked my hands from his grasp. "Harmon, that's ridiculous. You do realize you're not fifteen anymore, right? This isn't some kid's game."

His jaw hardened. "I'm painfully aware that this is not a game."

I couldn't hold eye contact with the pain I saw there, so my chipping fingernails became the subject of intense focus while I tossed his words around in my mind. Facts. I needed to stick to facts. What did we know? There was a dead senator, and so far, nothing had presented itself to suggest that his death was anything other than random. None of his enemies had come forth to claim the murder. I'd done research on him during the flight up from San Francisco. As far as senators went, he was very well liked by his constituency—even loved. He had been a proponent of the environment. In a state where Nature was a proper noun and a sentient aspect of everyday life, the people felt that Mansfield represented their best interests. He did have a few enemies, mostly within the logging community.

A small connection snapped in place, and I broke what had become an unreasonably long and uncomfortable silence.

"Harmon, the Rushings; Meg said Justin worked for a lumber company?"

"Mmm." He pushed up from the couch and started walking the length of the room, back and forth.

I sighed. We'd digressed to grunts as acceptable answers. He was still volatile; I'd need to be more careful with him.

"The senator," I continued, desperately trying to lock eye contact with a moving target as he paced, "He'd turned down a lot of lobbying groups and campaign dollars from the logging industry."

Harmon stopped and watched me in silent scrutiny as if I was a bug under glass.

I stood up, straightened my back, held my head high and ticked the points off on my fingers as I talked. It was a habit I'd picked up way back in speech and debate in high school. It always seemed to convey a sort of credibility, even to the most reluctant of audiences.

"First, we have a senator whom everyone loved. Especially in this area, where there are state beaches, parks and protected patches of wetlands in abundance. Historically, the residents have valued preservation, and the senator represented their ambition to keep the area pure. The logging companies, however, have pushed to encroach on the area for many years, claiming that the population increase demanded greater clearing, from which they could profit. The decline of jobs in the region, coupled with population growth, has many of the citizens—especially the younger crowd—leaning more toward the logging companies and their ambitions. Senator Mansfield won, but only by a slim margin. The logging industry is already jumping on the temporary instatement of the opposing candidate, Mali Deveraux, as interim. Ms. Deveraux is much more corporate in her leanings, with her campaign focus primarily on job creation."

Harmon had peeled a banana and was chewing slowly as if mincing my words between his teeth. "Or," he said, "it could be that the senator was just in the wrong place at the wrong time and was a convenient target to draw you out."

I rubbed my temples and shook my head, "Harmon, I need to solve this, and you're not helping. It's not like I'm the only public relations agent in the bureau! They could have called out someone from D.C. or up from L.A."

Harmon picked up the leather journal and turned it over, handing it to me with the cover showing. Three wolves. For a second, it looked like their eyes held a faint, white glow. "Have you ever had something like that happen before?"

I hesitated before taking the book. My insides churned, and I silently admonished myself. It was ridiculous that I was even entertaining this nonsense.

It was a book. But I couldn't help it. Something had happened that I couldn't deny, even though years of training screamed through me that I was giving in. I took the book in one hand, feeling its weight, like a burden on my soul, and turned it over so those wolves would stop looking at me.

"Ok," I conceded, "I can't explain what just happened, but I also don't see how it's related to a dead senator."

"And my grandmother."

"Yes, and your grandmother. I suggest we head out to the murder site, see what forensics has found, and start knocking on some doors. Let's take your box of memorabilia, maybe go through it some more, and see if we can find anything else that might give us some hints on why she was targeted."

"Just do me a favor," he said, pitching his banana peel into the trash like it was a three point shot.

"What's that?"

"Keep an open mind. I know you have both eyes wide open, but the information you see is running through a filter that I don't think will let you pick up what you need to see to solve this case. You're going to shut out information, or people, who would help or point us in the right direction."

I started to protest, and then a flash of memory crossed my mind. "That reminds me, actually, I met the press last night."

"I bet you were very welcoming." His sideways smirk made me laugh.

"Yeah. No. However, she was acting pretty odd. I've dealt with the press more times than I can count, and this is the first time one of them said she had no questions, but rather answers, and wanted to help."

Harmon shook his head, "And you just, what, shoved her off?"

"Harmon, she's the press!"

"And she offered to help. She said she had information?"

"I figured that was her trying to get her foot in the door any way possible. And literally, in the door! She was at my hotel, trying to get in!"

Harmon grabbed his coat and keys. "Let's go," he said. "I want to find this—what was her name?"

I had to strain to remember. The previous day had been a blur with more surprises than I was used to. I rubbed my forehead in gentle circles. "Martina Eccles."

"Let's find this Martina person, and see what she knows."

I glared at him, flipping my keys in my hand. "And what, exactly, do you think she'll do for us?"

"Think of her as a witness."

"Harmon, how often do you deal with the press?"

"Rarely," he admitted, opening the front door and motioning me through.

"They aren't witnesses. They're sneaky. Reporters will do anything they can to get a story, including faking knowing something. Most of them fancy themselves as investigators. Some of them probably could be. However, the majority of the time they get in the way and give the public way too much information about all the wrong things. They misrepresent facts and create headlines that are cringe-worthy. At the very worst, they interfere with the investigation and even create problems during litigation. Talking to reporters, beyond approved and sanctioned statements, is off limits."

I got into the car and buckled my seat belt. Harmon did likewise and glanced at me out of the corner of his eye. I could almost hear the wheels turning in his head. He was planning something, and I was almost certain it was nothing I'd want him doing. For the moment, it could wait. Sometimes it's best just to let things lie, and watch patiently.

"What's important right now," I said, in an attempt to ease tension, "is finding the best place around here to get a cup of coffee."

Chapter 8

The steaming cup that Harmon offered me took me to the south of France. Dark chocolate resting on a bed of fresh lavender blooms mixed with the bold jolt of roasted espresso. I closed my eyes and took a small sip, followed by a long, slow, grateful pull. "Oh Harmon, you got me. This is incredible. But don't look so goddamned pleased with yourself."

"I told you they were good!"

"Well, the *lavender mocha* was just something I was unfamiliar with. Consider me educated." I smiled around my cup.

"Like I said before," his grin took an edge of playfulness, eyes crinkling, "you should trust me."

I rolled my eyes and got back into the car. We drove back to the Key Peninsula, making occasional small talk, but mostly enjoying our coffee goodness in silence. Harmon's car was still parked at the Shoreline from the night before. He decided to get it on the way home, which put me in the driver's seat for the day. I was just fine with having that control.

Low, white clouds hung thick just over the tops of the trees, giving them the appearance of being brushed by cotton. It never ceased to amaze me just how low the clouds would form in Washington. Most people think of the sky as being something "up there," and out of reach. The Pacific Northwest often reminds people that the atmosphere reaches all the way to the ground. It is a fluid, changeable and fickle character that loves to interfere.

We rounded a corner into a thick fog bank. I instinctively slowed the car, but not soon enough. Movement flashed in the corner of my eye. The form of a man in blue flannel and jeans stood on the road, barely visible, enveloped in fog. I inhaled sharply, and my hands clenched the steering wheel as the tires locked under the pressure of fully applied brakes. The black ice under the tires was invisible and unexpected. My little rental car spun out of control, leaped the drainage ditch on the side of the road and ran up an embankment backward. We came to rest with the nose of the car firmly lodged in the ditch.

"What the hell?" Harmon swiped at the lavender mocha that covered his face. "What happened?"

"There was some idiot in the road."

"What are you talking about?" Harmon pointed outward, and I followed his gesture. The whole area was clear. No fog. No ice. No man straddling the yellow line. Just a quiet, country highway.

"You have to be kidding me!" I turned to Harmon, feeling my face flush hot. "We came around that corner back there, and the whole area was a fog bank."

"And you were calling me in for a psych review?"

I was about to lay into him when a slam against the driver's side door rocked the car up off its tires. I turned just in time to see a creature on two legs, with the body of a prizefighter, covered in hair like a mangy dog, and the head of a wolf, lunge at the car.

Harmon screamed in my ear, "Drive!"

I crammed my foot on the gas pedal, and the tires spun futilely in thick, wet soil. The car rocked again, and the window cracked. The beast placed hands to either side of the window, gripping the frame of the car door. It lowered its head. A wolf's head, with a man's eyes, charcoal with a side of menace. Steam blew from its engorged nostrils, fogging the window. A low, guttural growl emanated from deep within its belly that I felt more than heard. Yellow leather work gloves covered both hands. It reared back and sprung toward us, and I stepped hard on the gas pedal again.

The tires found purchase, and the car rocketed out of the ditch. The creature clipped the back end of the car, causing it to fishtail onto the road. I laid on the gas and sped away, leaving the beast standing in the roadway. In my rearview mirror, I saw it throw its head up into a howl.

"We have to go back." Harmon was shouting in my ear. "Turn around. That thing is going to kill again."

My hands shook over the wheel, and my feet failed me. I couldn't keep pressure on the gas pedal. The car slowed, and I edged off onto a pullout. We had probably driven a mile, perhaps a little more. If the beast was going to give chase, it wouldn't take long to catch up. I figured we had only minutes to figure out what to do next.

I turned to Harmon, tears in my eyes.

"You believe me now?" He asked, scanning the road.

"I think I might be starting to," I said, feeling bile rise. I looked toward the tree line, searching for movement, determined to distract myself so as not to lose my mocha right there in the car.

In the rear-view mirror, a motion caught my attention. A lone figure ran up the side of the road, heading directly toward us. A small shriek escaped my lips, and I put the car into drive and stepped on the gas. We lurched forward, the car clambering unsteadily. One of the tires was flat. Adrenaline flooded my veins like acid. Hard resolve and training took over, and I reached for my weapon. Harmon caught my hand. It dimly registered in my mind that he'd been shouting my name.

"What?" I demanded.

"That's not our wolf."

"What?" I repeated, but this time with disbelief. I turned around to see a tall, brown-haired woman in jeans, a turtleneck and an angora vest waving us down. "Martina!" I shouted, jumping out of the driver's seat. "What the hell are you doing out here? We need to get you to safety!"

The journalist spun to look behind her and then faced me again. "Looks like you're not going anywhere." She had the audacity to smirk at the deflated rear tire.

"We'll call for backup. Harmon! Call Schild. Have him send a unit!"

"Kess," Harmon said, pulling himself halfway into the driver's seat to see me clearly, "We have a problem."

Dark red stained his blue polo shirt in a not-quite-circular pattern. I ran to the passenger side, Martina on my heels. We pulled Harmon from the car and stretched him out on the road. A knife fell out with him, landing on the ground with a dull thud. Martina inspected it carefully, hesitating, but then picked it up and hefted it.

"Silver?" She asked.

Harmon gave a curt nod, his mouth set in a hard line. "I had it under my belt. Didn't think we'd get in a wreck. I guess it got me when we hit."

The muscles of his neck drew taut as he took ragged breaths. I pulled up his shirt and undershirt to reveal a deep gash just above the waistline of his pants. Hindsight being what it is, it occurred to me that we should have switched vehicles and taken the FBI issue cruiser out here instead of my rental. The self-admonishment must have come through on my face like a negative developing, because Harmon asked through gasps, "What's wrong?"

"Just ill-prepared. But don't worry. I can improvise." I wiped sweat from his brow and forced optimism onto my face, pulled my jacket off, and pressed it hard to his wound. He winced and squirmed underneath the pressure.

"Hold still."

His face contorted, "Yeah, easy for you to say."

"Um, guys?" Martina said, pointing down the road.

Our flannel-clad guest of honor was coming for his midday snack. "Martina! Get over here and hold this on Harmon. Keep pressure! And call for backup!"

I jumped up, pulled the knife from her hands and shoved my phone into hers as she took my place.

"This is silver, right Harmon?" I asked. He nodded, his eyes glazed over and he stared straight upward.

"Who should I call?" Martina asked, holding the phone in one hand and applying way less pressure than was required to Harmon's wound.

"Just dial 9-1-1!" I shouted. Our assailant was gaining ground by the second. He was close enough to hear his footsteps and his grunts. I hefted the knife, knowing I only had one shot.

I'd never been any good with thrown weapons, so I waited. And waited. He drew closer. I cocked my arm back, exhaled, held my breath and let the knife fly.

Like I said, I'd never been any good with thrown weapons. It glanced off his arm, butt end first, and skittered harmlessly across the road. Still, the silver content made him pause. He stopped long enough to glance at the knife, giving it the briefest of inspection.

A glow out of the corner of my eye caught me off guard. From the back of the car, Harmon's grandmother's book radiated green and white. Acting on instinct, I dove into the car and grabbed it. Flipping it open, I found the page I was looking for without trying. Words came from my lips, but I didn't know their origin. I was an antenna, and a wave of pure green energy washed over me, amplified through my vocal cords.

Silva,
Non potestas

Luna,
Non potestas
Ad quos eieci,
Antiquitas expuli
Bahomeha

The beast stumbled backward as if he'd reached the end of a rope. I held the book, studying it. My hands reverberated and glowed a soft, green luminescence that crackled with hairline bolts of white potential. I lifted my left hand, turning it over, eyeing it quizzically, all other thought abandoned. With my palm held out at arm's length toward the staggering beast, my eyes closed of their own accord. Light, heat, and energy shot from my hand toward the wolf. The creature screamed as if it was being crushed, harsh and forced, and it retreated into the woods.

Turning slowly on my heel, I saw Martina, still crouched over Harmon, mumbling softly to herself but looking directly at me. She wasn't making that phone call. I continued to spin involuntarily, my head swimming with exhaustion.

I wasn't aware that I'd blacked out until I woke up in my own hotel room, sprawled out on the bed with Harmon lying next to me.

Collapsing on a hard-packed gravel road does nothing for the complexion unless you are going for the whole zombie-thriller look. I sat up to face the mirror in the tiny alcove of a bathroom and prodded at the skid marks on my cheek.

"I know what happened back there." Her voice brought me up off the bed and onto my feet, reaching for my weapon. It wasn't on my hip. Martina patted it where it rested on the entryway table next to the armchair where she casually lounged.

"How did you get us back here?"

"My secret," she said, putting a single finger to her glossy lips as they curled up into a devilish smile.

I glanced at Harmon.

"He's not well," she said, standing. Her movements were executed with cat-like grace. In her standard attire, Pacific Northwest garb, one might mistake her for a Seattleite soccer mom. But only if she stood still. Nothing about her screamed "journalist." More like, "Contract killer."

"So, Martina, since you claim to be in the know, what happened?"

She pulled the book from a chair cushion and wiggled it at me. "*This* happened. I told you last night; I have answers for you."

The laugh that escaped was entirely sardonic. She had the common courtesy to reply with an affronted sneer. Still, I pressed, "No reporter has answers for the Bureau. Just problems. I thank you for your assistance in helping my partner and me to safety, but we can take it from here."

I opened the door and held out my hand. Defeated, she tossed me the book, which I immediately set on the bed. She left without another word, and I shut and latched the door behind her.

"Kessa," Harmon's voice was like water through sand, "come here."

I rounded the bed and sat beside him, placing a hand on his bare chest. His wound was bound with white strips of cloth stained with blood, both old and fresh. I figured out fairly quickly that Martina had used Harmon's own undershirt, torn in strips, to bind his wound. Her helpless act on the road had been just that: a ruse meant to fool us or distract us. Typical reporter behavior. I met his eyes, boggy pools of pale blue, and asked, "Are you in there?"

A strained laugh overtook him until it became a painful cough, ending with a mocking half-smile that crept across his face. "You called me your partner."

He placed his hand over mine. I smiled and didn't pull away.

Chapter 9

"She's still outside, you know," Harmon said out of nowhere. His eyes had been closed, and I had sat beside him for countless minutes, watching his chest rise and fall in gentle rhythm. The repetitive motion of his breathing invoked a trance-like state where I could ignore the past hour. Maybe even forget what I'd seen—what I'd done. Or at least, what had been done through me. The whole thing was a blur, and I wasn't eager to discuss it. Though I knew it was going to come up, and if Harmon was, well... Harmon... it would become the topic of conversation as soon as he could take half a normal breath.

"I know she is. I can hear her pacing. I'm pretty sure she took both our phones, and I checked the room line. It's dead. She's waiting for me to come out."

"So why don't you?" His breathing was still shallow, but he was managing to talk a little easier.

I gave another long look at the bandages that bound Harmon's injuries. The bleeding had stopped, but I doubted he'd be moving too quickly any time soon. I needed to get him to a hospital, but as far as I knew, we were still without a vehicle. I really had no idea how Martina had gotten us back to the inn.

Harmon shifted uneasily on the bed and let out a long, low groan. I tried desperately to think of some way to offer support for his attempted readjustment but came up pathetically empty handed. I was glad his eyes were closed because I was certain a sense of utter helplessness was written across my features. I'd never been very good at first aid, and this was way beyond the "apply a bandage" stage.

Daniel Harmon. This man, who was merely a childhood acquaintance, long forgotten just 24 hours' prior, was now my first and foremost priority. A lump rose in my throat at the realization of just how deeply he'd gotten under my skin. I wasn't aware that a person could irritate his self into my favor, but Harmon had done it, and I wasn't about to leave his side.

"You need to go find out what she knows," he said. "She obviously isn't just here from the press."

"I don't trust her,"

"Neither do I. But I do trust you." He patted my hand, still resting on his chest. "I know you can get us out of this. I could do with a little more medical care, here."

Guilt crept over me and gnawed its way down my spine. I'd had no faith in Harmon, yet it was obvious he'd believed in me from the start. "Harmon, I can't wrap my head around what just happened. I still have a murder to solve and the actual press to deal with. I have a job to do. But my primary goal right now is to get you properly cared for."

He smiled up at me, with his left cheek dimpling just slightly. "I do have to pee."

I couldn't help it. I dissolved into a fit of giggles.

"No, really Kessa. I do have to, and it's going to become urgent at some point soon."

"I know," I wiped tears from my eyes. I wasn't sure if they were from laughter, or if the stress was overtaking me. I patted his chest, "Ok. I'm going. I'll be right back. If you need anything—besides a bed pan—yell."

Martina was leaning against a bright blue Ford pickup, vintage 1960-something. The paint looked like it had been applied by a couple of teenagers with spray cans. Both side mirrors were missing. The grill was rusted where it wasn't full of holes. The emblem on the front read F-RD. The O had otherwise fled the scene of the crime that was her vehicle.

She picked at her fingernails, not bothering to look up as I approached. "You ready to talk?" she asked her hands.

"You ready to tell me who the hell you are, and give us our phones back?"

"Not exactly." She ran her hands down her hips, leveling her eyes with mine. Hers were pools of gray that brimmed with intelligent malice. I trusted her even less if that was possible.

I lost my cool. Before she knew what hit her, she was slammed up against the front fender of her piece of crap truck. I had a fistful of her angora sweater balled in my fist. Her mouth formed a perfect O, and I almost told her that her truck would be better looking with her shoved through the grill. Instead, I flipped her around, so her hands were spread across the hood of the truck, and pressed a hand firmly into her back, while I frisked her with the other.

Casual laughter emanated from somewhere between flesh and metal, and I pulled her back with one arm wrenched in a pressure-point lock. As I moved, she side-stepped, reversed the lock, and had me face-down on the ground with my arm wrapped up in her leg. She sat squat against my elbow, causing blinding pain to shoot down into my hand and up into my shoulder. Soil and rotting leaves filled my mouth.

"Can we agree to dispense with this unfriendly conduct?" she asked. Her voice was all schoolmarm, soft and condescending at the same time. "I'll let you up, but you have to play nice. We don't have time for you to be 'bad cop'. Besides, your good cop is damaged, and isn't going to get any better unless you make the right decision, right now."

As much as I hated to admit it, I knew she had me, quite literally, pinned. She was stronger and faster than she looked. I nodded against the ground.

"What was that?" she asked, allowing me slightly more leeway to lift my head.

I spat the leaves and dirt from between my lips and shouted, "Fine!"

She released her lock, and my pinky and ring finger went numb. I jumped up to my feet and shook my arm out, rubbing and grasping at my wrist. Damaging my trigger hand was not her brightest idea. Unless she figured I'd shoot at her. And at that point, I might have, given the chance.

"As I tried to tell you last night," she circled me, causing me to turn tightly on my heels, "I have more information than questions."

"Well, that makes one of us. I have questions, and if you want me to listen to anything you have to say, I'm going to need some answers." She nodded curtly by way of reply, which surprised me. I figured for some sort of argument out of her. "Ok then, how did we get back here?"

She thumped the hood of the truck, "Old Blue here. He gets me wherever I need to be."

"But," I said, still pawing at my sore hand, "you were on foot when we saw you."

"Because the truck was parked on the next drive up. Couldn't be seen from where you stopped. I was tailing you. Any other questions?"

"Yeah, that was mighty convenient."

She raised one eyebrow, "How's that?"

"You showed up right when we needed you."

"Well, then, count yourselves lucky."

I wasn't buying it. I'd been around enough cases to know that luck was never a factor. I was about to press her further on the point, but she abruptly changed the subject on me.

"That book you have. Do you know what it is?"

I shook my head. "It was Harmon's grandmother's journal. Harmon said he figured his grandmother might have been cataloging information about the area."

"Really. Does that make sense, Agent St. James? From your investigative point of view. Who records basic information in an indecipherable script? You encrypt the combination to a vault, not a list of trees and flowers."

I had to admit to myself that the same thought occurred to me when Harmon first handed me the book, but I didn't state my agreement out loud. I took the opportunity of the moment of silence that fell between us to study the woman before me. Like the night before, and each conversation since, she continued to dart her eyes back and forth, methodically, like she was watching a tennis match that only she could see. She had high cheekbones, dark, thick hair, and full lips. Her eyes, however, were an odd shade of translucent gray that reflected the low-hanging clouds. She was long and lean, and from her retaliation upon me, I knew the muscles under her jeans and sweater were hard and well trained.

"You're not the typical specimen of a journalist," I said, openly eyeing her up and down.

"I'm freelance, here for my own ambitions."

"And that, Watson," I smiled, happily referencing my favorite childhood hero, "is a problem. In fact, it's *the* problem. What do you get out of saving our asses? It has to be something."

"Yes, it is something, Agent St. James. But before I tell you what I get out of it, let's discuss your little light show, shall we?"

My calves went slightly weak at the thought. "I'd rather not."

"Well," She tossed her head toward the cabin, "if you want to save his life, you might want to change your mind on that."

"I just need my phone so I can get him to a hospital."

"That wound is deep." She clicked her tongue against her teeth. "He's going to need that fixed up soon. A bit foolish, don't you think, concealing a knife the way he was? Hopefully he doesn't die from *that* little bit of stupidity. However, he could succumb to yours. In fact, this whole town is at risk because you are so certain you have everything figured out. All these people around us are in danger because you have prejudged me, your attacker back there, and your entire investigation."

I bit down my anger at her accusation and clenched my fists into tight balls at my side. I can take a lot, but being patronized was at the top of my "not to be tolerated" list. After a couple deep breaths and a forced relaxation of my hands, I pressed her, "And what, exactly, am I missing here? What is it that you can offer me that no one else knows?"

"Finally!" She said, clapping her hands together, her eyes shifting wildly from gray to lavender and back again. "You finally asked the right question, Kessa St. James. What you are missing is your own self. Your own potential. You don't even realize it, but you could walk into that room right now, and heal your partner." I shifted uneasily, warily unconvinced. She placed a hand on my shoulder and continued, "Kessa, you're what we call an Adept of the Ancients. With a little help, I can show you how to access the Ancestral energy whenever you need it. I'm here to open the door to a world that you never dreamt was possible."

She was downright bubbly. I forced a single laugh. "Let me get this straight. Are you suggesting that something magical happened back there? And that somehow I was responsible for it?"

"That's exactly what I'm suggesting. Though *magic* isn't the best word to use. It's more of energy manipulation."

"This is ridiculous. I need you to either hand over my cell phone so I can call 911, or you need to drive us to the hospital so we can get Harmon the help he needs." I started walking back to the cabin, asserting authority, expecting her to follow. She didn't.

"The first thing you're going to do, is prove to yourself that this is very real by going in there, and helping your partner."

"That's what I intend to do. I'll break into the main cabin and use the caretaker's phone if I have to." I kept walking and put a hand on the door knob. It was searing hot. I pulled my hand away and turned to face her. She was right behind me, but I hadn't heard her move.

"We're playing this my way. I'd rather not do it like this, but we're out of time. I can't accomplish what you can. I'm not an Adept. You are needed, whether you want to be or not."

I appraised her sudden change in vocal inflection and posture through the trained eyes of an agent. When someone alters their own personality so many times in such a short period, it sends up a strand of red flags. You may as well attach a clump of balloons to the top with a banner that says, "Lies for Sale." A dissertation regarding her lack of credibility was dancing on my lips, ready to come out, when my phone rang in her back pocket.

"I'll take that now," I said, reaching a hand out.

She pulled it out, took a look at the screen, shrugged and tossed it at me.

"St. James."

"Agent St. James, this is Detective Schild." I breathed a sigh of relief. "We have the autopsy report back on the senator. Still waiting on Mrs. Harmon's. You want to come in?"

"I'd love to, but..." Martina had pulled my weapon, aimed it at me and was shaking her head slowly. I'd not felt her grab it from my belt. Her gaze lingered on the cabin door, and I thought of Harmon inside, waiting for me to secure him medical attention. "I need backup!" I shouted into the phone. "My location is..."

Martina yanked the phone out of my hand and clicked *End*. She threw it on the ground and stomped on it, shattering the screen. I lunged at her again, and she shifted. This time, I accounted for her skill and followed her movements. I went for my weapon, still in her hand. She bent herself back, contorting with unnatural flexibility, and sent me sprawling across the mud again. This time, she didn't restrain me but waited for me to come to my feet, flipping my service revolver idly over her finger.

"Kessa, you need to stop this. Just listen to me. Come inside. I can hear his breathing, and it's getting shallower. I have a sneaking suspicion he's getting worse instead of better." She turned the nob and swung the door open. I pushed past her to see Harmon, much in the same position I'd left him, but the bleeding from his wound had redoubled its efforts.

"Give me his phone," I demanded. "He's going to bleed out!"

"Can't." She perched on the chair like a hawk on a high branch watching over a hapless rodent as it scurried into the underbrush.

"Then help me!" I pleaded. I put my hand on his cheek. Salamander skin, clammy and cold, stretched tautly over his face and neck

She reached across to the bed and hefted Ginny's journal in one hand, and tossed it toward me. It landed within easy grasp. "Open it."

"What?"

"Just..." She rubbed at her temples, eyes closed. She was clearly frustrated. "Open it, Kessa."

"To where?"

"Use your fear and your determination. Picture what you want in your mind, and ask the book to respond to you."

"What the hell does that mean?"

She said nothing; just motioned toward the book.

Turning it over in my hands, I felt the odd vibration reverberating up my arms, through my torso and down into my legs. The sensation was becoming disturbingly familiar. My thumbs raced across the spine. Harmon gagged, and the gravity of his injury grasped me and pulled me in. He was going to die.

I opened the book. The ink on the pages took white-hot form, and I struggled to maintain my connection to the real world. Swirling patterns came to rest.

My feet anchored to the ground. I could see roots, like a mighty tree, shooting from my soles, burrowing down, down, down, to the center of the Earth. White light affixed itself like a pinpoint at the very top of my head and then tore open like a funnel. Silver and green strands of energy flowed from above, into the funnel and through my body, and shot out my right hand. The book in my left continued to thrum, matching the pace of my quickening heart. I closed my eyes and placed my right hand on Harmon's flank. His body bucked under my touch. I pulled back.

"Keep going," Martina stood directly next to me. I hadn't seen her move. When I glanced at her, I saw someone altogether different than how she'd appeared before. Her face was similar in shape, but her eyes had enlarged. Her ears drew up to points, and her fingers had lengthened. Her skin was much more pale, a pinkish-lavender, and her hair was stark white—almost glowing. She rested a hand on my shoulder.

"It's ok Kessa. You can do this." She nodded toward Harmon.

The energy flowing inside me felt warm and alive. I cocked my head, studied my glowing hand, and placed it over Harmon's wound once more. A tendril of green light swirled down my arm and pooled at my hand, cupped over the wound in his abdomen. He reacted just as violently, but I rode the wave with him. His pain became mine, and I cried out. My flank burned, and tears streamed down my face. His breathing settled and his cheeks flushed pink as I took the pain from him.

"Now think of what you want, Kessa. Picture it. See his wound, and now yours, healing."

I glanced down at my side. Blood seeped through my shirt. The gasp that caught in my throat was accompanied by a jerk away from the pain. Martina held me in place, both hands grasping my shoulders from behind. She pushed me down, keeping me from escaping.

"You have to finish this, Kessa, or you both die. Right here. Right now."

I nodded. Somehow, I understood. For the third time, my hand met Harmon's side. He didn't react, and my eyes went wide.

"He's still with us," Martina whispered, "but only just. It's now or never."

I closed my eyes and pictured him whole. Saw my own skin draw closed. The blood gone. I saw his crooked smile and the glint of malice in his bright blue eyes. The fifteen-year-old boy I'd known and the man I knew now, healthy. Happy. Whole.

The pain began to subside, and I wondered if this was what death felt like. I let go of the thought and swam in a sea of green and white energy. The intense rays gave way to a gentle flow, etched with silver, like ethereal ribbon candy. My heart felt like it was about to burst when my eyes snapped open.

Harmon sat up in front of me. The book fell from my hand. I unraveled the bandages from his torso. The skin underneath was pink and fresh, but otherwise unscarred. His mouth hung open, eyes wide and wondering. I was sure I had roughly the same expression on my face. He clutched me in a strong embrace, and we held each other, rocking on the bed, for what felt like forever.

"Kessa?" He finally said, pushing me back.

"Yes, Harmon?"

"You smell like shit."

I punched his shoulder but laughed.

"Ow! First you save me, and then you try to beat me up?"

We both laid back on the bed, staring at the ceiling. It didn't register until much later that Martina had left.

Chapter 10

Steam swirled around me as the hot shower rinsed away fatigue and grime. Confusion, however, clung to me like a second skin, refusing to wash away. I picked leaves and twigs from my hair and wondered at the last twenty-four hours. The sound of the cabin door opening pulled me from my trance, and I heard Harmon's muffled voice talking to whoever he'd let inside with him. I cut my shower short and was grateful that the room came equipped with a complementary bathrobe. The tiny shower room didn't afford much space for personal effects such as clothing. But then again, the designer of the cabin probably never figured on the rather impossible scenario I had playing out before me. I stepped out of the bathroom and peeked around the corner. Harmon stood in the doorway, laughing with Detective Schild.

"Hey, guys?" I asked around the wall, not wanting to step any further into the room. "Would you mind waiting outside a minute?"

"Oh, sure Kess." Harmon flashed a smile at me that I knew was mine alone. Butterflies lurched in my stomach, and I silently admonished myself. He was my partner, we were still Bureau, and we had a case to solve. I had to keep that very much in mind. Nevertheless, I couldn't help remembering the trailing moments of whatever it was that I had done to heal him. The green and white energy flowing between us had changed something deep inside both of us. I didn't know to what extent, but I was determined to keep it filed close at hand, for additional investigation as time allowed.

I emerged from the cabin moments later, dressed with my service revolver in its belt at my hip. Fortunately, Martina had been decent enough to leave it and Harmon's phone behind. The chilly November air gripped at my wet hair and ran all the way down my spine. Strangely, though, I wasn't shivering with the cold. Rather, it felt inviting and natural. Another file opened in the cabinet of my mind, and I shuffled the odd sensation away for future questioning.

"Schild," I said, "sorry about the call earlier. I..."

"Harmon explained."

"He did?"

"Yes, Kessa," Harmon said. "I told him we got a flat and walked back here, and then about the bear." He nodded at me, like *please, just go along with this.*

"You agents, always so hush-hush and full of secrets." Schild chuckled and wiped the cold from his nose. "Backup for a bear? Either I don't have the right clearance, or you two are proper city folk. If you want, hop in the cruiser, and I'll take you back to get your car, Harmon. The Shoreline, you said?"

Harmon and I nodded in unison. Schild raised a single eyebrow—a gesture that made it very apparent that he suspected we had a lot more going on than investigating a case. The truth was, we did. Just not what he was thinking.

"I'll just go grab—my purse is still in my car. Down the road. With the bear. Never mind, let's go. I'll ride in the back." I hurried to Schild's cruiser and let myself in.

The back seat of the cruiser smelled like old dust and layers of sweat. I leaned my head back on the rough gray vinyl and closed my eyes, silently chiding myself for my reaction to Schild. Seriously, I couldn't have sounded guiltier if I'd tried. I had to pull it together.

Schild took the driver's seat, and Harmon hopped into the passenger seat. Seeing him lively and active struck me as surreal. Not an hour ago, he was slipping from life, bleeding out internally. I'd saved him, but I still didn't know how. My only answer to that question was kept captive by Martina, and we had no idea where she'd gone. Her truck had disappeared just as silently as she had. I pondered the idea that maybe the truck flew away with her cackling at the wheel. An entertaining thought, but doubtful.

"I have the autopsy report here," Schild said, handing a file to Harmon. "Figured I'd bring it along, assuming I'd find you both alive and well."

I leaned forward against the metal bars that separated the good guys from the bad guys in the cruiser. The fact that they still had metal mesh, and not bulletproof glass, was a testament to the quiet nature of the area. Harmon held up photos so I could see.

"It says here that the lacerations were consistent with claws and contained amounts of hair and skin foreign to the senator." Harmon flipped through pages.

"Correct," Schild said. "We went over the results carefully, and it would seem that an animal was involved in the attack. Cause of death was, as you can see there," he thumped the page on Harmon's lap, "exsanguination via the aortal artery. Maybe someone with a dog, which brings our current suspect list to one: Justin Rushing. He's still MIA, and now his wife has gone missing as well. The kid is supposed to be with his grandparents. We have a unit headed there today to question them."

"What's the motive, though?" I asked. "We have means and opportunity, but why would Justin kill a senator?"

"Our best guess is Rushing's involvement with the logging industry."

I caught the corner of Harmon's eye and he frowned and shook his head. "I don't think Justin has it in him. But I have to say, looking through this, he's our only lead."

"Not the only lead," Schild countered, "just the only one that makes sense."

"How's that?" I asked.

"Forensics came back. The DNA test on the hair samples found a relative match."

"That's great!" Harmon said, grabbing the report. His eyes scanned it quickly, and he flipped the paper over and back.

"What's wrong?" I couldn't see the paper clearly.

"The match," he said, "is me."

"What?" I tried to get closer to the bars to read over his shoulder, and was quickly reminded that police cars are purposely designed so you can't see what's going on in front when you're in the back.

"It's a relative match," Schild said, "which is why Harmon is sitting up here with me, and not back there in cuffs. But it means a direct relative of his could be a suspect."

"The only relative I have—*had*," he corrected, "was my grandmother. Considering she's dead, I don't think she's a viable suspect."

"Not to mention, Harmon was with me when Ginny was attacked."

"Right," Schild wiped his brow as he turned the cruiser onto Highway 16, "Harmon's not considered a suspect for just that reason. Do you have any other relatives, though?"

"Literally *none*," he said through gritted teeth.

"According to the report, you might have a long-lost brother or something."

We rode in silence through the Harbor to the parking lot across from the Shoreline. Harmon's car was still there and in one piece. After the past several hours and all that had happened, I'd half-expected it to be stripped, or maybe just boosted altogether. I gave silent thanks for small favors.

Harmon expressed his gratitude out loud. "Thanks, Rick. I'm glad you still have my back." He clapped Schild on the shoulder before extracting himself from the cruiser and opening a door so I could do likewise.

"Schild," I asked, "how did you know where we were?"

"I guessed," he said, a sheepish smile dimpling his round cheeks. "Figured the first place to check for you would be at a known location, and I started with your hotel. I guess I'm not that bad of a detective, huh?"

"You rock," I said with a smile. "Call us if you get anything else."

As the cruiser sped away, Harmon turned to face me. I wasn't ready for the conversation I knew he wanted to have, so I walked toward the car and said, "Let's go meet up with the unit interviewing Meg's parents."

He grabbed my arm. *So much for my diversionary tactics.*

"We'll go talk to Meg's parents, but you and I are going to talk along the way." His assertive tone startled me and was a firm reminder that he was, in fact, a federal agent.

I gulped, but then steadied myself and met his firmness with my own, trained confidence. "Harmon, I will tell you what I know, but please understand that it isn't much." My boldness wavered, and the last few words flowed about as effortlessly as molasses straight from the refrigerator.

He placed his hands lightly on my shoulders. "We won't figure this out unless you talk through it. I'm here to listen."

I gave him a tight smile and a nod and opened the door of the cruiser. He startled me by grabbing my free hand. His eyes searched me for a moment, his face softened. Without the sarcastic smirk, he was ridiculously good looking. I felt my face flush at the thought, and for the briefest of moments, I could swear I sensed a feeling of insecurity coming from him. The sensation ceased the second he spoke.

"Kessa, I just want to thank you. I'd be gone right now if not for you." He looked down at the ground. "Twice."

"Twice?"

"Today, obviously." He shook his head like he was trying to eradicate the memory. "I still don't understand what happened there, and I'm kind of glad for that. But yesterday…"

"Yesterday I tried to call you in," I interjected.

"Exactly." I felt my brow furrow, and he continued, "If you hadn't tried to get my badge, I wouldn't have sobered up for, well, who knows how long. In fact, I really want to go across the street, into that bar, and down to the bottom of whatever bottle they'll hand me."

His eyes clouded over. I held his gaze in lockstep. A swirl of energy inside me, green and glowing, etched with silver, caught me off guard, and my whole body shuddered.

"What is it?" he asked, his face painted with concern.

"Nothing. I think. Harmon, I owe you an apology. A big one. I was sure you were nuts, and now…" I fought to find the right words against the logic in my mind that shouted 'No!' at every implausible occurrence of the past day, and my very central role in each. "Let's just say, I got way more than I bargained for in this case, and at this point, I'm completely out of my element."

"I'd say you're very much in your element, and you're fantastic at what you do, even when you don't know you can do it." He released my hands and tucked a strand of my hair behind my ear. His warm touch sent a jolt of excitement down my spine. Green and silver energy, wanting desperately for release.

I broke our eye contact and studied my hands intently. When I looked back up, he was gazing pensively across the road and out across the bay. The inlet of Gig Harbor spread out from behind the restaurant, deep blue waters dotted with pleasure craft and wakeboards. A ridge of dark-green pine riding up a high ridge divided the water from the horizon. The peak of Mount Rainier jutted out of low-lying clouds, looking impossibly massive. The light breeze played in Harmon's hair, and my stomach flipped. I forced the emotion of the moment from my mind and focused on the case.

"Our priorities," I said, holding up two fingers. "First, talk to Meg's parents. And second, find Martina, and get some answers. For both of us."

We got in his boat of a cruiser—the FBI doesn't know the meaning of "economy car"—and started the engine.

The silent ride through the Harbor grew awkward. I busied my mind by focusing on the daily life of this little town. Kitschy cafés and art galleries lined the waterfront drive, and periodic gates led to rows upon rows of mooring. Masts by the hundreds rose up behind the squat buildings. A large public dock sat centrally to the town, edged by a large, grassy park and a historic boathouse painted gray-blue with barn-red trim and a red roof. Even on a weekday, the town bustled with people window shopping, jogging, or lounging by the waterfront. An occasional break in the architecture allowed for a quick glance across the harbor, where mansions sat stately above the shoreline.

"I feel like we're inside a postcard," I remarked, as we passed a group of people with artist's easels erect, painting the scene before them. "Is it always like this here?"

"Yeah, Gig Harbor doesn't realize that the world outside itself exists. And the Key Peninsula even more so. There is a definite 'way of life' around here that doesn't match reality." I felt a subtle shift in the air around us, a feeling of resolute determination, and I realized it came from Harmon. He continued, "But then, what *is* reality, anyway?"

"I know you want to talk about what happened at the cabin." My voice was smaller than I'd intended, and my stomach knotted. I gathered my thoughts for a moment before continuing. "I've never been one to back down from a challenge, or avoid some uncomfortable reality. Hell, I'm an FBI agent. You know how it is. It's not an easy road."

He nodded in understanding and let the silence speak his desire. He wanted more.

"Martina said I'm an *Adept of the Ancients*," The words hung in the air for a moment. "I don't know what that means at all. I just know that somehow—and yes, you were absolutely right—I'm connected to all of this. Do you have any idea what any of this means?"

"Some, but not all," he admitted. "Back when I was a kid, when we first met, I did a lot of research into the life of our wolf friend. I have to admit, though, none of what I ever found covered what happened today. Most of what I read was folklore and superstition. There was a fine line discerning fact from fiction. Your cousin tried to help before they moved, but he tended to want to use *Dungeons & Dragons* manuals as a viable source."

We both laughed. "Well, Mark didn't have both feet in reality, that's for certain."

"No, but he was good for comic relief. And a good friend. It was a sad day for me when they moved away." The road slipped under us in silence as nostalgia washed over us like a warm breeze. "My grandmother, on the other hand, constantly told me to stop poking my nose in where it didn't belong. But then she would leave a trail of breadcrumbs for me to follow. She knew something, and I think she always hoped I'd discover whatever she was hiding. But she was afraid, too." Harmon's voice became strained, "I think she lost her life because of what she knew."

"Well then, we need to make sure she didn't die in vain. We will piece this together, find Martina, and figure out what the hell is happening. I'm just not sure what to put in my report."

Harmon's smile turned conspiratorial, curled up like the Grinch. "Oh, I'm excellent at snowballing Field. I can give you pointers."

I sighed, "Harmon, I don't operate that way."

We pulled up the long driveway of a 70s-vintage box of a home that was more windows than wood. The manicured grass yard, edged with dozens of barren rose bushes, must have been absolutely stunning in warmer months. In the chill of November, the shrubs sat dormant with browned leaf tips, waiting for spring's renewal.

Harmon shifted the car to park and gave me a side-eyed glance. "You're going to have to change the way you do things. If we call this in and give them what we know, we'll *both* be up for psych review. And then the senator's family—and me—we'll have nothing. No justice. No closure. Nothing." He balled his fists and moved to slam them into the steering wheel, but pulled back at the last second before turning to me, catching my shoulder as I opened the car door. "I'm asking you again, Kess: Trust me. Please."

I avoided looking directly at him. His words rang true, regardless of how much I disapproved. My mind wrestled for options and came up blank. I finally met his eyes, set with resolve. I felt completely unsure but spoke the words anyway. "I trust you, Harmon. What choice do I really have?"

Chapter 11

The door had opened before we had a chance to ring the bell. Harmon stood at the threshold while I hung back at the bottom of the steps. The back yard was considerably smaller than the front, with a squat, wire fence enclosing an area that only the smallest of dogs would find as an adequate running space. Appropriately enough, a miniature pinscher sprinted back and forth, warning us with his high-pitched bark that he would do us some serious damage if we were a threat. I stifled a laugh and continued to survey the area while Harmon greeted the senior Rushing.

"Paul," Harmon said, using a skilled, Bureau-approved cadence and tone in his speech, "we need to ask you a few questions. May my partner and I come in?"

Paul Rushing filled the doorway, with arms crossed over his barrel chest. White caterpillar eyebrows drew down in a V that matched his scowling mouth. "I'd rather we just talk here, if you don't mind, Danny."

Harmon nodded curtly and stood aside. Rushing Senior stepped out onto the porch and closed the door behind him. My continued scan of the yard drew my eye to a small outbuilding barely in view behind the dog run. I made a mental note of the shed, knowing we might be coming back to search, and resumed listening in on Harmon's conversation.

"So then where is Zach, if he's not here?"

"He's with friends."

"Do these friends have names?"

"Of course they have names, but you don't need them unless we're suspects. Is Zach a suspect, Danny?"

"Mr. Rushing, I'm Agent St. James." I stepped up closer to offer a handshake that he didn't take. "I'm in from San Francisco Field to provide public relations support on this case. We already have the press poking around, and I'd rather we talk to Zach before they do. If they get to him before we do, you're going to have a mess on your hands. We deal with this all the time, and we can help you through the rough spots."

His forest green eyes met mine and darkened a shade. "You just let me decide what my family can handle."

"Mr. Rushing," Danny said, "Right now, you're not a suspect. This isn't a threat, but that can, and most likely will change if you don't cooperate. Your grandson is the primary witness to the death of a United States senator. The body was found on your son's property. We can have the whole family brought in, and we can have Zach taken into custody. You don't want that to happen."

Rushing shifted uncomfortably, his eyes darting from me to Harmon and back, and then to the shed. It was subtle, but I caught it. Harmon did, too.

"Something back there, Paul?"

He pushed through us and bolted for the back yard.

Harmon gave chase, running after Rushing, and easily overtaking him right before he reached the tree line that edged the property. He clasped a hand on Rushing's shoulder in an attempt to stop him, but Paul spun hard, bringing his fist around in a solid roundhouse. He caught Harmon in the gut, knocking the wind out of him. I drew my Glock and yelled, "Stop!"

Rushing's eyes grew wide, and he dove into the trees. I ran in pursuit, catching glimpses of him as he darted down a deer trail. The bands of greenbelt that ran between houses in the area made for a lot of natural beauty but did nothing for the ability to tail a suspect. He knew the woods far better than I did, and within moments, I was standing alone, spinning in circles, shouting his name. No answer came save for the angry screams of a Stellar's jay from above my head. I trudged back to the yard, or so I thought—I'd emerged at the next house over and had to pick my way across the front of the tree line—and found Harmon just recovering from the sucker punch.

"You lose him?" he asked through gasps.

"Yeah, we're going to have to call for backup, and have this place watched. We need a warrant on the shed, too. Gig Harbor was sending a unit over anyway. They should be here soon."

Harmon stood buckled over with his hands resting on his knees. He heaved a deep breath and nodded in agreement, tossing me his phone.

I clicked the phone on, pulled up the recent calls and dialed Schild. After hearing my brief explanation, he said he'd send a team to stake out the house and start the paperwork for the warrant.

"What next?" I asked, handing Harmon his phone. He was upright and recovered, and scanning the tree line for Rushing.

"According to your list, we need to find Martina once our backup arrives."

I sat down on the front porch step, and Harmon sat beside me. The steps were narrow, and his body was close to mine. An energy jolt threatened to rise up inside me again, but I mentally shut it down.

We sat in silence until a Gig Harbor patrol car rolled up the driveway. Once they were briefed, we took our leave with their promise of a call once the warrant was served and the shed was searched.

"Let's head back to my cabin," I suggested, once we were back in the car. "It's where Martina keeps turning up. Maybe we'll get lucky."

Harmon repeated, "Get lucky, huh?"

Embarrassment mixed with annoyance rose within me. "You know what I mean, smart-ass."

"Guilty as charged," he said with a laugh.

Dusk brushed the shores of the Burley Lagoon, painting the water in hues of pink and orange. The sky reflected the colors across wisps of clouds in a dark blue sky. My cabin came equipped with a small wooden deck, adorned with two Adirondack chairs and a round table barely big enough for the two mugs of steaming coffee that sat between Harmon and me. Watching the sky darken, sipping coffee, became a dream-like alternate reality. The death of the senator, the fugitive small child, the possibility of a werewolf, and myself wielding magic: it all seemed a million miles away. Harmon sat in an easy silence beside me, nurturing his coffee with eyes closed. For that moment, I pretended it was all a dream, and we were just a couple of friends enjoying the evening.

Reality came crashing back into place when Harmon jumped from his chair, drawing his weapon. He'd obviously heard something I didn't, and I came to his side, drawing my gun. Martina rounded the corner, still in her jeans and angora. Harmon didn't lower his weapon. Neither did I.

"I've been waiting for you," she said, looking at the small deck with a frown. She ignored the gun barrels tracing her movements, climbed the porch steps, and perched herself up on the railing with liquid agility.

"We have some questions for you, and you're going to answer," I said, allowing all of the authority I could muster to course through my voice.

"I should hope so," she smiled, looking at each of us in turn. "Kessa. Danny. Your weapons are not necessary. Please, have a seat and be comfortable."

"I'll be the judge of that," I said. Harmon, however, lowered his weapon. His eyes glazed over as he sat back in his chair.

"Harmon!" I snapped my fingers at him, but he didn't seem to notice.

"He won't remember this conversation, Kessa. This is between you and me, and the others." Her eyes danced around again.

"What are you looking at?" I turned my head but saw nothing. "And what did you do to him?"

She ignored my questions. "Kessa, I'm here to help. I can only open the door, though. You will need to walk through. I will do all I can, and in exchange, I will help you keep the press off this case. We both want that, don't we?"

"How can you possibly..."

She fidgeted with her Seattle PI press badge. "I can be any one of great many things. We can create whatever reality you want. But you already know that, don't you?" She hopped down from the railing, ran a finger up the barrel of my Glock and pushed on my hand. I felt my arm slack against my will. "You know you can alter your reality. Tell me, Kessa; what did you feel? What did you see, when you healed your partner? Please just answer. I need to know so I can help."

I sighed and sat back down. "I felt his pain," I admitted. "And like I was..." The words escaped me, and I sat with mouth open, unable to adequately express the sensation.

She sat on the deck, legs crossed, leaning forward with her hands on my knees. "Tell me, Kessa."

"The Earth," I said slowly. "I was rooted to the Earth. All the way to the core. And energy coursed through every cell in my body. It was like someone turned a hose on my head, only whatever came out wasn't water. It was warm and dry, and it went through me instead of over me. And I could control it."

I shook my head. No, that wasn't right. "Not control," I said, and she smiled brightly, "I could wield it like it was another limb."

She clapped her hands and jumped back up. "Exactly!"

"Exactly, what? I really don't know how to take all this."

"You're doing great," she reassured. "What else?"

"The energy was colored. Green and silver. Maybe some white. What does this mean?"

"Rest easy, you'll know in time." She stood to leave, and I shot up from my chair to catch her arm.

"What are you?" I asked.

"In time," she repeated. She snapped her fingers, and Harmon finished a sip of coffee that he'd been taking for several minutes.

She disappeared around the corner, and Harmon casually turned to smile at me, not showing any sign that he'd witnessed what had just transpired.

"Something wrong?" he asked.

I shook my head but said nothing.

"Well, looks like Martina isn't going to turn up." He stood up, brushing his slacks back into place. "It's getting dark. We should probably call a tow for your car. We need to get my box out of the back, too."

I nodded over my coffee, still unable to find words.

He looked around, and back to me, scratching his head. "Did I miss something?"

"Yeah," I said, "You did. You missed Martina. She was here, and now I'm more confused than I was before."

I filled him in as best as I could.

"So I was just totally out of it?" He asked. "I don't think I like that at all. But, I have a bit of a confession. I'm sure I've seen her before. It's like something out of a dream. From when I was a kid."

I was hugging myself and forced my arms to relax to my lap. "She's probably local."

"No, you know it's not that simple. When I was very young, I snuck out of bed one night because I heard my grandmother talking to someone. Even when I was a kid, I wanted to be a spy. It's why I joined the Bureau. Sneak around and catch people *in the act*." He smiled sideways at his own memory, and I couldn't help but match his grin. He continued, "Martina was there, on my grandmother's sofa, and they were talking about my grandfather. Remember that locket?"

I nodded.

"She was telling my grandmother that she had to keep the locket on at all times; that it would protect her. But not to ever submerge it in running water. Never could figure out why."

"The stream," I blurted out.

"What?"

"Do you remember that day? We were running from your wolf, but when we jumped the stream, you stopped. You said they can't cross running water."

"Good memory," he said. "I figured you had forgotten everything you could about that day."

"I tried," I admitted. "But in reality, it's like it happened yesterday. Especially being back here."

Long shadows of towering pine trees crept across the water as the daylight faded, and suddenly I felt uneasy.

"Let's take this inside," I said.

"I'm thinking, continue this over pizza? I'll order one up."

"Sounds great. I'm pretty sure I could eat a whole pizza myself right now."

Back inside, he flopped onto my bed. I perched uneasily in the armchair and studied him as he ordered our dinner. My stomach knotted at the visual memory of the last time he lay on that bed, dying under my hands.

"I'm going to stay here tonight," he said, tossing his phone on the table and kicking off his shoes.

"Is that so?" I asked, one eyebrow raised.

"You have no phone. You have no car. I noticed when we came back into the cabin that the caretaker for this place still isn't home. You have no backup and..." He picked up the room phone, "Yep, still dead. So either I take you home with me, or I stay here. The pizza is on its way, and it's getting late. It'll be easiest if I just stay. We can pick it up in the morning."

Butterflies threatened to burst through my stomach wall. "That's ridiculous, Harmon. You can just come back in the morning."

"Not a chance," he said, rolling onto his back, hands clasped behind his head, and feet casually crossed.

"I can take care of myself."

"I know you can. I told you years ago, if I was going to get in a fight, I'd want you by my side. That still stands." He sat up quickly, tossed his legs over the edge of the bed and brought his face awkwardly close to mine. "I just have a bad feeling, and I'm not going to ignore it. This gut instinct has saved my ass more times than I can count. We'll both be safer if I stay here. So I'm staying."

Before I could protest to the lack of personal space, he was already laid back on the bed, fumbling for the TV remote. I gave up the fight and crossed over to the bed. "Move over."

He slid to the edge of the painfully small double bed. I lay down next to him, trying to avoid any bodily contact. As Harmon absent-mindedly flipped through channels, my brain alternated between wanting to enjoy the moment, to being grateful that he had my back, to thoughts of what our directors would think of this highly inappropriate moment. By the time the pizza arrived, I'd quelled the tide of jitters inside enough to relax and eat. Shortly thereafter, Harmon fell asleep at my side like we were an old married couple. No words, no ceremony, and apparently lacking the extreme discomfort I felt. I watched him breath, gentle and slow. The myriad of conflicts within me gave way to simple gratitude. I felt safe with him beside me. With that thought held firmly in mind, sleep came easily.

Chapter 12

I stepped lightly through the forest, my bare feet feeling the ground between my toes. Cold and soft, ribbed with moss and tiny twigs, but none so sharp as to pierce the skin or even cause the mildest discomfort. The path I walked lead deep into a forest of old growth pine. Sunlight filtered through emerald boughs, streaming in shafts, dotting the forest floor. Each tree radiated a gentle green glow. A feeling of déjà vu crept through me. Every step brought me closer to my unknown destination, yet I knew I walked the right way, and I felt an insistence that told me to hurry despite my desire to walk deliberately and soak in the beauty of my surroundings.

The ground beneath my feet swirled with silver energy swirled like a low-lying fog as I walked. It licked up my legs, warming and welcoming with every footfall. Birds twittered in high branches out of sight, and far off in the distance, a lone owl hooted softly. My mind told me I was dreaming, but something deep within my soul stirred and nagged at the reality of the setting.

The trail ended at a vast meadow, where a lone grandfather alder stood sentinel toward the center. Martina emerged from behind its trunk. Her features had changed slightly. She stood taller and leaner. Her arms bore swirling tattoos that wrapped down each hand and disappeared into her palms. Similar markings framed her brow, and curved along the right side of her face, down her neck and onto her shoulder. She wore a light blue, shimmering shift. Her smile told me I was in the right place, like the receptionist flashes when you arrive at your doctor's office right on time.

"Kessa, you made it. I wasn't sure if I'd be able to pull you across this way." She spread her hands wide. The alder tree behind her rained autumn leaves down around us as if on cue. A cocktail scent of dew-covered grass and peat moss rose from the ground.

"I'm dreaming," I said.

"You are sleeping on Earth, but you are also here. There are those of us who can transport humans between worlds."

"Sorry, but where is here?" I glanced around the glade, and almost asked why it felt familiar, but thought better of it. Dreams often feel familiar, I told myself.

"You are in The Ancestral Land. It's an alternate, but overlaying reality to your own. There are many, but this is the one to which you are tightly bound. It's one of the realms of the Fae, and the eldest among the planes of reality."

"Uh huh. So, then what are you, and what does that make me?" I crossed through the damp grass to the alder and laid a hand on its wide, white trunk. Warm energy flowed up my arm like a soft electrical current. I pulled away reflexively and looked up into the soaring boughs overhead, so dense with autumn leaves that I couldn't discern the height of the tree.

"I am faery. You are Adept. You're also stubborn. I figured bringing you here might convince you to stop reasoning and start listening."

"So you're telling me that this is Fairy Land, and I'm somehow part of it?"

She nodded, "If you want to think of it that way, you can."

I laughed. "This is quite the dream."

Martina pinched her brow between slender fingers and closed her eyes. "Kessa, you doubt deeply and dismiss quickly. If this is all just a dream, what harm is there in letting go and believing for a moment?"

When she opened her eyes, they had shifted in color to dark amber. She rested her hand on the alder for a moment, then pulled back. White mist swirled around her fingers, pouring toward her from the trunk of the tree. She motioned for me to follow suit. I shrugged my shoulders and placed a hand likewise on the trunk. When I pulled away, the same energy followed. A surge of peace rushed through my body. I felt centered and powerful. My throat constricted as tears welled in my eyes.

I cleared my throat and shook my hand. "Okay, I'll play along. This is Fairy Land..."

"The land of Fae," she corrected. "The Ancestral Lands. Specifically, we are in the Grove of the Ancient."

"Ok, land of Fae. You're... faery?" She nodded at my slow deliberation and waved me on. "And that makes me.... faery as well?"

She shook her head, "No, you are human. But you are an Adept of the Ancients."

"You keep saying that like I have any clue what it means. How about you explain it? You can even use small words."

She laughed and placed a hand on my shoulder. It should have felt like a condescending gesture, but I was willing to assume that she was by far superior in knowledge of where we were at the moment, and a nagging insistence grew within me. I needed to know more, even though the admission railed against every bit of reason my brain screamed at me.

"You are able to bridge the worlds, and harness the energy of the Ancients," Martina said. "It doesn't make you one of us, but it does allow you some powers of the Ancestral Lands."

"Like healing Harmon," I said, barely above a whisper.

"You care very much for him," She smirked.

"Leave that out of it."

"Whatever. What is important is that, at that moment, you accepted both your bond to the Earth and your gift of Fae. You acted as a bridge when you channeled the energy to heal Danny."

"But the book did that. I was holding the book."

"Books like the one you held do assist in opening the doorway," she agreed, "but you still have to possess the ability to use such a device."

I shook my head. "I'm not sure I follow."

"Think of it this way," she said, "whoever created that book was Adept. More appropriately, he or she understood and accepted that gift. The power granted to an Adept is infused deep within such a device, and another Adept—regardless of how skeptical—can access and harness the energy there."

Silence hung between us as I mulled over her words.

"I need you to accept your unique ability, Kessa," she continued. "That's why I had you explain what you experienced. You have to realize that it was you, and not the book. You rooted to the Earth. You reached across planes. You saved Harmon's life."

She sat in the grass, and I followed suit. Tiny flowers sprang to life around us, then transformed into glowing, winged creatures draped in petals with delicate wisps of arms and legs, and glowing white hair. They rose up and fluttered around us. Martina held out a finger and one of the flower people perched like a little bird.

She brought the faery close to her ear, listened, nodded and then returned her attention to me.

"And that was?" I asked.

"Flower faery. They are the messengers of the Grandfather Tree. He extends to you a greeting of the highest compliment."

I turned to the tree with a weak smile and waved. "Um, hello."

A light breeze lifted my hair around my face, tickling my nose. I felt my pulse quicken at the unexpected exchange, and I refocused on Martina. "So, tell me, Martina, if that's really your name, why do you need someone like me? Can't you just flit down to Earth and use magic?"

"It's not that easy." Her mouth turned down in a frown, and her eyes grew distant like she was watching a movie of the past play in her mind. "I can come to Earth, but my magic is... limited. There was a time when the path of the Fade provided open doorways between all realms. We were able to walk freely between the planes, but things have changed. Most of the faery find passage difficult, and only those who have adapted are still able to travel to Earth."

"So, you don't really work for the press, do you?" I asked.

"Actually, I do." Her mischievous grin and shift in tone made the hairs on my neck stand at attention. "How else can I keep up with all the changes on Earth? I find your modern world fascinating." She waved her own statement off. "But what does it matter? I have to do something to keep me abreast of the movements of Earth, so I write stories about your kind."

"Makes as much sense as anything else that's happened in the last day."

"Kessa, you need to believe that you are here, now. There is much to be done, and little time for you to learn. There is a dark force that threatens your world. The two deaths you are investigating are just the beginning. Much will be lost unless you accept who you are. And only then will you be able to stop the blight from spreading."

"Ok, sorry. You lost me. Blight?"

"What you call 'werewolf' is actually one of the Fae. They are beings that squat inside a human host like a parasite, enjoying and exploiting the human form, but they are demon spirits. The one who possesses your buddy on the Key Peninsula is an elder among his kind. He is older that you can imagine, and has walked your realm for nearly forty years, gaining the complacent trust of his host and strengthening his bond between the worlds."

"We only have one werewolf," I said, sitting more upright. "A blight makes me think of something that spreads."

"Yes, exactly. He has figured out how to increase his influence and bring more of his kind forth from the depths of Fel, the lower realm of Fae."

An insistent itching crawled up my back, and I pawed at it absently. "How? I thought your powers were limited."

"They are, but he's somehow found a way to become a bridge, much like you. Only he isn't drawing from the Grandfather Tree. The place he pulls his power from is different."

"Evil?" I asked, reaching to scratch below my shoulder blade as the itch made its way closer to my neck.

"What is evil?" she asked. "He is what he is. He acts in accordance with his own will to survive and perpetuate his kind. He is, in that respect, like any other life form. All life springs from Fae. Some strive to maintain a balance between the worlds. Some do not. And some want to return to the old ways when the realms stood connected."

"So, which do you want?" I asked.

She flashed a quick, forced smile. "I want what's best for all of us."

I scratched at the base of my neck. The itching turned to a burning. "I'm assuming what he wants and what we want are entirely different? And we wouldn't benefit one bit from him getting his way?"

"Very astute," she said. "But your time here runs short."

The burning slithered into my right ear, and I heard my name being called, over and over, far off but insistent. My eyes grew wide as I felt the dream slipping. As the Grandfather Tree faded from sight, Martina fished in her pocket handed me a chain that held a smooth, green stone. "The Earth Stone will help you call on your Ancestral energy. Remember who you are, Kessa."

I nodded and slipped the pendant around my neck. It felt lighter than when I'd held it in my hand, and it flashed in brilliant lavender, causing the hairs on my arms to stand at attention like I'd walked into a blast of cold air. My eyes closed and my teeth clenched involuntarily. I felt dizzy like I'd just gotten off a ride at the fair. When I opened my eyes, Martina was gone.

Blackness swirled in on the vision of the Grove of the Ancient until there was nothing but night and the sound of Harmon's voice, incessantly calling my name. He shook my shoulders, insistent and demanding. Something else beyond his shouts, loud, banging, grinding, brought me fully out of my dream state. My eyes opened to Harmon's face inches from mine.

"Kessa! Wake up!" In the darkness I could see the whites of his eyes, wide with panic. Glass shattered, and we both turned to see the beast's face in the moonlight. His deep, throaty growl erupted through a spray of foaming spittle.

My mind wouldn't wrap around the sudden displacement from the dream to reality. Harmon's full weight pressed against my chest as he fumbled in the dark for our weapons in the drawer of the bedside table. I heard the familiar racking of a slide and three quick shots rang in my ears, deafening all other sounds. He pulled me to my feet and shoved me toward the door. Before I had time to register the fact that I was up and moving, we stood outside, and he held the door shut.

In the dark, his lips moved, but my ears rang in tinny uselessness. I shook my head and yelled—or at least I thought it was yelling— "I can't hear you!"

He pulled me to him, pressing his mouth up close to my right ear and shouted, "We need to get to the shoreline and into the water. It can't get us if we're in running water!"

Claws raked against the inside of the door. My hearing returned enough to recognize the sound of shredding wood. Harmon tossed me my weapon, and I widened my stance and took aim at the door.

"On 3," he mouthed.

I nodded and blew out half a breath to steady my hands.

He held up fingers in the night. One. Two. Three. Harmon stepped back, and the door flew open. At the sight of our attacker, I fired a three-round burst. At close range, he was an easy target. The shots flew true and struck mid-torso. It was the type of defensive shots that would drop any assailant.

Except this one.

He staggered backward into the room, but the rage-filled howl let us know that all I'd really done was piss him off.

"Run!" Harmon screamed, pushing me into a sprint. High tide pushed the waterfront within a dozen feet of the cabin. Harmon overtook me and splashed into the Burley Lagoon with an involuntary cry. Seconds later, my shriek matched his as frigid water enveloped my feet, sending incapacitating jolts up my legs. I stumbled and fell at the shoreline, landing face-first in the salty, muddy water. A clawed hand wrapped around my ankle and dragged me backward.

"Harmon!" I pawed at the ground, desperate for a handhold, but came up with muddy clumps of boggy marsh. Pain seared across my leg as the beast latched a second paw around my ankle. I twisted and kicked.

The fiend dragged me closer, up onto the shore. Its massive weight fell upon my legs, pinning me. It dug claws into my wrists, holding me fast with its face so close I could taste its hot breath. To my utter shock, it spoke. Low and gravely, and accented with growls. "You shouldn't have come back. You have no idea what you're involved in here. Leave while you can, or you won't make it out alive."

"Like hell!" I twisted my arms, and bucked my waist, attempting a backward roll, grasping for the beast's arm. He fell forward, flailing. His charcoal eyes went round as he hit the water. He propelled himself up and backward, screaming out in pain.

As I pushed myself deeper into the water, the beast turned and dove back through the cabin window. I took the opportunity to look around for Harmon. He splashed toward me and pulled me out deeper still.

My teeth chattered uncontrollably. "We need to get out of the water," I said. "I'm already losing feeling in my toes."

He pulled me to him. His body was equally cold, but pressed together we found a small amount of warmth. The creature re-emerged from the cabin, clutching something in its hand, which it held up to us.

"Is that my grandmother's journal?" Harmon asked. The moonlight didn't give enough light to see clearly, but I knew it was the book. It glowed faintly in the beast's hand.

"Yes," I said, "and we can't let him take it." I pushed through the water with a singular purpose and no plan of attack. Harmon grabbed my shoulder.

"We can't beat him. Not like this."

The beast turned and ran past the cabin, into the forest beyond, with the book clutched in his claw. We waded back to the shore once we knew he was gone. My feet were so numb I had no idea of what I might have been stepping on. Our clothes sagged with freezing water and clumps of mud as we dragged ourselves back inside the cabin.

"Looks like it only took the book," I said, glancing around the room. Shattered glass littered the carpet and part of the bed. The decimated door would be good for making toothpicks, but not much else. My suitcase had been tossed, but a quick survey showed that the beast wasn't interested in women's clothing.

"We need to get out of here," Harmon said, grabbing up my clothes and shoving them back in the suitcase.

"Where?" I asked.

"Well, we know it won't cross the water, so I'll bet it can't get over the bridge. Just to be safe, though, I think we should go back to my place. We can regroup. Get you a new phone. Take hot showers. Maybe a stiff drink. And your arms..."

I held up my hands and studied my wrists. The beast had clawed chunks of skin away in our scuffle, and fresh blood pooled around the deep scratches. "The water was so cold; I don't even feel it."

"Well, we need to get cleaned up, and we need a plan. We need to call for backup, and get units out here."

"And tell them what?" I tossed my hands in the air. "That a psychopathic demon spirit is inhabiting one of the locals, causing him to look and act like a werewolf, and that's who killed the senator?"

Harmon laughed uneasily, "What the hell are you talking about."

The whole dream came flooding over me, and frustration rose inside me like a capped fountain. "Nothing. Just a dream. I think I'm losing it."

Harmon cocked his head sideways and pointed at my chest, "What's that?"

I reached up to my collarbone and felt the smooth stone hanging on its delicate, silver chain. I inhaled a gasp and turned to the mirror. The Earth Stone.

I sat on the bed and looked up at Harmon. Tears flooded my eyes. The fountain burst, and I couldn't hold back. He sat beside me and wrapped me in his arms, letting me cry against his chest.

"This isn't right," I finally said, clamping down on the stress and fear, "I don't believe in these things!"

"You're going to have to fill me in, Kess," he put a finger under my chin and lifted my head to look me in the eye. "I'm lost here. But let's go get cleaned up. You can tell me on the way. We can work this out."

"He has the book," I said. "We need to get it back."

"That's the least of our worries right now."

"No," I said, feeling bile rise in my throat, "it's what worries me the most."

<h1 style="text-align:center">Chapter 13</h1>

Sometimes, you just have to overlook your own discomfort in order to garner a bit of solace out of what turned out to be a very bad day. I found myself squashing my inner voice, which was highly disapproving, as I stepped out of Harmon's shower and wrapped myself in a black towel. I wondered silently why bachelors always have black towels. In my sporadic and mostly-failed dating life, upon the rare occasion when I made it long enough with a potential mate to have the opportunity to use his shower, one hundred percent of the towels I'd wrapped myself in had been black.

I admonished myself again. I wasn't dating Harmon. He was my partner in an investigation, and nothing more. I was using his shower because our suspect had completely trashed my cabin, and I'd emerged from the fight covered in sea water, mud, and my own blood.

An inkling of thought crossed my mind, now that I had a chance to step back and analyze the events of the day. The biggest unknown suddenly fell around the whereabouts of the caretaker for the tiny little group of cabins that comprised Shari's Bed and Breakfast. One would think, through that entire ruckus, Shari would have at least popped her head out to see what all the noise was. That is, assuming she'd come home at some point before the attack. I searched my memory, trying to recall if I'd seen her car, but it obviously hadn't been on my mind at the time. I tucked the concern away, earmarked with high priority, so we could check in on her first thing in the morning.

Harmon's hand on my shoulder nearly brought me out of my skin, and worse, just about made me lose my towel.

"What the hell are you doing in here?" I demanded, pulling my wrap tighter around myself.

"Easy, ferocious," he said with a laugh. I didn't see the humor in the moment, as was evidenced by my scowl of disapproval. He held out a steaming mug and forced a protruding pouty lip. "I bring gifts from the coffee gods. Figured you might want to warm up on the inside. I'll leave you to it."

He set the cup on the counter and stepped back out of the bathroom, closing the door behind him. My mouth hung agape for a moment, but I just shook my head, locked the door and let the towel slide to the floor so I could warm my insides without fear of further intrusion. The steam in the bathroom caressed my still-cold skin. I hurriedly dressed in an old Prince T-shirt and flannel pants. Harmon still needed to get in the bathroom to warm himself, and I was half afraid of what he might suggest as the alternative to a hot shower to do the job.

I emerged from the bathroom to find Harmon lounged out on the bed. He had changed when we first got back to his place, and he'd scrubbed the mud out of his hair in the kitchen sink while I showered. "All yours," I said.

"Nah, I'm good. Join me?" He sat up and patted the bed.

"Harmon, I don't think that's a good idea."

"Not like that, Kessa," he scrunched his nose. "Just, come sit. And plan. And maybe fall asleep somewhere where we won't get chased, beat up or potentially eaten."

I couldn't help but laugh, and decided *what the hell*. It wasn't like it was the first time we'd been in bed together. I set my mug on the bedside table and propped a pillow up against the mahogany and leather headboard.

"So, what's our plan then?" I asked, sitting cross-legged, still uneasy with the idea of getting too comfortable.

"First, tell me about that new necklace that just appeared," he said, indicating the Earth Stone around my neck.

I pulled my knees up and hugged them. He sat up, cross-legged to face me, and put a hand on my arm. "What is it, Kess?"

"I wish you wouldn't call me Kess," I said. "My mom's name was Tess, and it brings back a lifetime of annoying confusion."

"Ok, fine, but tell me, what is that? Where did it come from? You didn't have that on when we went to sleep. Or at all, from what I recall."

I took a deep breath, and looked into his eyes, studying his intent. I exhaled slowly and shrugged. "You wouldn't believe me if I told you. Hell, I don't believe it, and I was there." I lifted the stone from my chest and let it thunk back down on the chain.

"This is me you're talking about," he said. "Remember? The kid in the woods? Believer in werewolves? The one you were going to call in for psych?"

"Yeah, sorry about that," I said, feeling guilt well up within me.

"Forget it." He gently squeezed my arm. "Just tell me."

Something in the way he looked at me, into me, broke out a tiny little piece of the wall inside me that I had always struggled to maintain. It held me back from trusting so many times. It had always served me well. But I couldn't keep the truth from Harmon. How he had earned that level of trust I so quickly I couldn't comprehend. But the fact of the matter was, I had no one else to tell. If I called it in as an official report, my career would end. My handful of friends back in San Francisco were all Bureau, and we rarely interacted outside the office. I was the perpetual loner, now carrying a burden I didn't understand. The opportunity to mull through it with someone presented itself in Harmon, and as his expression beckoned me to confide in him.

The shock of surprise hit me when I realized I didn't want to share this one with anyone but him.

I relayed the dream, trying to recall every detail. The sights, sounds, and smells of the forest around the Grandfather Tree. The tree itself—himself—and Martina. How she'd changed, and what she'd said. About the beings of other realms, passing between worlds, and the idea of accessing levels of energy that were akin to magic. And me being a part of it all, somehow gifted. I concluded with the itching, burning feeling of being pulled from the dream, and Martina handing me the stone, and me placing it around my neck.

When I finished, Harmon laid back on the bed and closed his eyes. "So what you're saying is, instead of freezing ourselves in the water, you probably could have done something with that stone? Something like accessing magic to save us?"

I felt annoyance rise in me. "It's not like I'm used to this, Harmon. I don't think, 'Hey, we're in danger. How about I whip up a spell?' I don't even have a clue as to what I can do with this yet."

"I get it," he said. "Sorry."

"Besides," I continued, "whatever I channeled to heal you was through the book. I haven't even attempted to call up energy without it. All I really know is that I'm exhausted."

"Get some sleep," Harmon said without opening his eyes. "We'll figure it out tomorrow."

I laid down beside him and gave in to my exhaustion.

Awakened by the smell of sizzling bacon, I bolted out of bed. Daylight streamed through the window, and I glanced at the bedside clock. Nine-thirty. My mind immediately returned to Shari's Bed and Breakfast, and Shari, or the distinct lack of her presence.

"Well good morning!" Harmon chimed as I emerged from the bedroom. His expression changed to one of concern as he registered my urgency. "What's wrong?"

"Shari," I said. "The woman who owns the bed and breakfast. Where was she last night? Why didn't she come out at the utter destruction of her property? Was she even there?"

"Heavy sleeper?" He suggested, handing me a plate full of breakfast. Bacon, an omelet, toast, hash browns, and a glass of orange juice.

"Doubtful anyone could sleep through all that noise," I said, sitting down and taking a bite. He circled around the breakfast bar to join me, shoving a stack of unopened mail onto the kitchen counter below the bar to make room for his plate. "At any rate, we need to get back over there, assess the damage, and come up with some sort of cover story."

He paused chewing and gave me an incredulous look, "Kessa St. James, are you suggesting we *lie* to the police?"

"What do you propose? We tell them we were attacked by a werewolf?"

He laughed and shook his head, "You are seriously wound up this morning."

The customary irritation level that belonged solely to Harmon rose within me as I opened my mouth in retort. He held up a hand, "I'm just giving you crap. I know we need a cover."

"Maybe just breaking and entering?" I suggested.

"They'll ask why we didn't call it in. And then they'll ask where you were."

I chewed my lower lip. "That could present a host of problems, for both of us.

I could say I stayed in Tacoma. That I had you drop me off at a hotel near the mall so I could replace my cell phone."

"It's weak, and it won't work. I took the liberty of calling in for a new phone for you from Seattle Field. A courier should be here any time now."

"Thanks." I smiled, taking a sip of my orange juice. "I agree it's not the best cover, but maybe the Gig Harbor police won't know Bureau procedures?"

"Well, we can start there, and then try to pick our way through it. I don't like lying to Schild. He and I go way back. Used to run track together at Peninsula High. Ran after a few other things, too, if you know what I mean." He waggled his eyebrows at my frown.

"I think what's important right now," I said, changing the subject, "is me figuring out whatever this is that I'm able to do. I get the feeling it has something to do with the forest. It's deeply rooted in the Earth. And the Grandfather Tree, I couldn't help but remember, is the exact type of tree that circled your grandparent's old home. Remember how the clearing around the house was ringed with aspens?" He nodded, taking a bite of his toast. "I think I need to go there, Harmon."

"That house isn't there anymore. It got torn down."

"But what about the grove? Is it still standing?"

"Who knows?" He said. "But that doesn't feel very safe. We have no weapons against that creature."

"Where did you get that silver knife?"

"You're going to laugh. I got it at the mall, in one of those engraving places. It was some silly ornamental thing, just a letter opener. But it had a high enough silver content that I figured it would do some damage."

I winced at the memory of the damage it had done.

He placed a hand over mine and looked at me like he'd read my thoughts. "It's fine. I'm still here."

"I still don't know how I did that, Harmon. Or what else I'm capable of. I have no idea." I focused on eating to avoid having to say anything else about it.

Harmon rose from his chair and wrapped his arms around me. He had showered at some point while I slept; he smelled like pine and oak. It was intoxicating, and for a moment, I found myself resting my head on his chest, accepting the comfort he offered. Suddenly embarrassed, I pushed myself away and straightened my shirt, looking everywhere but at him. He met my darting eyes and drew me in with his smile.

"If you need to go to the grove, that's where we'll go. You have no idea what you're capable of right now, but I promise you, we'll find out."

I wanted so badly to believe him. Conflict ripped at my stomach, and I nodded silently. I fingered the stone hanging at my breast and wished for the last two days to start over. If I'd had the chance, I'd have followed my own advice, even to the detriment of my career, and I'd have avoided all of this.

Chapter 14

My new phone rang about ten seconds after I'd thanked the courier from Seattle Field and shut the door. Harmon had seen to it that the phone was programmed with my same number. I recognized the incoming call immediately. My district office was on the line, presumably wanting answers I didn't have to give.

"St. James, where the hell have you been?" Crase didn't even give me a chance to answer properly. I could picture him, pacing in his office, one hand tucked in his belt, the panel of his suit jacket slung behind his arm, and the phone dwarfed by a massive, dark-skinned hand, squashed to his ear. The stubbly moustache that cropped up moments after he attempted to shave would quiver, and the vein at his temple would look like it was about to burst. I'd seen him angry, and it was never pretty. Even from several hundred miles away, I wanted to shrink into myself.

"Sorry sir, my phone got destroyed. We had a car wreck."

"And did you partner's phone also get destroyed?" He didn't let me answer. I may as well have been fourteen all over again, explaining to my father why I was coming home late from the movies. "We know about the car. It was towed by a detective Schild yesterday. We've been trying to track you down. Neither of you answers your goddamned phones now? I thought I had two dead agents."

"Sir, I can explain."

"Save it, St. James. Have you turned on your television lately? You had one job. Control the press. Apparently, according to you, that means let them run wild with speculation."

"Hold on, let me turn on the news." I crossed the room and looked around for a remote. Harmon pointed silently, and I opened a drawer in the single table that adorned the end of the couch. The TV was set to CNN, which was fortunate. Less searching translated to less time on the phone with my very agitated director.

"Whoa, boy," I said. I brought a hand to my head and watched the media circus unload the clown car. "Animal attack? That's what they decided to go with? And the Rushing family keeps wolves now? Sir, I'm so sorry. We had a bit of an incident yesterday, but we're on track. We're still waiting on Virginia Harmon's autopsy, but we know the cause of death for Senator Mansfield. We have a potential suspect and motive, and we've staked out one residence. I'll send over a full brief in twenty."

Crase's silence was even more intimidating than his ranting.

"Sir?"

Heavy breathing came across the line, and I braced myself for the onslaught, or perhaps a demand for my badge and gun. What came next surprised me.

He spoke with quiet resolve, albeit strained. I could tell he was talking through clenched teeth, probably rubbing his temple with a forefinger. "You will go out there. You will hold a press conference. And you will give them an *approved goddamned story!*" I pushed the phone from my ear as he screamed the last three words before he unceremoniously hung up on me.

I tossed the phone on the couch and sat down with my head in my hands.

"I heard 'approved goddamned story' from here," Harmon laughed, flipping a dishrag over his shoulder, a smirk decorating his face while he cleaned our breakfast plates.

I glowered at him, hoping to dissuade him from being so perky. "We need to get a handle on this Harmon. It's not funny."

"Oh, come on. It's a little funny." He turned off the kitchen sink and rounded the breakfast bar to get a better view of the TV screen. "Wow, they really know how to spin a story, don't they?"

"I've seen worse," I admitted, leaning back on the couch and covering my face with a throw pillow. I tossed it away immediately. "*Ack*, Harmon, don't you ever clean in here?"

He shrugged, "Why bother? You're the first guest I've entertained in a *long* time." His over-animated facial expression on the word "long" made me laugh.

"See!" He flopped down next to me and patted my knee. "Humor. It's good for you."

"I need to file a report," I said. "We have to follow up with Shari, and make sure she's unharmed and taken care of. We need to call a press conference."

"Easy, girl." He held up a hand to stop me. "Let's handle one thing at a time. I'll call Schild for the press conference and have him pull some strings out at the civic center." He reached for his phone on the end table.

"Wait," I grabbed his arm, and he stopped and looked at me with a hint of exasperation.

"Didn't you just say to call?" he asked as my silence stretched on.

"Just what the hell are we going to tell these people? We still haven't figured that out."

His smile turned upward on just the left side of his face—the expression I had come to understand precluded a statement that would undoubtedly irritate me. He didn't fail to deliver. "I'm just going to make it up as I go along."

I growled and pushed his mildewed throw pillow back over my face; dust be damned.

After filing my report, which consisted of a quick email typed into my phone comprised of not much more than I'd already said to Crase, I changed as fast as I could and ran a brush through my hair. I frowned at the sight of myself in the mirror. I still had scratches on my face from being shoved to the ground. Fortunately, I had slacks and long sleeves to wear, because, between the bruises and the claw marks, I looked like an accident victim. I was tugging self-consciously at the sleeves of my blouse when Harmon slid in behind me to the sink to brush his teeth.

"I called Schild. He's setting up a press release. He'll text me the time and location in a few, but said it should be sometime this afternoon." He placed both hands on the counter and let his head hang for a second before continuing. "Same cause of death for my grandmother. Same DNA results, too."

"So, our killer is somehow related..."

"To me, yes."

"Do you have any relatives at all? Anyone even half-related?"

He turned and leaned back against the counter, crossing his arms and staring much further away than the confines of the tiny apartment bathroom allowed. "I had an uncle, but he disappeared years ago. We're pretty sure he died. The body found in his torched garage was beyond identification, but the size was about right."

"But that could be a lead," I suggested. "Maybe he had kids you didn't know about?"

"It's a real long shot. That was when I was a kid. He was my dad's brother, and he was a bit of a loner. We think he killed himself right after my parents died."

I studied his face, trying to extract what might be going on inside his head. His brow drew together and the little laugh lines that framed his mouth deepened, but reflected no joy.

"I'm really sorry," I said, placing a hand on his shoulder.

"Forget it," he said. "It's all ancient history anyway. We need to go out to the old Harmon property and see if we can figure you out."

"Yeah, that'd be a good idea."

He lifted the green stone from my chest and examined it. "What are these etchings? Any idea what they mean?"

"Etchings?" I asked. "It's just a green stone."

I studied the pendant in the mirror. Shallow carvings in spiral patterns covered the entire back of the stone, and delicate wisps curled around the edges to frame a circle on the front, the center of which contained a triskele, identical to the one that was etched on Harmon's grandmother's journal. As I held the stone and focused on it, a pale, green glow emanated from the spiral patterns, rising up and enveloping my hand like a mist. A low, humming vibration made the small hairs on my arms stand at attention. My surprise at the swelling energy gave way to comfort. I felt warmth through my body as I twisted the stone, manipulating the energy field.

"Do something with it, Kess," Harmon said.

I faced Harmon and willed the flow away from me and over to him. It followed my command, sliding up his arm. He jumped back but then settled as the it wrapped its way over his shoulder, down his spine, and returned to me at my bidding. I released the stone, and the glow faded.

His mouth hung open, and he reached out for the stone again, picking it up off my chest and examining it carefully. "What the hell?"

"I have no idea." I couldn't help but break into a huge smile. "I don't have any idea what just happened, but I think I like it."

"Can you heal this?" Harmon asked, tenderly brushing the side of my face with the backs of his fingers. My stomach flipped like the girl whose crush just finally noticed she existed, and I thought he smiled in response. It had to have been my imagination.

I studied his face, searching for more hints behind his eyes. He was infuriating, unprofessional, and unpredictable. And yet, he had kept me safe, he had my back, and if I truly gave him the credit he was due, he had not once let me down in the two days we'd been partners. Granted, two days is a pretty small sample set, but I realized that for all of his quirks I knew I could count on him.

"You healed me up." Whatever moment of closeness we'd been sharing abruptly ended as he grabbed his toothbrush. "I just figured maybe you could touch yourself up there before the press conference? Otherwise, you're going to be on national news looking like you got ran over."

"I can try."

I took the charm in my hand again and felt the flow of the energy. "It feels different from when I channeled energy from the book," I said.

"Well, what did you do when you healed me?"

"Mostly panicked."

We both laughed.

"Try thinking about what you want," he suggested.

I closed my eyes and concentrated, picturing myself healing, enveloped by green, flowing warmth. The energy stayed at my chest, unwilling to move. It wrapped my hand and danced gently around my wrist. But unlike before, there was no feeling of deep connection with the Earth. No rooting of the soles of my feet, or opening at the crown of my head. The intensity faltered, fizzled and died on my hand. Opening my eyes, I saw I was still just as scarred as when I started.

"How did you get it to come over to me?" Harmon asked.

"I just thought about it. Really, I was just playing around."

"Try that. Maybe you're overthinking it. Just send it up to your face first?"

With eyes closed again, I tried to coax the glow back into my hand and up my arm. My face contorted with frustration.

"Come on!" Harmon said. "Go on, green thing. Go on!"

I dropped my hand to my side and glared at Harmon. He broke into a full belly laugh.

"It's not a dog," I said, "and this is really frustrating!"

"You're right." He forced his face to a serious expression, giving him a rubbery appearance. That broke me. I fell over the sink laughing.

"I give up. I have no idea what I'm doing. For being so *Adept*, I certainly suck at this. The only thing I can think is that Martina was there. Maybe she's helping me more than she's letting on?"

Harmon shook his head, and his expression darkened. "I don't trust her."

"I don't know what to make of her," I said, "but she's the only one who really knows what's happening here."

"And that," he shook his finger at me, "is why I don't trust her. What information has she given you about this idea of being Adept? Or about herself, for that matter?" He rubbed his temples. "Usually I can get inside people's heads pretty quickly and figure out their motives. It's what I do. But I can't read her at all. Not that she's given me much of a chance."

"Yeah, I don't like her little trick of sending you to sleepy-town while she gives *just me* information. And not much information at that," I said.

"Exactly." Harmon crossed behind me and leaned against the doorframe. "So let's figure out what you can do, and how you can do it, without her involvement."

"Maybe it needs some sort of urgency to work." I idly fidgeted with the stone at my breast.

"It works well in a fight. We've seen that twice now."

"Yes," I admitted. "I guess if it only works when the chips are down, I can live with that. I just need to remember it's there for me."

"That would have been helpful last night," he said, his voice flat.

"Would'a, could'a, should'a." I sighed. "Well, hopefully, we can have a nice, easy press conference, and then track down our killer. Then I can get back to San Francisco and be out of your hair. Maybe keep that promise I made myself all those years ago."

He cocked his head to the side, "What's that?"

"I told myself I was never coming back to Gig Harbor when I was a teenager. Now I understand why."

He frowned. "But then I never would have had the opportunity to make you that fantastic breakfast. And you never would have tried a lavender mocha." He paused, looking down at his feet, and quietly added, "I wouldn't have had the chance to get to know you."

The silence stretched between us. I decided I needed to brush my hair again, vigorously, and whip it up into a ponytail. After a few very uncomfortable seconds, he cleared his throat, "What I mean is, we make a good team. You're a good partner."

His phone chimed, and it was a total 'saved by the bell' moment. He scrambled to read it. "Press conference at noon inside the civic center. It's nine forty-five now. We're going to have to get moving. We'll have time to make a quick stop by Shari's on the way."

"Let's try not to lose a car or destroy a building today, shall we?" I said in a vain attempt to lighten the mood between us.

His sinful smile stretched from ear to ear. "Sounds boring."

Chapter 15

We pulled into the driveway of Shari's Bed & Breakfast not knowing what to expect. The last thing I figured I'd see was Martina's truck, but there it sat, off to the side where it had been while Harmon had nearly died.

"Why the hell is she here?" I asked, feeling the hairs rise on the back of my neck.

"Who?"

I looked at Harmon, and pointed back, but my hand dropped. The truck was gone.

"Martina's truck was there. Didn't you see it?"

Harmon looked at me from the corner of his eye. "You sure you didn't hit your head last night?" He parked the car next to Shari's little white Volvo and leaned back against the driver seat headrest.

"I have a feeling someone is messing with our heads again," he said.

"Yeah, I get that feeling, too."

"See why I don't trust Martina?"

I nearly launched into a diatribe about how she was the only help I had, and that I was feeling hopeless but was interrupted by Shari tapping on my window. In startled haste, I flung the door open, and she jumped back more nimbly that I'd think was possible for someone of her stature.

"Oh, blessed be, you're safe!" she said, clasping her hands over her mouth. Her thick, blonde hair was pulled off her face and gathered into a bushy knot at the base of her neck. She wore sweat pants and a zip-up hoodie.

"Yes, and thankfully so are you," I smiled at her, but a thousand questions bombarded my thoughts all at once. I settled on the one I was most interested in having answered first, turning my attention to my cabin. "Did you call the police?"

The cabin door hung half-way off its hinges, the wood splintered and shredded around where the knob was once mounted. Large chunks of door frame lay scattered around the cement slab that served as a front stoop. There was no scene tape. No tracks besides those from our struggle. Nothing. I knew the answer to my question but wanted to hear what she had to say.

"I figured you *are* the police. If they needed to be called, you'd handle it."

Harmon and I shot each other a quick look. His expression said *I don't buy it.*

"Where were you last night, Miss..." Harmon asked, stepping out of the car and coming around the hood to flank me.

"Evans." Shari's smile turned playful. "I had a date. She was a hottie."

Harmon snickered, and I glared at him. "What time did you get home, Miss Evans?" I asked.

"About an hour ago." She kept her impish grin plastered to her face, and her attention trained on Harmon. He stifled another giggle, and I shook my head.

"What did you do when you got home?" I asked.

"I went inside, and I called your director. He's pretty unhappy with you, so you know," she said.

At that, Harmon completely lost it. He fell back against the car, guffawing. Shari seemed to delight in his appreciation for whatever humor he was finding in this conversation. Why he was laughing was beyond me.

"Your partner certainly is the happy type," Shari said with half a smile. "I like happy types." She looked at me for only the briefest of seconds, and then returned her gaze on Harmon. But in that tiny moment, Harmon stopped laughing, if only for a fraction of a second. As soon as she trained her focus on him, he fell into a brand new fit.

"What's going on here?" I asked, crossing my arms.

"Whatever do you mean?" Shari asked, a broad but humorless smile spanning her tanned face. She fixed her eyes on me. Harmon sat on the ground, shaking his head. For the briefest of seconds, I thought her eyes shifted from chocolate brown to lavender and back.

I grabbed her by the hoodie and shoved her up against the car. "I said, what the *hell* is going on here?"

Shari put her hands up in surrender. "Sorry! Guess you don't like happy types!"

I felt Harmon's hand on my shoulder. He pulled me off of Shari and turned me toward him. "Kess, what the hell?"

"I..." My mind whirled and the previous few moments ceased to make sense. I shook my head to clear my thoughts.

"I'm so sorry about my partner, Miss?" Harmon's voice sounded like a far-off echo.

"Evans," I heard Shari repeat.

"We will look into this break-in. I'll send over a unit later today if that works for you."

Words formed in my mouth, but it refused to open. *Don't let her walk away.*

I reached for the power within and found it surging and pulsing just behind an invisible dam. I poked and prodded and tried to edge around the wall, but it wouldn't flow through that barrier that seemed limitless in its expanse. The world outside was just as distant, like fog over glass. The conversation between Shari and Harmon faded to near silence, and their lips moved in slow motion. She turned and walked away, sauntered up her cabin steps and closed the door behind her.

"What?" I asked. Harmon was talking. I was pretty sure the word hadn't actually come out of my mouth.

"Snap out of it!" He had me by both shoulders. "What's happening? Kessa!"

Urgency rang in his voice. I finally found words nestled in the haze that shrouded my mind, but I spoke like tree sap through cheesecloth. "You let her walk away."

"Who?" Harmon asked.

"Who do you think?" Slightly easier to speak, the power behind my words returned. "Shari! She was here. And you were talking."

"No one's home, Kess."

I looked over at Shari's cabin, and her car was gone. My fists formed balls, and I felt a shudder rock my whole body. I inhaled deep and slow, and let the breath out fully. The power inside me bubbled and churned, threatening to let loose. The wall holding it back was suddenly gone. I was back in my own control.

I turned to Harmon and grasped his shoulder. "Tell me exactly what you think happened."

"You're starting to scare me."

"Shut up and just tell me!" I yelled, giving his shoulder a shake.

"That's the Kessa I know and love." He laughed nervously. "But you're still worrying me. We just got here. No one home. No sign of police being called. No Shari. And then you just froze."

"She was here, Harmon."

He gave me a blank look as I recalled my version of the prior moments.

"What the hell happened, then?" he asked after a long pause.

"Honestly, I don't know. But whatever Shari is, it's similar to Martina. The shift of color in her eyes—I've seen that before. And Martina mentioned the 'others' a couple times. I have a feeling this place has some sort of connection to the other side, and I'm starting to feel surrounded."

"I don't like that they can get inside our heads," Harmon said, scanning the ground for tracks or anything that might corroborate my story. "Profiling is my job, not theirs," he added without a hint of humor.

"Tell me about it. I've seen Martina do it to you, and now I've had it done to me."

"Only difference," Harmon said, tapping the side of my head once, "is that you remember all of it. Hazy as it may be, at least you know what happened. I've really got nothing."

"We'll just chalk that up to a slight advantage," I said. "Maybe if we can figure out what they are, and what they do, we can find a way to shield you from it."

"Maybe." Harmon's tone said that he sincerely doubted our odds. "Let's just get out to the press conference."

Chapter 16

The Key Peninsula civic center looked more like a retirement home than any community building I was used to. In San Francisco, facilities like these easily accommodated groups in the thousands, if not tens-of-thousands. The small, rectangular building, with its gray, shingled sides trimmed in faded blue stood on a vast expanse of lime-green grass. Flanked by native forest, the center reflected the area's rugged realism. It, like its surrounding people, didn't try to be anything other than exactly what it was. I could picture the hall hosting spaghetti dinners and square dances. The lawn was, no doubt, a favorite locale for farmer co-ops and flea markets on sunny summer weekends.

The parking lot hosted news vans from every channel parked haphazardly, in no way respecting the faded white lines. Crew members teemed about their vehicles, running cables and adjusting antennas. Reporters stood uneasily in dress shoes and slacks on packed gravel, talking into microphones the size of grapefruits while camera crewmen balanced massive video cameras on their shoulders with practiced ease. A pair of helicopters circled above, carefully avoiding each other's path. Harmon drove around to the service entrance of the building in an attempt to avoid the awaiting throng. They would have their chance, but reporters were not known for their patience, and would take advantage of an early opportunity at a story. The local police force guarded our entrance to ensure secure passage into the hall.

Schild met us at the rear door and escorted us inside. The potpourri of cinnamon and pine gagged me with its potency. The first Christmas adornments hung on office doors. "I guess the season of joy starts early around here," I commented.

"Earlier every year," Schild said. "They have you in the main hall. Should be big enough. That's one hell of a crowd."

I mumbled a wordless agreement while struggling to pull the strings of a credible story together in my mind. Harmon and I had discussed what we should say on the drive. Everything we came up with felt contrived, with more holes than Swiss cheese. We had commented on how most of the FBI's official reports were similarly constructed, and that the press would most likely just take it as our typical snowball job.

The small raised stage featured a lectern, much like those used by college professors. A potted tropical tree next to the podium, with its broad, dark-green leaves, looked very out of place given the surrounding conifer forest. A pull-down screen hung on the wall, configured for video from an overhead projector. I took my place behind the lectern and put on a practiced "FBI official" expression. Harmon stood at parade rest to my right with a matching look on his face. He had elected to wear a suit and tie for the occasion. The effect was startling. He actually looked professional.

Schild fidgeted at my left, clearly unused to the type of event about to be hosted. He asked, "You ready? Should I open the doors?"

I nodded my approval and scanned the room quickly, making note of the exits. The door behind us led back to the car. In the event of an emergency, that was our first choice of escape. The main, double-doors presumably opened into a foyer, which would no doubt empty onto the front porch of the building. An entrance with hinged saloon doors opened through the inner wall, with a sign above that read 'Kitchen. Staff only please.' Three large windows on the outer wall provided a view of the parking lot. The room itself was large and empty, without even the benefit of folding chairs. It was a not-so-subtle hint to our representatives of mass media that this was not going to be an all-day affair.

The doors opened, and reporters by the dozen filed in and took their places around the room. I scanned the crowd and found who I was looking for: Martina managed to push her way to the front. She smiled, and I gave no response save for an eye-contact acknowledgement of my notice of her presence.

The room buzzed with low conversation, and a sea of digital recorders emerged. I held up a hand, and silence spread across the room from front to back.

"Earlier this week, Senator William F. Mansfield's body was discovered on the Key Peninsula near the intersection of the highway and 84th Street." A blast of camera flashes threatened to blind me as I continued. "The official cause of death is exsanguination, with the suspected murder weapon being a sharp, square metal implement. As of yet, the murder weapon has not been found. Additionally, the body of local resident Virginia Harmon was found in her home with similar wounds and the same cause of death. Autopsy reports confirm that Ms. Harmon died approximately twelve hours after Senator Mansfield. The senator's body was discovered by a local child, who, by request of his family, will remain anonymous. We appreciate the press's cooperation with this family. We are currently investigating possible suspects, and will provide more information as facts become available. The Bureau and local law enforcement ask that you please refrain from speculation at this time."

As I finished talking, hands shot up across the room. Fielding questions was the part of the job I hated the most. Reporters were famous for their lack of tact. But I did my part and pointed at a slender woman in a form-fitting red blazer in the front row. Her voice recorder, which she held at arm's length toward me, bore a national news affiliate sticker.

"Rumor has it that both victims were covered in claw and bite marks. Can you confirm the possibility of an animal attack in conjunction with the official cause of death?"

I stifled the urge to sigh. The only way these people got this information was through blabber-mouth rural cops who don't understand what it is to investigate a high-profile case. "I cannot confirm an animal attack. Next question?"

A white-haired man in a gray suit, his teeth too perfect, pushed his way to the front. "The Rushing family has good reason to be rid of the senator, seeing as how Justin Rushing is part of the Lumber League. Are they suspects?"

This one had done way too much homework. "We cannot discuss local residents or possible suspects at this time, as we are still investigating. Next."

My words caught in my mouth as the double doors at the back of the room flew open. An elderly man pushed through. He stood tall and his very presence commanded attention. He wore jeans and a blue flannel shirt that sparked fear deep inside. It was the same outfit worn by our wolf, down to the mud-encrusted work boots. In his left hand, he held Ginny Harmon's journal. His right, gloved hand clutched a silver chain, from which a locket dangled.

Harmon's face twisted up in confusion. "Kessa," he whispered, "that looks like..."

"Our wolf, I know. Only now he's human?"

He shook his head and ran a hand through his hair. Before he could speak, the man opened the journal and started chanting. Low, deep and rasping, his words coursed through the room. A hum of energy crackled. The crowd of reporters regarded him with interest, turning video and voice recorders toward this intruder. Some pushed through, trying to get a better view.

Martina hopped up onto the stage. "This is not good," she said.

"You think?" I asked. "We need to get these people out of here."

"I don't think we're going to get that chance."

As the man chanted, the book began to glow. But, where it had shone green and white for me, his words brought forth a swirling inky blue. From the locket, a stream of midnight circled in the air in front of him, stabilizing into a swirling vortex. A stream of black, like semi-transparent tar, issued forth from this portal he'd created. It pooled on the floor and took form. The creature stood waist-high on all fours, with a wraith-like body and the face of a feral dog. It was a being of pure energy, smooth and ethereal, and yet radiating strength. Cries of shock and horror erupted from the journalists, who scrambled backward over each other, trying to distance themselves from this unfathomable nightmare.

The beast let loose a howl that sent the crowd into a frenzy of screams and shoving. Several people darted for the kitchen. One stocky camera man fought with a window that probably hadn't been opened since it was installed. Voice recorders and cell phones clattered to the floor as the beast lunged. It overtook an Asian man and began pawing and biting at his torso. A tentacle from the beast's mid-body raised up and changed form into a long, angular spike, which it plunged into its victim's heart. No blood flowed from where the beast struck, but the screams elicited by the attack made it clear that the beast was cutting deep into the man's soul.

Martina screamed in my ear, "Kessa! Use your Earth stone. Call on the Ancestors. *Now!*"

As I reached for the stone at my neck, I yelled at Harmon, "Take him out!"

Harmon was standing stock still, his mouth open. Schild had long since bolted through the kitchen doors. The elderly man at the back of the room held up his locket and continued chanting, issuing forth another black beast from the portal. And another. And another. They circled their prey—the handful of reporters who were unlucky enough to be at the back of the crowd trying to push into the kitchen—and they latched on.

I felt power surge from my Earth stone. My eyes blinked slowly, and my vision changed. A haze floated on the air like someone had forgotten to open a chimney flue, but there was no smoky smell. Martina resonated a rose-colored glow. Her features changed abruptly to a lavender-colored, tall and lanky body. Her almond-shaped eyes and high cheek bones were similar to what I'd seen on her in the Ancestral land, but she lacked the swirling tattoos and lithe figure.

The beasts that circled the remaining reporters glowed with a hazy, shimmery darkness. Our attacker shifted in this spectrum, alternating between the form of a man, and the form of one of the circling beasts.

"What am I supposed to do?" I pleaded at Martina. My shout attracted all the wrong attention.

One of the beasts ceased its assault on the woman in the red blazer and turned its azure gaze directly on me. It stalked toward the stage with singular purpose. Harmon leveled his gun and fired off two shots. The screams from the remaining reporters became more frenzied at the sound of gunfire. The bullets whizzed straight through the beast and embedded into the floor.

"Ask for help, Kessa! They won't help you unless you ask!"

The beast edged in closer, circling like a wolf around rabbit's nest. Its extra appendage curved and danced. It fixated upon me and closed the distance.

Harmon jumped from the stage, intent on grappling with this unknown foe. I shouted for him to hold his position, but he ignored me and persisted with his futile attack. His arms failed to grasp the neck of the beast, but the creature's paw struck Harmon's face with full force, rocketing him backward. It pounced and clamped its powerful jaw on his shoulder. He writhed under the mass of the creature, gritting his teeth and flailing to grab hold of the incorporeal form of his attacker.

I held the stone in my hand and squeezed my eyes shut. "Ancients, I need you. Now! Please! Help me!"

The silliness I felt at my own words was quickly erased by the flood of power that welled within me. I held out my hand, upright and cupped, and watched with awe as a cold, white flame licked up my fingers. With my palm outward, I pushed the energy at the beast. The creature's spike pierced the surface of Harmon's chest just as the blast of white fire propelled it backward against the wall. Harmon's agonized scream flooded my ears, and I watched him writhe on the floor.

The man intensified his chanting, and the beasts pulled back for the portal, retreating one by one. For a moment, I thought my show of bravado had dissuaded him from further attack.

I really hate it when I'm *that* wrong.

The victims of the beast were all that remained in the room with us. Wet, cracking sounds, accompanied by rasping cries and groans arose from the lot of them. Their bodies contorted and disfigured, with arms and legs lengthening and joints protruding at odd angles. Thick, grey hair sprouted from their limbs and torsos, and their faces warped into dog-like snouts, round eyes, and pointed ears.

The Asian reporter, who had fallen first, was also the first to rise in his new werewolf form. His jaw dripped with thick, white spittle as he locked his attention on me.

The elder ordered, "Kill the women, but keep the man alive." The newly risen beast rushed forward on command. I held out my energized hand and let forth another blast to counter his attack.

He dodged my bolt with the dexterity of a trapeze artist. He sprang up into the air, pushed off the wall and landed in a crouch before me, his chest heaving. The others were completing their transformations and turning to attack as well. The one before me took a swipe at me, and I ducked backward, attempting to harness another magical discharge. My avoidance wasn't as good as I'd thought it would be, and pain erupted from my abdomen. The beast's claws shredded fabric and skin alike. It came for me a second time, and I tucked and rolled as Martina delivered a solid kick to the back of its head that sent it splayed and stunned onto the stage.

"There's too many of them!" she shouted.

"Damned straight!" I replied.

"Get us out of here!"

A vision of escape entered my mind, and suddenly I understood precisely what she wanted me to do. I focused all of my energy on the closest window and let loose a blast of power. The window, the wall, and part of the floor disintegrated at my insistence. Martina dove past me and scooped up Harmon like a rag doll, throwing him over her shoulders in a fireman's carry. We sprinted out the newly-made exit with the sound of scrambling claws, yaps and snarls chasing behind us.

"This way!" She shouted.

Her blue truck sat parked like it had been our planned escape vehicle. I didn't remember seeing it among the vans in the lot earlier.

She chucked Harmon into the bed of the truck, and I jumped up over the edge. She dove into the open door, and the engine roared to life. The tires sprayed gravel toward one of the beasts as she clambered onto the bumper. The woman in red, her blazer now hanging in shredded pieces, held the tailgate with one clawed hand as she swiped at me with the other. I harnessed the energy still coursing through me and directed it at her torso. I intended to lose her from the back of the truck as we sped out onto the main road. Instead, I lost both her and the tailgate.

Harmon started to sit up, and I pushed him back down.

"Stay still, we're safe for now."

I noticed he had a faint energy aura much like the beasts that were now fading in the distance behind us. I watched him closely while we bumped down the highway, wondering if he was going to start changing into one of those beasts. His chest heaved with labored breaths, but he seemed otherwise unaffected.

"You still with us?" I asked, tentatively.

He pawed at his shoulder and chest. "I think so. That thing, though. It got me."

"No, I got *it*," I said, suddenly feeling accomplished.

"I don't feel right."

"You'll be fine, but that was a pretty nasty attack." I winced at the very recent memory of Harmon screaming in agony. "Just keep your head down. Rest. I've got you covered. Not sure where we're headed, though."

I banged on the sliding rear window, and Martina craned a hand around to open it. "What's next?" I asked.

"I was hoping you had an idea. I'm just driving."

"The grove," Harmon said. "Tell her to take us to my grandparent's old place."

While it seemed like the worst idea in the long dark history of bad ideas, something deep within me said to listen to him. I'd spent a good deal of time at the beginning of this case doubting him, and he'd gotten beaten up a few times now. I owed him one.

I nodded and gave her brief directions to my uncle's property, then on to the power line road just beyond that led into the woods where the old house had stood in its clearing. Whatever was there might give us some answers, or might just be another dead end. At any rate, the property was abandoned and promised a decent hiding spot.

Again, I hate being so very wrong.

Chapter 17

The power line road that once served as an access conduit to the older properties of the Key Peninsula was the only stretch of well-kept ground in the area. Thick overgrowth masked decades-old driveways and long-forgotten trails. Harmon sat up at attention as we passed under an impossibly tall electrical tower that hummed with pulsing energy. I wasn't sure if it was just me, or if I was feeling the electricity.

"Here," Harmon said. I banged on the window, and Martina stopped the truck.

I hopped out of the bed and offered Harmon my hand.

"I'm fine," he grumbled, stumbling to the ground. He caught himself on the truck's bumper to steady his stance, and then visually scanned the thick salal undergrowth. "It's right around here somewhere."

Martina climbed out of the cab and aided us in our search for the ages-old driveway. "We might just have to push through the undergrowth," she said.

"Wait, what's this?" I pulled some bushes aside to reveal a decaying for-sale sign. "The bushes aren't quite as thick here. This might be it."

"Grams talked about selling this place. Looks like she tried. Though it doesn't seem a whole lot of people took notice."

We waded through the scrub until crossing a trampled trail. "Is this the trail that led to my uncle's house?" I asked. Harmon nodded, and I pointed at a distinct shoe print, "looks like it's been used recently."

"The grove is right through here. I had my tree stand over that way." He pointed up and to the right. Far up in the trees, the remnants of a cobbled-together wooden structure hung from branches that had dismantled it through years of slow growth. We followed Harmon as he led us through the alder ring and into the clearing.

The dilapidated little white house stood right where I remembered. Beside it, a rusted-out Caterpillar backhoe had become more of a planter for weeds than a useful piece of construction equipment.

"I thought you said the house was demolished," I said.

"I thought it was."

We crossed to the tractor. Harmon ran his hands up the metal cowl, fingering at the rust holes. "Abandoned, and by the looks of it, for a long time."

"That might be abandoned," Martina said, "but the house, not so much."

Wisps of smoke trailed from the little stone chimney that still stood at attention above the sagging roof.

"I have an exceedingly bad feeling about this," I said.

"Yeah, same here," Harmon agreed, jogging over to the window. "Déjà vu, huh?"

I nodded, remembering we'd had much the same conversation the first time we'd visited the grove together. Only on that day, it was me who had noticed the chimney smoke.

Martina sidled up beside me and nearly whispered, "Change your sight like you did at the civic center. You need to look at his aura."

"I know," I said. "I saw it in the truck. Whatever that thing was, it got him. He knows it, too. But for some reason, he didn't change with the others."

"It's uncommon, but it can happen, that one can be touched by a Fae demon and be afflicted, but not entirely overtaken. It's a lot like planting a seed. The essence will grow, and it will become either a thorn bush or a blossom, depending on what was planted, and how deep it's rooted."

"I'm not sure what that means."

"It means that to eradicate the Fae energy within him, he's going to have to choose. Because it's a demonic affliction, it will tempt him with strength and power. If he gives in, the baowal energy will overtake him, and he'll change."

"The what?" I asked.

"Baowal. They are Fae beings from the Fel region. That's what came through the portal and attacked Harmon. That's what's afflicting the townsman and those reporters. And that is what is coursing through your partner, searching his psyche for darkness so it can latch on. Tell me, do you know of anything in his life that might be causing fear, hatred or anguish?"

"Well, his only living relative just died, so I think the answer to that is a resounding yes."

"Kessa," Harmon shouted from beside the window, waving me over.

Martina and I gave each other a shrug and plodded through the thick weeds to the side of the house.

"Oh my god, Harmon," I said, peering through the window, "it looks just like it did when we were kids!" My heart stuck in my throat and for a moment I was fifteen years old again. With the exception of the window now being completely broken out, everything was identical to how it had been.

Yellow wallpaper dotted with white daisies peeled from the walls. Mold spread across the corners and roof-edge of the walls. Slat-board floors sagged under years of ill repair. A plaque hung on the stone hearth with five arrows, tip to fletch in a star pattern, surrounded by a circle of braided twigs. The fireplace smoldered as it had the first time I'd peeked through the window, with the same black cauldron hanging above glowing embers. My stomach turned at the same, sweet smell from the brew that I remembered all too well. Like someone had set a pot of potpourri in water and forgot about it for several months.

"It's like we never left."

"Not exactly," he said. "Take a close look at the cauldron."

The swing arm over the fireplace was still the same, but the pot that hung from it was now permanently affixed. "Looks like someone welded it in place."

"I guess our wolf-man didn't like you disrupting his culinary practices all those years ago?" Harmon offered.

Martina poked her head up beside me and immediately recoiled, her hand flying to cover her mouth and nose. She choked and gagged, bent over at the waist.

"Desecration of foxglove in iron," she choked.

"You have any idea what that means?" Harmon asked.

"None," I replied.

Martina slid along the side of the house until she was away from the window, and sat with her back against the wall, feet tucked underneath her. She flopped her head back and closed her eyes, taking greedy breaths of clean air. "Foxglove is sacred to the Ancients. The energy of the brew is meant to desecrate the Ancestral spirit in this grove, disallowing our aid here." She looked directly at me. "Your powers will be useless inside this grove as long as that cauldron stays heated."

I fingered the stone at my throat uneasily. "So when these guys come home, if we're still here, we're going to have to fight them fair?"

"Looks like we get to find out," Harmon pointed.

I followed his gesture and saw them approaching from the far side of the grove. Nine wolf-like figures—if wolves walked upright and wore tattered clothing—stood in the clearing in a V formation with our familiar werewolf leading the pack. They looked from one to another, until the one to the right of the leader let loose a chilling howl. The others picked up the chorus, but none made a move.

"We're toast," I said.

"Maybe not," Martina countered. "I can get both of you through to the Fade, but it's risky. They won't be able to cross without releasing their embodied spirits from the host, and they won't take that risk. We, however, will end up in the Fade."

"Is it a better option than getting shredded alive?" I asked, as the pack dropped to all fours and slowly stalked toward us.

"Possibly," she said. "We definitely have a slim chance of getting both of you through alive."

The pack broke into a trot and fanned out, forming a perimeter and trapping us against the building.

"I guess that sounds like a plan," I said. "Harmon?"

In my deep concentration concerning any plan for escape, I'd failed to notice that Harmon's expression had gone feral. His eyes clouded over, and he crouched with one hand on the ground, looking at me with hunger in his eyes. His lips pulled back, revealing clenched teeth.

"Harmon!" Martina shouted. "Snap out of it! Concentrate!"

She sprung to her knees and grabbed his face with both hands, looking eye to eye at him, her face mere inches from his.

The wolfs closed in on us, walking zig-zag patterns, presumably to show that they had us trapped. Their eyes never left us, and their yaps turned to growls as they edged closer. I pulled myself closer to the wall.

"Martina, we have to do this—whatever it is you're going to do. They look like they're about to spring!"

Martina slapped Harmon with hard across his cheek.

"What the hell did you do that for?" He demanded.

"Good, you're back with us. Now grab my arm so I can get us out of here!" She pointed toward the pack as they ran forward in long strides.

We latched onto Martina, and she began to chant. A dark chorus of wolf song rang out across the glade as they bore down on us, springing their trap. The foremost wolf leapt, and the others followed suit. I instinctively went to reach for my gun.

"No!" Martina yelled, "don't let go!"

The first of the wolves reached us. I closed my eyes and braced for impact.

Suddenly, my stomach wretched into my throat as I felt the sensation of falling upward. The back of my neck felt like it was going to erupt and my mouth ran dry. The world spun, and I reached out to brace myself against the wall, but it was gone.

I opened one eye tentatively, then the other. The three of us were in the glade, but the air had taken on that wispy, hazy appearance I'd experienced on my first visit across the realms.

"We're in the Fade," Martina said, "and we need to move. There are many beings here that will sense your presence and come for you."

"From the Fel region?" I asked.

"Some, but most are denizens of the Fade."

"What is this place?" I asked.

"Think of it as a series of passageways between the worlds," Martina answered. "It grows from the root of The Ancient, and it spans across the realms. But there are many dwellers here, and they prey on humans. Your lore is full of stories where the faery of the Fade have trapped and kept mortals indefinitely."

"Come away, O human child?" Harmon asked. "I always thought that was just an awesome poem."

"It's very real," Martina said. "Yeats' own capture and escape inspired his famous verse. And while some of the Fae folk might give you the paradise that Yeats described, others will delight in your eternity of torture. Most just want to use you for their own personal gain."

"Sounds pleasant," Harmon said. "Let's move."

The barren path beneath us stretched into the hazy visage of the house. Martina led us directly through it as though it weren't even there. As we ran, I realized that the Earth objects stood shrouded, much as when a graphics artist applies a transparency filter. Solid objects became illusory doorways. However, the ground beneath never failed to catch our footfalls, and it appeared much more opaque. Eventually, the earthly constructs gave way to a pathway running between impossibly tall trees. Looking behind us, I was surprised to see that all traces of the grove had vanished.

"We've picked up a tail," Martina said, glancing over her shoulder. "Whatever you do, don't interact with anything here! And don't accept anything from any of the faery. Not even a flower or twig, and especially do not eat any food or drink offered. Taking a faery offering solidifies their hold on you and makes you complacent to them, regardless of their demands."

I looked back but saw nothing following us. Martina's eyes saw more than ours did; I was certain.

"We're interacting with you," Harmon said. "What makes you so special?"

Martina leveled her gaze on Harmon, ceasing her constant scanning. "I'm helping Kessa, am I not? Have I harmed you? It's my choice to assist you. I could keep you here, too, if I wanted."

"You gave her the Earth Stone, though, correct? Does it grant you some sort of control over her?"

"Harmon," I said, "we don't have time for this." Irritation flushed my cheeks, and I wrapped my fingers protectively around the stone.

Martina and Harmon faced off, and I felt his anger and distrust. The sensation startled me; it was like I saw through his eyes for a brief moment and understood exactly the depth of his distrust as if the feeling were my own.

Red alert bells sounded in my mind, but before I could speak, a tall, thin, grayish-green being slid out from between the trees, blocking our path. Its skin, if you could call it that, gave the appearance of smooth yet peeling tree bark. Its acutely angular face held a long, branch-like nose. Deep green leaves sprouted from gangly arms and legs. Its mouth sat askew. Eyes of moss green radiated from deep within sockets that could only be compared to tree knots.

"You have one among you who is tainted," the creature stated, speaking to Martina alone. "He is a danger to the Fade, and to all other planes in conjunction. He is of the Fel. Do you take him there now?"

Martina bowed gracefully. "Great Sentinel, he is yet to be tested. He is afflicted only partially, and he knows not yet what challenge lies before him."

"Are they talking about me?" Harmon whispered, glancing over at me nervously.

"Yes. Shush."

"I shall take him from you, and deliver him myself," the tree creature stated, holding out a branchy finger.

"Excuse me, do I have a say in this?" Harmon asked, stepping forward. Martina stood from her bow and straight-armed Harmon across his chest, causing him to stumble backward.

"You protect this abomination?"

"He is within my sphere of control."

"Like hell, I…"

Martina sucker-punched Harmon, causing him to double over with a grunt. He took the hint and decided not to press it any further.

"And the other?" The creature turned his gaze upon me. "She wears an Ancestral relic. Is she yours as well?"

"I have taken it upon myself to serve as her advisor. She is a fledgling Adept."

The creature brought a hand to its mouth in contemplation. One eyebrow arched with a crack. "And why do you pass through the Fade?"

"Baowals have entered the physical realm. We only pass through to make an escape. This one seeks the Ancestral Lands," she motioned to me, and I bowed awkwardly, "and a blessing of passage from the Grandfather Tree. The grove on Earth in which the baowals reside is desecrated, thus untethered from the Ancestral Lands. It now links with the Fade. I request your assistance and approval of passage, Grand Sentinel, and promise that I shall keep control of my charges."

She bowed deeply again and looked over at me. I took the cue and bowed as well. Harmon was late to the party, but followed suit, though he watched me intently. We stood like that for what felt like an eternity. Finally, the tree-being spoke.

"You shall have passage, but do not bring the tainted one back to the Fade without him first deciding. As we speak, nyads draw close. They know him by his scent, and would release him upon us. He would wreak havoc on the balance here."

"You have my unyielding promise."

"Keep your promise true, young one. I sense that you are tested, too. You may rise."

Martina stood upright, and we both did likewise. The Grand Sentinel held out an arm, issuing us forward.

When we were out of earshot—not that it had ears, per se—I asked, "What exactly are nyads? And more importantly, where are we going?"

"Nyads are faery of the Fade who cause strife and anguish to anyone who passes through. They are ancient beings, and the war with them has raged for longer than humans have walked the Earth."

"So, they would be the ones to enjoy torturing us?" Harmon asked.

"Precisely."

"What did he mean about you being tested?" I asked Martina.

"Better yet, tell us again how you're not attempting this faery mind control after telling that walking stump we were your *charges*," Harmon said. I didn't argue; the thought pressed on my mind as well.

Martina avoided eye contact and quickened her pace to a jog. "Taking on an Adept is tasking," she finally answered, "and Harmon, I don't think you would have enjoyed the trip to the Fel with the Sentinel. I had to say something."

I didn't buy it, but for the moment I chose not to argue. Something didn't add up, but I couldn't put a finger on it. At that moment, I'd have given anything for just a few moments alone with Harmon to mull over some thoughts, but that wasn't going to happen.

Silence stretched among the three of us as we continued on the path. The forest of silver trunks stretched up higher than the eye could see. The first boughs grew no closer than fifty feet overhead, covered in a dense mesh of the same gray-green needles that padded the trail. Pockets of dim light dotted the path, but we mostly walked through a hazy dusk. The time of day was impossible to discern, and I wasn't sure what the source of the light even was.

"Is anyone going to explain this *taint* to me?" Harmon asked.

Martina sighed. "You were attacked by a baowal, and now you're afflicted. However, it was not able to overtake your soul and fully possess you like it did the others. You have not been fully assimilated. The connection, however, is within you, and you will need to choose."

"Forgive me for being dense, but I don't get it. Choose what?"

"You have to figure out if you're one of the good guys, or one of the bad guys," I said.

"More or less," Martina agreed. "The power you'll start to feel will be deliciously tempting," Her mouth pulled into a razor of a humorless smile. "It will grant you with new abilities, and you'll feel like you have an edge. It'll tell you that you want what it has to offer, that you need it. But in the end, it's you who are desired. To beat it, you're going to have to withstand the temptation, and actively choose to release it from your soul."

"Okay, well, I choose to release it now. There's nothing tempting about this at all. I feel like an emo teenager."

"It's not that simple," Martina said. "You have to choose while it is tempting you. It's done so once already."

Harmon looked genuinely perplexed. "It has? When?"

"Don't you remember getting smacked upside the head?" I asked. Harmon shook his head.

"I'm sure he doesn't," Martina said. "You will need to maintain complete awareness. The affliction within you—the taint—will seem to fit naturally, and the longer it's within you, the more a part of you it will become. It is like any Fae energy, born of natural elements. And thus, detecting its presence is difficult. The taint is now a part of your aura—the very energy that makes up your being."

Harmon grinned, "So it's kind of like giving up a bad habit?"

"In the simplest terms, I suppose so."

"Well, I managed to quit smoking. I'll kick this, too."

As the two of them talked, their voices faded into the background. A gentle tune, sweet and lilting, filled my mind. The scent of fresh blueberry muffins caused my mouth to water, and I was suddenly five years old in my auntie's kitchen, sitting on the floor by the oven. Green and gold linoleum sprang up beneath me, and I waited, tracing circles on the floor with my finger. My mind registered it as vaguely curious, but those muffins were almost done. I just had to wait a few minutes. Auntie always said I was impatient, and that I needed to learn how to wait. I was going to show her!

A ring of fat blue mushrooms cropped up around me in a nearly-complete circle, and I sat twirling a finger in my hair, contemplating them. The little gap in the ring served as a doorway for a squat, round gray creature with apple dumpling cheeks. He wore a blue mushroom hat and carried a basket bursting with steaming-hot pastries. Auntie's muffins rode on top like first prize. I reached a chubby hand out, eagerly anticipating the treat that had become our Saturday ritual while Mommy was catching up at the firm.

The funny little baker grinned; sharp teeth glinted with a thin sheen of saliva. He presented the muffin on an open palm, and I strained to grasp it.

Pain shot up my arm as Harmon grabbed my hand in a full dive. My head cleared as we tumbled together and slammed up against an invisible barrier at the edge of the mushroom ring. From the corner of my eye, I caught sight of Martina, delivering a round-house kick to topple the basket from the arms of the grotesque little faery standing just inside the ring's entrance.

"Run!" Martina yelled. "I can't hold this one off for long!"

"What the hell is that?" I asked.

"Nyad! Run!" The creature grappled Martina and shoved her to the ground.

Harmon pulled me to my feet, and we sprinted through the opening of the ring while Martina grappled with the faery.

"Keep running, up the path. Same way we were going!" She flipped the nyad over, and it immediately retaliated. It was faster and nimbler than its podgy stature suggested, and it landed a blow squarely into Martina's stomach, doubling her over.

"We need to get out of here before we don't have the chance," Harmon said.

"What about Martina?" I protested, but only lightly. I certainly didn't want to slow my escape.

"I'm sure she can handle it. This is her turf, not ours."

We rounded a bend in the trail, and directly ahead stood the tall white alder from my dream. I ventured a glance behind us. More than a dozen nyads tore up the trail toward us.

"We've got company," I said through labored breaths.

"Keep moving! I don't know how close they need to be to do whatever it was they just tried on you, and I don't want to find out!"

Harmon bolted into a full sprint, and I struggled to match his speed. He started to pull away but slowed when he realized I couldn't keep up. He let me overtake him and stayed just behind me. The clambering sound of dozens of feet grew louder behind us. The Grandfather Tree edged closer.

When we crossed the threshold into the Ancestral Lands, the air around us shifted. It became warmer, and a sudden tranquility crept over me. I came to a dead stop.

"What the hell are you doing? Run!" Harmon grabbed my hand, but I pulled back.

"You can stop. We're safe now."

"But…" Harmon turned and saw that our pursuers stalked about the trail head, shouting silent insults through a barrier that was impenetrable to them.

"They can't cross over," I said.

"And you know this because?"

"I have no idea," I admitted. "We're allowed to cross planes, but for whatever reason, they can't. Don't ask me how I know. I just do."

I hadn't realized how cold the Fade had been, but the goose bumps on my skin were a testament to the fact that we had just encountered a change in air temperature.

"Let's get to the tree," I suggested.

"And then what?"

"I have an idea."

In all honesty, I had no clue if what I'd planned would work. I'd only been in the Ancestral Lands once before, and it was entirely Martina who had brought me in and sent me back out. I strained to look past the throng of hungry nyads, clambering over each other for a better look at us, their prey. There was no sign of Martina on the trail.

I ran for the tree, even though the creatures couldn't reach us. Running away felt appropriate. At the base of the massive trunk, I knelt down and grasped the Earth stone. "Grandfather Tree, great Ancestral Spirit, please come to my aid."

Nothing.

"That isn't working," Harmon said.

"No shit!"

"It sounded ridiculous."

"You have a better idea?"

"How did you get out last time?" Harmon asked, poking at the tree. "Is there like a secret knot or something?"

I laughed without humor. "That would be something, but I don't think so. Last time, I just woke up. But my body was there, and I guess my soul was here?"

"Is that a question? Because I don't know the answer."

I sighed. "I know you don't. But neither do I, Harmon. I didn't even believe in this type of thing until this morning!"

"Well, I do, and I always have. But that doesn't mean I want to be a permanent resident." His breathing intensified and his shoulders tensed.

"What if I can't get us back?" I asked, more to myself than to Harmon.

"No. No! That's not acceptable. There has to be something you can do." I felt his anger in waves like desert heat pouring off the sand at midday.

"Harmon, you need to calm down. You're ramping up again; I can tell. What are you planning on doing?" I asked, exasperated.

"Maybe I can shoot those things. Then we can go back the way we came."

Harmon drew his weapon, and the milling mass of nyads came to a standstill. A shocked gasp rippled across their numbers, and then they pushed against the barrier, gnashing their teeth and swiping with their claws. Harmon's pupils dilated, the black centers nearly engulfing his crystal blue irises. He turned the weapon over in his hand and looked from me to the nyads and back. I felt his internal struggle along with him.

"Harmon?" I asked tentatively. He glanced up and to the left and began mumbling.

I grabbed his shoulder and shook him. "The taint, Harmon! You need to resist it."

He looked at me with a flash of confusion, his brow wrinkled. His eyes darkened another shade. He slowly raised his weapon, and pointed it directly at me, his lips curling into a wicked smile.

I put my hands up. "Harmon. It's me. Kessa. Your partner. Put your gun down, Harmon. You don't want to do this."

Harmon craned his head back to one side, and his mouth ripped into an open gape. A furious, pained roar erupted from the depths of his lungs, and he spun, emptying his clip into the mass of nyads. The bullets flew freely through the divide between the realms and struck home in several of the creatures. They lunged backward, scrambling for cover behind trees. Harmon cried out and continued firing long after his clip was empty.

I pushed his arm down. His chest heaved as he turned to look at me, his black hair plastered to his forehead with sweat.

"You in there?" I asked, my voice wavering.

"Kessa? What happened?"

"Nothing good, I'm afraid. But it could have been a lot worse. I don't think you actually killed any of those creatures. Thankfully you didn't kill me, either."

We sat at the base of the Grandfather Tree, using the spacious trunk as a backrest.

"I guess we just wait here," I said. "I hope Martina didn't die on us back there, or we're going to have one interesting existence from here on out."

"We totally failed," Harmon said.

"How's that?"

"We lost a car and destroyed a building today."

"At least we're consistent," I said.

Neither of us laughed.

Chapter 18

It wasn't until Martina crossed the boundary from the Fade that I realized the nyads had given up their chase, presumably losing interest after figuring out that we weren't going to go wandering back into their huddle. Martina dragged herself up the trail, clutching one arm. Deep green blood oozed from the gashes that lined her skin. She walked with a limp, carrying her right foot askew.

"You made it," she said with a relieved sigh.

"So did you," I was equally pleased. "We tried to get out of here, but I have no idea how."

"Just barely made it. Nyads aren't known for their kindness when they don't get their way. But then again, neither am I."

"Can we get out of here?" Harmon asked, still sitting against the base of the Grandfather Tree with his eyes closed.

"Yes, we can, the same way we came in."

"So you're saying," Harmon stood and leveled his gaze with Martina, "If you had bit it back there, we'd be stuck here for the very short remainder of our lives?"

"There are others who might help," Martina said, a dismissive air overtook her voice. "One would eventually have been called to your aid by the Sentinels."

"You mean that tree thing that wanted to toss me into a deep, dark pit? The one that you said you were protecting us from?"

"The Fae realm isn't gentle, but the beings who monitor the Fade do live by a general truce and code of conduct. They see threats as something to be immediately eliminated in order to maintain the balance. No one creature rules over another, but the Sentinels are charged with the elimination of intruders, especially when they are perceived to be a danger."

"And so those nyads were just doing their thing? They're not a danger?"

"Harmon," I said, resting a hand on his shoulder, "It's okay. We're safe now. Let's just get back to Earth. We have a big problem there we need to go deal with."

"At least now we know what we're fighting," Martina said.

"Speak for yourself," I said with a laugh that lacked humor.

"The creatures that came through the portal are called baowals. They are the source of your werewolf legends. They are a being of the Fel that survive off of the life energy of an Earth-bound host. Kessa, when you grabbed the book and chanted to hold off the one on the road, the last word you spoke was a name. I started to suspect baowal involvement then because I believe the name you spoke is one of their alphas."

"They function like a wolf pack?" I asked.

"Simply put, yes. They are demonic in nature, and constructs of the Fel. All life follows patterns, and those creatures just happen to share similar traits with Earth-bound wolves. They also stray from wolf behavior considerably. For example, they are genderless. Thus there is no mating. But they do form packs, and those who are the strongest are named, which could benefit us."

"So there's a way to fight them?"

"The realm of Fae is all about balance," Martina held her hands out like she was giving a lecture on a school field trip. We complied with her gesture and looked around. "Just as the Sentinels are charged with removing threats to the balance in the Fade, others are tasked with reining in the havoc that would be spread by some of the more malevolent creatures. In an effort to maintain that balance, the strongest beings of the realm are given names that can be used to control them. Whoever wrote in that book knew this particular being's name, and inscribed it somewhere within. The book itself is bound with the magic of the Ancestral Lands. I got a look at it while you were unconscious, and it's written in the Ancestral language. Where did you get it?"

Harmon held up his hand, "From me. It belonged to my grandmother. I found it in her attic years ago. Also..."

He caught my eye; the strained lines around his mouth told me his brain chewed on something that he couldn't quite articulate. I felt the confusion within him and tucked the sensation away.

"Also, what?" I asked, after a long pause.

"Nothing," Harmon said. "Can we just get out of here?"

I nodded but knew there were a couple conversations we'd have to have soon. First, the fact that I could suddenly feel what he felt, and second, whatever it was he kept trying and failing to tell us.

"I think that's probably a good idea," Martina said. "Like before, take my arm, and make sure you keep your eyes closed."

The air back on Earth felt dense and wet, and the sounds and scents nearly overwhelmed my stomach. I hadn't realized just how sparse the Fae realms had been in terms of sensory input. We stood on a small rise just above the parking area for Shari's Bed & Breakfast. Police tape wrapped my cabin's door, but otherwise, the parking lot was empty, and Shari's car was likewise missing from in front of her bungalow.

"We need to get back to the civic center and get your car, Harmon," I said.

"Call a cab?" Harmon offered.

"No need," Martina said, pointing us back toward the parking lot. Her blue abomination of a truck sat at the ready.

"That's a good trick," I said.

"One of the few still available to me on Earth," Martina sighed. "Long ago, we had stronger magic on Earth. We were able to defend ourselves and others. But that's long since passed."

"Hence your working through the Adepts?" I asked.

"You learn quickly, Kessa. Certain people have it within themselves to reach through and draw on that Fae energy though it tends to be a little unpredictable, as I'm sure you've noticed."

"Considering I destroyed a regional landmark today? Which reminds me, I need to call my director. I'm sure he's heard what happened, and I'm also certain he's ready to have my head." I pulled out my cell phone and clicked it on. The time on the clock caught me off guard. "Wait, how is it only moments after we left the grove?"

"Time works differently in the Fae realms, and I'm able to control the *when* of when I pop into Earth, as long as I don't break the rules of time." I gave her a perplexed look, and she clarified with, "I can't go back in time, and I can't go forward. I can just make time pause for myself and my fellow travelers if that makes sense."

I nodded. "I guess. But we came out at Shari's."

"Right," she said. "I can't control the where. If I'm coming from the Ancestral lands, I show up right here. Other Earth locations put me into the Fade like we experienced. I tend to stay close, and I typically choose to shift here. I like to avoid the Fade."

"For good reason," I said.

She fixed her gaze forward, "I just like to keep my eyes open."

We scrambled down the hill through ferns and huckleberry bushes. The cab of the old Ford was a tight fit for the three of us, but we squeezed in anyway. I sat in the middle with nowhere to put my feet.

"We are going to need some silver weapons," Martina said as we rode down Highway 302. "You won't be able to kill the baowals, but you can banish them back to the Fel."

"And what happens to the people whose bodies they've inhabited?" I asked.

Martina's mouth turned down, "Separation from the host typically doesn't end well. They will most likely die."

"Unacceptable," Harmon said, his voice harsh.

"I agree that loss of life isn't ideal," I said, "But you know as well as I do Harmon, occasional sacrifices for the common good are necessary."

"Not in this case. Not with the head wolf, anyway. There has to be some way." His face took on that look of taut frustration again. I knew the time for our pending conversation had come.

"Harmon?" I asked, placing my hand on his arm. "What are you not telling us?"

He blew out a long breath and rested his head against the truck's window. "Your head wolf—mister alpha demon what's-his-name?"

I nodded, "You mean the one who attacked us at the cabin, took your grandmother's book and unleashed a pack of hell? What about him?"

"That's my grandfather."

The world circled in on me, and I felt my mouth go dry. I wasn't sure if the hopelessness filling me was my own or Harmons.

"The relative DNA match," I said.

"Yes, the match. When we saw him without his wolf's clothing at the civic center, I recognized him instantly. He looked like an older version of the pictures hanging in my grandmother's home."

Silence fell between us as we all pondered this information.

Martina finally spoke, "I know of very few survivors of a banishing, but it has happened."

"Well, he has to be one of the survivors," Harmon said, glaring across the truck.

"We will do everything we can." I gently rubbed his arm and felt him tense. Everything about him radiated anger; it flowed off him in waves. My phone rang, and I was very thankful for the excuse to stop discussing our predicament.

"St. James," I answered.

"Agent, it's good to hear your voice." Schild's voice strained with tension. "We couldn't find you after the attack and feared the worst. Where are you? We need you back at the scene. It's all clear now."

"We're nearby and headed back that way now. I'll fill you in when we get there."

"Any idea who set off the bomb? I was facilitating an escape through the kitchen entrance. We expected to see a blood bath from the screaming. There wasn't a single body in the aftermath, but not everyone has been accounted for. We have eight missing. I'm not sure if we managed to get through that with zero loss of life yet."

I rolled my eyes; he had bolted like a scared rabbit. But who am I to judge? "I'll give you a full report when we get back. We'll be there in?" I glanced at Martina, and she held up one hand. "Five minutes."

After clicking end, I shook my head, "This is so beyond my ability to reason. I have no idea what I'm going to tell him."

"Pin it on one of the missing reporters," Harmon offered. "They're as good as dead anyway."

I felt myself bristle at the thought, and at the realization that it was our only decent option. "I don't like the idea of lying to our partners on the force, or to our superiors, but I'm not sure there's any other way."

"If you think of one, I'm all ears," Harmon said.

"Schild saw your grandfather, Harmon. It's going to be difficult to keep him out of this. I'll lie only so far. There were no witnesses to the explosion except us. But Schild was right by my side when your grandfather—what's his name, anyway?"

"Lawrence."

"When Lawrence came in, there were a lot of witnesses. Not just Schild, but the surviving reporters. He was on film. I'm sure some of them are already airing the footage."

Harmon swore under his breath and leaned his head back against the window. "You realize, that means our faery friends are also on film and are being released as public knowledge."

"Yes, that thought crossed my mind. I'm very surprised my director hasn't called to chew me a new one yet."

"And how are we going to explain her involvement?" Harmon asked.

"I was right next to you when that reporter in the red dress set off the bomb, and you very heroically ushered me to safety," Martina said.

"We can easily say that she ran out the back with us, and her truck happened to be nearby." I turned to look at Martina, who nodded in agreement. I noticed that the gashes she'd garnered in her fight with the nyad were nearly healed. "You're going to be questioned," I said.

"No problem. I'll tell them I was panicking and didn't see anything except Harmon directing me out of the building."

"That'll probably be sufficient."

We pulled into the civic center parking lot, which was much less populated. The few news vans that remained were being combed by police. Some of the squad cars read "Tacoma Police." They'd called for backup. I couldn't blame them.

Schild squatted down on the front porch of the center next to a brunette woman who cried into a handkerchief. "Ms. Austin here says her camera man is among the missing. That makes eight total," he glanced at Martina, "It was eleven until we got hold of you three."

"This is Martina Eccles, a reporter with the PI," I said, "If it wasn't for her, we might still be among your list."

"Three less missing. That's good." Schild wiped his brow.

"Let's go talk inside where we can sit down," Harmon said.

I followed his line of sight and realized that the woman sitting beside us had taken a keen interest in our conversation. Reporters. I shook my head.

Turning to Martina, I said, "Thank you for your help. Can you please wait around for just a little while? We may have some questions for you."

She smiled a little too conspiratorially, and I hoped Schild didn't notice. It was something that either Harmon or I would have caught immediately. Thankfully, Schild wasn't quite as astute.

I wasn't sure exactly what I'd expected, but the state of the hall wasn't it. There was no blood or evidence of a physical struggle. If it hadn't been for the giant, gaping hole in the wall, I'd have thought nothing out of the ordinary had happened.

Schild seemed to pick up on my thoughts, "Weird, isn't it? There's nothing. Bomb squad is on the way to do their investigation. But there's no explosion crater. I'm not a bomb expert by any stretch, but typically there's some sort of downward compression with a bomb. This looks more like it was done with artillery, but I don't remember anyone having a shoulder-mounted RPG, and there's no ammunition casing. There was just some old guy with a book and a necklace, and then chaos." He shuddered at the memory.

I crossed over to the wall and made a show of inspecting the damage. "Definitely some sort of projectile, I'd say. We'll let the experts weigh in, though."

"Have you confiscated the footage?" Harmon asked.

"We thought we got it all, but I've been informed that some leaked. One of the news stations aired our suspect."

A string of obscenities escaped Harmon's lips as he paced. I could sense his anger welling inside him and took the opportunity to explore the sensation. It wasn't mere intuition or observation; a piece of the anger roiling inside him made its way to me like I was picking up a frequency. I felt the taint overtaking him again, and I could sense his rage right along with him.

"Harmon, why don't you go get an official statement from Mrs. Eccles?" I suggested.

He stepped through the blast hole and stalked across the lawn without as much as a backward glance, still talking to himself.

"Odd," Schild said, watching Harmon as he crossed the grass.

"How's that?" I asked.

"His reaction seems odd; overblown for a simple press leak. Aren't you guys used to that sort of thing?"

I hoped my smile wasn't as weak as it felt. "We've been a step behind this whole case. It's just getting to him I think."

"Well, maybe I can help out. Maybe not the way you want, though. I do have some information about the senator's case. The warrant came through, and our stakeout lasted all of about twenty minutes. Paul Rushing definitely had reason to run, but not for anything related to the senator. Let's just say his shed had more grow lights than power tools."

"What about Justin?" I asked. "He turn up?"

"We caught up with him as well. Turns out they had a greenhouse on their property, too. He and his dad had a little side business. He's being questioned now, but I don't think it's going to turn up anything to do with Senator Mansfield."

"Sounds like a dead end." I agreed.

"However, the man who burst in here—he looked familiar. I can't place it, but we have Tacoma running photo analysis. Any idea who he might be?"

I gave a noncommittal grunt, redoubling my examination of the splintered remains of the wall.

"Well," Schild continued, "We did find a link between Mansfield and Virginia Harmon."

"Oh?" This was definitely good news. Something I could give back to my superiors, anything at all, would be better than trying to explain Adepts and faery realms and baowals.

"Turns out, Mansfield was looking for retirement property and stumbled across Mrs. Harmon's plot that she'd put up for sale years ago. Some piece of land up off the power line road, I guess. He had put down an offer, and according to the real estate broker, Mrs. Harmon had accepted. They were in escrow."

"So our killer would have some vested interest in the property," I said, not intentionally out loud.

"My thought exactly," Schild agreed. "We're sending a unit to investigate the property."

"No!"

Schild recoiled at my sudden exclamation. "Excuse me?"

"I just mean, Harmon and I need to be out there as part of that investigation."

"Well, you'd better hurry because my unit is on their way now."

I started to run for Harmon when my phone rang. "Crase," I swore, letting it ring. On the fourth ring, I picked up. No matter how much I wanted to, I couldn't just ignore a call from my director.

"Yeah," I said.

"Is my call I inconveniencing you, Agent?"

"No sir, sorry. We've had an incident."

"You think I don't know that? It's all over the news. What the hell is happening there, St. James?" His initial irritability shifted somewhat with his last question to something ringing with more curiosity. Maybe even concern.

"We're still investigating. We have Tacoma in for backup and they called in the bomb squad."

"Some Detective Schild called, and Agent, I'm a bit confused. You're going to have to explain to me why you didn't call in an attack on your cabin. Were you present at the time of the attack?"

I pinched the bridge of my nose. The answer hit me in a flash. "I was outside, getting some air. It was a smash and grab, sir. He didn't get anything, though, because he didn't expect me to be armed."

"St. James, you're a better agent than this. You call it in. You know that. It could have something to do with the case. Anything and everything could be related."

I shook my head and suppressed a laugh. If he only knew just how related everything was, and on how many levels. "Sorry, sir. Won't happen again."

"Well, the caretaker is a bit irate with the Bureau, but we'll take care of her. You just solve this case, and we'll try to get whatever that is off the air from our end. Just try not to give them any more media fodder, will you?"

"Absolutely not, sir. We are on the edge of a break, I think."

"Good to hear."

I thought Crase was going to make his goodbyes, but his voice came through with an edge of hesitation. "What are those shadows on the film, anyway?"

"I haven't been near a TV, sir. Can't tell you. I'll take a look, though." It was an honest answer. My stomach churned with guilt. I don't give my director half-truths. "I need to get going, sir. We are following that lead. It's a connection between Mansfield and Virginia Harmon. Real estate deal."

"That's the agent I know. Get on it, St. James. And no more mishaps. Got it?"

I mumbled an agreement and hung up, my conversation with Crase taking an immediate back seat to the crisis of the moment. A Gig Harbor police squad car was headed into danger, and they had no idea what they were up against.

Chapter 19

Harmon and Martina were in a heated discussion when I approached them. He held a sealed water bottle in his hand. His picking at the label intensified as Martina lectured him. They both stopped talking when they saw me approach.

"You guys talking about what to get me for my birthday?"

"We were just discussing the finer points of protecting not just humanity, but the boundaries between realms, and how it factors against the loss of a single life," Martina said.

"We're not killing him," Harmon's eyes flashed an amber color on the word "not" and I took a reflexive step backward.

"And we were also discussing his affliction," Martina added with an offhanded flick of the wrist.

"Well, we have to think fast and come to a consensus now. Schild just sent a unit out to the old Harmon property."

"What?" they both shouted in unison. Harmon chucked the water bottle at the ground so hard that it cracked open, spilling its contents in a single gush.

"This is insane," he said, tossing his hands up and pacing. "We're not ready. We don't have any sort of plan except *go kill everyone.* We don't have the right type of weapons."

"Harmon, stop," I said.

To my surprise, he ceased his pacing and stared at me expectantly. I took a breath and gathered my thoughts. "You're a profiler, Harmon. Right now, you're not necessarily thinking through things clearly, but I need you on this. Your field office said to trust you. I didn't want to. But then you went ahead and earned my trust anyway. Now I need you to listen to me."

He huffed a breath, and the veins in his neck rose and presented the anger that coursed through him. "I don't hear you offering any reasonable suggestions."

"*You* are my reasonable suggestion. Harmon, you're afflicted. He thinks they tagged you. He thinks he *has* you like he owns the rest of his pack. They operate like wolves, right?"

Harmon nodded.

"Okay then, I need you to get in there play the part. Join the pack and sniff around, as it were."

His chest heaved, but he didn't respond, so I continued.

"There are two beings in one body, the demon, and Lawrence, and both of them have connections to you. If you can convince the demon that you're choosing him over us, and if you can simultaneously appeal to whatever part of your grandfather is left, you might be able to break through and gather some intelligence. But you're going to have to keep your cool, and you're going to have to use your training. Get inside his head."

"Kessa, that's brilliant," Martina said. She turned to Harmon. "You need to see if you can appeal to his family bond. Get him to tell you the demon's name, and carefully memorize it. Pronunciation is key. For Kessa, it rolled off her tongue because she was being controlled by the Ancients through the book, and through the spirit of the author who already knew the name. You won't have that help."

Harmon looked Martina over from head to toe, grinding his teeth. "Martina, I need a moment with my partner, please."

She looked like she was about to complain but then conceded. "Sure, I'll be in the truck."

Harmon waited until she shut the door. He pulled me several more feet away before speaking. "Kess, if I go in there, I might not come back out. Not because I think he'll kill me. The thought of going in there is like the answer to every question I have. I *want* to go in there. I don't need to be a profiler to get inside his head. He's already in mine."

"I know how you feel," I said.

"No, you don't..."

"Actually Harmon, I do. Ever since I saved your life, and even more so since you got hit by the baowal, I can feel every emotion you feel like it's my own."

He barked a single laugh. "I thought it was just me."

"What?"

"I've been sensing you, too. Just you, though. No one else. I've been trying to figure it out."

We let the idea sink in for a moment, and I shook my head. "Let's table this. We know it's there, we've acknowledged it, and outside of a whole lot of potentially embarrassing complications, we might be able to use this connection to our advantage. Maybe I can help you fight the taint when it threatens to overtake you."

Harmon clutched one of my hands, and I felt my stomach flip at the unexpected touch. He smiled knowingly, and I grimaced. "See?" I said. "Embarrassing complications. Can you stop that now?"

He let go of my hand. "Sorry, I just want to know where I stand on all fronts before heading in there."

"So you're going?"

"Martina's right. It's a good idea. I'm not too keen on how quick she jumped at the chance to nail down the alpha demon's name."

"She wants to banish him," I said though I didn't feel as sure as I'd tried to sound. Harmon picked up on my doubt.

"You can feel it, can't you? She's hiding something. She has some stake in this, and we're not privy to the full reason for her involvement. I need you to get it out of her while I'm in there."

"I agree, but I'm not sure what else I can do but just go along with her for now."

"Use your investigative skills. Watch her for tells. Ask the right questions. Get her to trip up on her inconsistencies." Harmon reached for the stone around my neck, and my fingers met his at my chest. "She gave this to you," he said.

I nodded.

"Don't use it. Just a hunch. I don't think you need it, and I know we don't need her."

"I give it a fifty-fifty chance I'll walk back out of there," Harmon said once we were back in the truck.

"Isn't there any advice you can give him to sway the odds?" I asked Martina.

Martina fixed her gaze upon me, much like a kindergarten teacher would with a wide-eyed student. Somewhere between kind and condescending. "You need to learn that the faery don't take sides. In the case of an Adept, such as yourself, I respond when driven to do so. I showed up because I sensed your presence and your affinity for my plane. You have asked for assistance, and I've responded." I started to protest, but she held up and hand and continued her lecture. "Danny needs to decide for himself what is true to his soul. You can't decide for him, and neither can I. His energy is Fel, and such is his affinity. I cannot get involved."

"Well, I guess it's now or never," Harmon said. "We'll find out what kind of man I am soon enough. Let's go."

Harmon drove, which I thought was probably for the best. It gave him something to do while brooding.

I watched him out of the corner of my eye, feeling the torment within him. The fact that I could feel his emotions—not just assume what they were, but actually experience them to some extent—underscored my own shifting reality.

I thought over our plan, and worry gnawed at my belly. I didn't want to lose Harmon to the pack. In the brief moment our eyes met, I understood: He reminded me that I wasn't the only one picking up vibes.

Wonderful. That's all I needed. I had to get my mind off of Harmon before he figured out the full extent of the conflict that had been troubling me in the quiet moments we spent in close proximity.

For a moment, I closed my eyes and searched inside myself. Somewhere deep within my soul, a thrumming energy pulsed and churned like water coming to a boil. I reached for it gently, probing it with my conscious mind, asking it to come out and play. Immediately, I felt a vibration in my fingertips, as if I'd touched a low-current wire. I knew I could do something with it, but I wasn't exactly sure what. But I was certain that I didn't need a stone or a book or Martina to reach the magic inside me. It was right there, and it was mine to use as required. The revelation was at once exhilarating and terrifying; a chill ran the length of my spine as I shoved the sensation back opened my eyes.

The power line road slipped under us in silence as Harmon maneuvered his FBI cruiser over the uneven terrain, and it occurred to me that the trees glowed faintly.

The undergrowth below radiated an emerald sheen from the surface of the leaves. Even the sky shimmered. More evidence that the magic inside me was growing.

"Martina," I said, not without a bit of hesitance, "Is it just me, or is something happening, you know, in the magical..."

"The Earth's aura is shifting here, yes." She arched an eyebrow. "You are seeing it?"

"Is that a good thing? Or a bad thing?" I asked.

"The Earth is trying to defend herself from corrupt energy. She's striving to maintain balance."

"We're stopping here," Harmon said, throwing the car into park. "I'm going in on foot. You two are hanging back."

"Not happening, partner. We can tail behind, and stay just outside the grove."

He held up his phone, dialed my number, and let it ring. "I'll leave it on speaker in my shirt pocket. Stay quiet. You'll be able to hear what's going on. You'll know if I need backup."

"I don't like this," I said. "We need to be closer."

"If we step inside the influence of the energy field, they'll know we're there," Martina motioned at the tree line with a sweeping wave. "The whole area is teeming with energy. I'm pretty sure you know that."

Harmon met my eyes, and the near-constant anger he'd exhibited since getting hit subsided just enough for him to revert to the sarcastic man I'd come to know. "This was your plan. Stop freaking out. Besides, you need to hang back and handle Schild and his boys when they show up. Stall them."

"How am I supposed to do that?"

He flashed his smirking smile, "Pull jurisdiction on them. Tell them we're taking over this part of the investigation."

"Harmon, that's stupid," I huffed. "That's movie cliché bullshit, and you know it."

"They'll probably believe it. These are very small-town cops we're talking about here. And they want nothing to do with this. That much was evident by the way Rick fled at the first sign of danger earlier. His biggest worry out here is setting a speed trap. He's way out of his element." Harmon tapped the side of his head. "You don't need to profile that one too hard."

"Fine," I conceded. "But I'm coming in there at the first hint of danger."

He placed a hand on my shoulder. "I wouldn't have it any other way."

Harmon turned and looked Martina up and down like he was inspecting livestock. He needn't say a thing; his radiating hatred hit me like a truck. I tucked the sensation away; he was using our link to warn me again that he didn't trust Martina. She couldn't hear his thoughts, nor could she sense his emotions. He gave me a long look, and I tried to send across a feeling of appreciation. I hoped he understood that I'd gotten the message.

He turned away and loped across the tree line, disappearing from view. Martina glanced my way. I shrugged and turned my attention to the phone in my hand. The line crackled with his footsteps and picked up his increase in his breathing. We knew when he reached the edge of the clearing from the slowing of his movement.

"Lawrence!" Harmon's voice was only slightly muffled by his shirt. He was talking extra loud for our benefit. "Lawrence Harmon, I'm your grandson, Danny. I know you're in the house. Come out and talk."

A long pause gave way to the sound of grass crunching underfoot. My pulse quickened, and it took every bit of willpower I had to stay put. Martina seemed infuriatingly nonplussed, picking at some bit of something on a fingernail. I wanted to ask her if we were boring her, but the words caught in my throat when the sound of Lawrence's voice reminded me the phone works both ways.

"Daniel. I'm glad you decided to visit. It's been a long time." His voice was low and hoarse like he'd been getting over a case of bronchitis, but in no way did he sound menacing. Quite the opposite, actually. Had I not known the reality of what Harmon had just walked into, I could picture a happy reunion between grandson and long-lost grandparent.

"I think you know why I'm here," Harmon said. I knew his tactic. He was trying to draw Lawrence in and gain his trust by allowing him to discern the reasoning for Harmon's visit on his own. He could decide if Harmon was there as the grandson or as the afflicted.

Lawrence's reply made the hair rise on the back of my neck.

"You're law enforcement now, aren't you?"

"FBI, yes," Harmon admitted. "Been an agent for a little over five years now."

"Let me guess: Profiler. And you're here to figure me out."

"Why would you think that?"

I heard rustling—the crunching of dry grasses underfoot. I guessed it wasn't Harmon, even though he was known to pace. This sounded more like the slow circling of a predator with cornered prey.

"You've watched me for years, Daniel. You had that little perch up there, where you'd sit while I was held captive. For a while, I suspected it was Ginny who'd sent you. But no, you were there because you were curious, weren't you?"

"I didn't know it was you," Harmon's voice sounded strained.

"Of course you didn't. Ginny would never have told you the truth. She'd never let on who I was. She was always scared."

"What did she have to be afraid of? Something you'd done?" Lawrence had given Harmon an angle to work with, and his questions began to reflect composure and skill.

Lawrence laughed, and it turned into a cough. "Something I did? Certainly not. More like something she did. The gift of baowal was hers to me. I'm how I am because of Ginny's dabbling."

"Is that why you killed her, Lawrence?"

A growling response from Lawrence made me want to abandon my post and sprint toward the trail head. Martina must have sensed what I was about to do, because she reached out and grabbed my shoulder. I struggled to free myself, but she blocked my path. She signaled the phone in my hand, put a finger to her lips and motioned a button press. I wanted to give myself a giant facepalm. I tapped the phone screen to bring up the keypad, and I pressed the "Mute."

"Ginny Harmon was an Adherent," Martina said, her eyes wide.

"And that is?"

"Like an Adept, but gifted with energy from all of the realms."

"Oh, that can't be good."

"Oh, but it's very good. That book you had was written in the language of the Ancestral realm. Ginny also dabbled in the Fel region. I'm betting she has other journals. Probably one for each realm."

"Why would that matter to you? Aren't you *Of the Ancients*?" I asked.

Martina looked startled for a second, and then smiled, "Of course, but it's always good to know your enemy, right?"

I was about to point out that Ginny Harmon wasn't the enemy when Lawrence's voice cut in again, and we both fell silent.

"Daniel, you approach the world from the point of view of a cop. There are good guys, and there are bad guys. You've decided I'm on the latter end of that spectrum." I heard Harmon try to speak, but Lawrence continued, "Just a moment, let me finish. Ginny and I were doing good work back then. We found a way to protect the land. Remember the force field? The one that you and your friends experienced that day? I can put that up now, wherever and whenever I need to. I can turn the tide of the destruction that is ravaging this land. But this grove needs to stay intact. This area is sacred. Ginny was going to sell it to that liar of a US senator."

"So you killed them both," Harmon pressed with a practiced lack of judgment. "You secured this area for yourself by taking them out of the equation."

"I didn't kill Ginny." Harmon senior's voice rang with sadness and then changed to a cool stoicism. "Daniel, follow me over here. Yes, here. Place your hand on this tree. Can you feel that?"

After a pregnant pause, Harmon said, "Yes. I feel it."

"That is Fel energy. You feel it because it courses through you. I wanted you fully turned today, but it would seem you're simply touched by the gift that your grandmother gave me so very long ago."

"What does that mean, *she* gave *you*?"

"It was Ginny who made this all possible. She had access to a realm of power that I'd only dreamed. She was able to create her own reality. Her practice brought forth the baowal. They are those you saw today—my protectors, sworn to aid me in the glory of the defense of this land. But Ginny didn't have it within her to continue the work she started. She shut me out, locked me up, and denied my existence. She kept you from me though you found me yourself."

"I thought I'd found a werewolf."

Hacking coughs interrupted Lawrence's response, "Myth. Legend. I control when I change. There's no moon required. I have access to Fel magic, and so it shall be for you as well."

A wet, cracking sound filled the phone, accompanied by a single gasp from Harmon. I took off at a sprint, not caring whether Martina was behind me or not. The sick sound of breaking bones and ripping flesh filled my ears and blinded my senses. I'd heard the sickening sounds before, just recently, while watching eight journalists lose the lives they'd known. Lawrence was becoming the beast within, and Harmon had gone silent. My fear became stark reality as I crossed the threshold of the grove. Harmon lay unmoving at his grandfather's feet.

The changed form of Lawrence Harmon turned his attention my way and arched his back to loose a howl. The chorus echoed once, twice, then by many as the pack picked up the song. They came from the trees at equidistant points, surrounding the grove. I'd sprung their trap, and it struck me that we'd given them exactly what they wanted. Harmon was the perfect bait to lure both of us into their domain. I reached for my weapon in vain, knowing that it would be useless against this enemy.

As I drew on the wolf form that was Lawrence, pain erupted up my neck and skull, and the world went black.

When I came to, I stood bound and held in the old Harmon house. Watching a werewolf change back to human form was disturbing, but not in the bone-crunching, sickening manner of witnessing the change to the beast. It was a slow, gentle and wholly unnatural shifting. Hair disappeared. Muscles shrank. Stature and posture changed. And at the end of the silent process, when Lawrence Harmon stood before me in his grandfatherly form, wearing only the loose, elastic-waist shorts he'd worn as the beast, my mind could only hold on to the vicious potential of the lethal killer that was merely one thought away.

"Miss St. James, I believe we have a misunderstanding between us." The elderly Harmon interlocked his fingers and cracked his knuckles as he sat upon the failing wing chair. The floor beneath him bowed in response to his weight, frail as he appeared.

"How's that?" I asked, struggling against the duct tape that bound my wrists in front of me. A tall, lean man with dark skin and charcoal eyes held me in place. I assumed he'd carried me across the grove and into the cabin, where he proceeded to slap me back to consciousness, followed by roughly yanking me to my feet. Gauging by the pain exploding across the back of my head, I wagered that he'd also caused me to black out, probably while he was still in wolf form.

"Cinder here says you had Danny wired," he made a *tsk* noise and continued, "You were listening in on our conversation. Not very honest behavior, Miss St. James. It doesn't inspire trust."

"Trust," I growled, twisting my hands. "That's a funny concept coming from a murder suspect," Cinder clamped down on my wrists, and an involuntary yelp of pain escaped my lips.

"Why would I be a suspect?" Lawrence rose from the chair and approached, stopping inches from my face. His graying eyebrows drew down into a look of consternation.

I scoffed. "You'll get caught, Lawrence. Your DNA was discovered on both bodies. You're Harmon's only living relative. There's no one it could have been except you."

"Ah," he held up a single finger, right in front of my nose, "that is where you're mistaken. And therein lies our misunderstanding."

"Explain," I said with a practiced level coolness.

"You're one to make demands," he laughed. "Feisty. I can see why Danny has taken a fancy to you."

"He's my partner."

Cinder laughed behind me, and Lawrence echoed him. I felt like the reject, left out of the joke.

Lawrence ignored my affronted frown. "Your involvement with my grandson is problematic but not nearly so dangerous as your dependence upon the woman you call Martina."

"Martina saved our asses from your pack."

"*Martina* drew us out and caused us to attack."

I drew a deep breath and let out a slow exhale. "Care to tell me how that makes any sense?"

The elder Harmon paced the floor, reminiscent of Danny's typical behavior while he was thinking or irritated. He stopped in front of me and spun sharply on his heel, coming to parade rest. It crossed my mind to ask him if he was former military.

"You place your trust in the wrong allies, Miss St. James. Such is the way with law enforcement. You make assumptions, and you're usually right. So you go on the overall assumption that you're always correct. You only change your mind with evidence and procedure. And yet, you're into something now that baffles your mind, aren't you?" He paused, cocking his head to gauge my reaction. I gave him nothing, staring straight ahead. "Your training fails you, doesn't it?"

"Lawrence," I said, like tiptoes through a room full of thumb tacks, "why don't you let me loose and we can all talk about this. It sounds like you have information you'd like to give."

He barked a single laugh full in my face, his hot breath and spittle accosting my cheek. "You're working with *her*."

"Martina?" I asked.

"Who else? You're a child. Unfortunately, you're a dangerous whelp."

Lawrence's gaze reached past me to Cinder. The look they exchanged caused the skin to raise on my arms.

"Are you two... communicating?" I asked. Curiosity had gotten the better of me.

"Martina is not what you think she is. Nor are we what you presuppose." Lawrence said, crossing back to his chair and perching in such a way that looked as if he were about to spring forward at any moment.

"So give me something here, Lawrence. Let me in on all of this mystical double-talk. Like you said, I'm a cop, but I'm out of my league. Let me go, level with me, and I'll see what I can do for you."

"You really are used to being in control, aren't you Miss St. James?" Lawrence said, his words stinging with condescension. He raised the stone at my neck and let it fall back to my chest. "You've chosen an alliance, and unfortunately, you sealed that decision before you had all the facts. You've taken it upon yourself to desecrate your own soul, and you had no idea it was even happening. Had you but come to me first..." He let the thought trail off to mix with the heady aroma that arose from the cauldron over the fire.

It was my turn to sneer. "Yeah, we tried that as kids. Nearly got us killed."

"I wasn't the same back then," he stood and began stoking the fire, "and I admit, I wasn't in control. Ginny had every right to keep me quarantined. But I'm not that man anymore."

"No, now you just kill off senators and loved ones alike, and force affliction upon eight unsuspecting news reporters."

Cinder's voice behind me made me jump; I'd nearly forgotten he was there. "No one forced me to do shit. I chose this. So did my brothers and sisters."

"You couldn't have known what was going to happen," I said.

"The Alpha approached us and sought those who would be willing to be pack. Only those who knew and had accepted were joined."

I met the elder Harmon's eyes, which held a menace of a smile. "You see? No harm done." He stood, cross-armed and waiting for my response.

"He may believe what he's saying," I asserted, "but you know as well as I do that you set that thing after your own grandson. Harmon was never approached or asked. You tried to capture him. He's said it himself that the—thing—that's inside him wants him to play along. But he's obviously stronger than this lot here. Good job brainwashing the rest of your *pack*, though. I'm sure you make a fine alpha, but your grandson is the better man. Better hope Harmon doesn't decide to accept what's in there, or you might just wind up out of a job."

An eye-flash of communication ran between Lawrence and Cinder; pain erupted across my head once more. The room spun, and me with it.

Chapter 20

Waves, the color and texture of ink, washed over me and over me. I rolled in their depths, tasting brine and campfire smoke. Pine and oak. Wildflowers, sweet and rich, sprung to life, grew to seed, withered and died, all along a shoreline just out of reach. The waves pushed me toward solid land, but then pulled me back away before I gained footing. My head went under, and I swallowed sea water.

From somewhere deep inside, my voice spoke softly. *If you don't wake up, you're going to die.*

"How do I wake up?" I whispered to my own disembodied spirit. "I don't know how."

Just open your eyes. You have to move.

"But where will I go? There is nothing else. Just the waves."

Harmon needs you.

"Harmon is dead. Am I dead, too?"

Harmon needs you. He is alive, and he needs you now.

The voice stilled, leaving me to the rocking of the waves. With the cresting of the flow, I pushed my arms out and willed myself to swim. As I kicked and struggled, my hand grasped the shore. Smooth pebbles gave way, and I lost my grip and ebbed with the tide.

"Just a little harder," I said to myself.

Pulling with all my strength, I grasped for the shore and heaved myself up onto dry land. As I rolled from the waves, my eyes opened.

The dark room around me reeked with a pungent smell that brought forth images of rust and death. My eyes adjusted slowly, and my limbs registered an even, dull pain at their farthest reaches. I tried to move and realized I could not. My hands and feet were bound tightly together. A piece of tape covered my mouth.

I felt cocooned in the confinement of an old-style bathtub filled with just enough water to cause a panic to rise within me. I heard the trickle of the faucet and knew that it was still running. When I tried to sit up, pain erupted across my chest and back; I had at least one cracked rib.

Fighting against my restraints, I managed to pull my hands slightly apart to determine that my wrists were still bound with the same tape. More tape now covered my mouth. My motion brought forth splashing that I was afraid would alert any nearby guards to my struggling. I fought against my quickened pulse to slowly, methodically bring my wrists close in front of my eyes.

My vision had adjusted enough so that I could see the bonds clearly in the small amount of moonlight that filtered through the tiny bathroom window. I pushed at the tape across my mouth, rubbing it with my bound hands. The waterline inched over my cheeks, and I strained my neck and shoulders upward, still pushing at the tape until it curled up enough for my fingers to grasp a corner and pull. With my mouth free, I took the tape at my wrists between my teeth and pulled slowly, gently, until I was released. After freeing my feet, I gingerly rose from the tub supporting my weight with my arms and took a survey of myself and my surroundings.

I had been relieved of my service weapon and phone, but that much was to be expected. I took stock of my myriad aches and pains and realized I'd not been handled gently. My head felt like I'd been on an all-night bender. Deep breathing was nearly impossible because of my aching ribs. I gently touched each spot that was tender, feeling up my legs, down my arms and across my chest.

My eyes grew wide in surprise. The Earth Stone still hung on its chain on my neck. I mentally reached for the magic power within, and found it walled off, as if behind glass. Wrapping my hands around the Earth Stone, my stomach churned. It hung cold and lifeless at my breast. Having no power of my own and nothing from the amulet felt like a limb had been amputated. I reached out again, trying to gather life energy, but none flowed. The land beneath and surrounding the house was dead to me, and I, in turn, felt the life force draining from me slowly. Too much time spent in this forsaken house, I realized, would end me as sure as the water that had been intended as my grave.

A commotion outside the bathroom made me freeze in place. I crept to the door on tip-toe and listened.

"There are six squad cars. The police are in the tree line trying to figure out how to get through the barrier." It was a woman's voice speaking.

"No matter," I heard Lawrence say, "They won't get through."

"The other woman still hasn't been found," A male voice added.

"That could be more problematic," Lawrence said. "She may yet figure out how to counter-weave the barrier. Find her."

"What of the Adept?" the woman asked. I held my breath.

"She's been dealt with. A shame, that one. She has potential, but she follows the wrong lead."

"And your pup?"

"He'll come around. He's been given the gift and the choice. He's a smart whelp. I'm certain he'll join the pack.

"And if he doesn't?" the male voice asked.

Snarls and growls erupted through snapping jaws. Lawrence must have felt his leadership was in contest. The other yelped and squealed, but pressed no further.

"Go now," Lawrence said, "And find the Ancestral demon. Kill her when you find her. The Ancients will claim her and do with her as they will. The young Adept is lost to them, tainted by the influence of Martina and her ilk; they will want nothing to do with her. We will claim this region for the Fel and place it solidly under the protection of the Elders. Its human population is ample and resourceful. This region will prosper. But first, we must eliminate the Ancestral faction."

The two others in the room mumbled their agreement, and I heard a door open and shut. After listening closely for several minutes, I surmised that Lawrence had left the house with his two pack members. I cautioned a glance out the door and confirmed my suspicions.

The living area, dimly lit by oil lamps, still housed the same old chairs that had stood by the fireplace for at least fifteen years. From the cauldron over the fire, smoke scented of rotting foliage and sulfur wafted through the room. Normally, the olfactory nerve deadens an offensive odor once it is deemed non-threatening. The fact that this particular scent only grew stronger spoke volumes. I felt more unbalanced with each breath.

Pushing through the stench, I edged up to the cauldron and cautioned a glance inside. The mixture swirled like a galaxy—if the stars had been replaced with globs of something vaguely flesh-like. The cauldron hung permanently affixed to the swing-arm, and the fire beneath smoldered through layers of coal and wood. I didn't understand the full significance of the pot, but it definitely had something to do with the power over the grove. I grabbed the fire poker, and scattered the tinder beneath the cauldron, extinguishing the flame.

There was a small door off the main living area that stood partially shut. Listening at the threshold, I heard soft snoring. I pushed the door open to see Harmon lay sleeping on a narrow bed. His labored breathing punctuated a restless sleep of twitches and thrashes.

"Harmon," I half-whispered. "Wake up. We have to get out of here."

He opened one bloodshot eye, then the other, and rolled to his back with a painful groan. A look of confusion etched deep into his face as he took me in. "You're dead," he said with matter-of-fact resolution.

"Obviously I'm not. And I don't want that reality to change anytime soon, so get up."

"Where's Lawrence?" he asked, pushing himself to sit. He dropped his legs over the side of the bed and propped himself up with one hand.

"He left with some others. What happened to you? You look like hell."

"I feel worse." He looked at me long and hard, and I felt the conflict that etched itself in deep lines on his forehead. "You need to go. If he comes back, he'll kill you, or worse."

"What could possibly be worse?" I asked.

"He'll make me kill you. And I probably will."

"Ok, sorry I asked. Harmon, get up. We're leaving."

I reached out to grab his hand, and his lip pulled back in a snarl. "Get out Kessa, before I do something we'll both regret."

"If you would regret it, why would you do it? You've already pissed me off plenty in the last few days, but this one takes the cake. You're coming with me."

His defiant air deflated and he looked at the floor. "I wish I could, but I can't." He ran his hands through his hair, letting silence fill the room, then looked back up with renewed hopefulness. "How about if you stay here?"

I wanted to ask him if he was stupid or just crazy. I wanted to kick him and scream at him. Instead, I took his hand. He looked at me with a longing that cut deep into my soul. "Harmon, I have to go. You can come with me, or you can stay. You know it's your choice. That much has been made clear."

"You have a choice too, Kessa. Become one of the pack. Lawrence will turn you; I know he will. You're strong and smart. Stay, and I'll ask him to turn you."

"So you've made your decision then? You're going to let the baowal win?"

"What's so wrong with that? My grandfather is strong and confident. He says he's protecting the land."

"What about the people?" I pressed. "Did he protect those reporters?"

"He made them protectors, Kess. He made them strong. He took this land back from the senator, and now he has a force to protect it."

"And what about the senator? What did he do besides decide to retire? And your grandmother? How can you follow that man after he killed two people in cold blood?"

"He didn't kill anyone." Harmon looked out the window, but I felt his anger.

I sat down on the bed next to him and took his hand. This time, he didn't move away. "Harmon, you know what Martina told you in the Fade, that you'll be tested, and you'll have to decide which path you will walk. How do you know you're on the right path?"

"How do you?" he asked, his voice edged with irritation.

"Martina opened a new world to me that I had never dreamed was possible. I'm not exactly following her lead, but I do appreciate her nudge in the right direction."

"And what do you know about her, Kessa?" He studied me in silence. "Think about it. She shows up when it's convenient. She's tried to convince you that you need both her and her trinket to harness your magic. But I saw you draw it up right there in my bathroom when she was nowhere to be found. She pulled us into the Fade and nearly got both of us killed. Lawrence and the pack weren't coming after us; they were going after her. She said herself that the faery were manipulative and conniving. I don't think she's given us any real reason to trust her. Lawrence said she killed Grams and Senator Mansfield."

"Harmon, that's ridiculous," I said, but an edge of doubt cut through me.

"Is it? How do you know she didn't?"

"I'm in this for the people I've sworn to serve and protect. From what I've seen, Lawrence—or whatever inhabits and controls him—is using people. Those creatures he yanked from the Fel region have an appendage that matches our murder weapon. He didn't give those reporters a choice. I'm still fully in control of myself, even if I don't understand everthing that's happening. I know it's still my decision. You have a choice, too. You need to think really hard on that, and ask yourself why you went into the Bureau, and if this reality truly sits well with you. You say Martina is manipulative; you believe your grandfather when he says he didn't kill Ginny, even though all evidence points to him. You forget who you are, Harmon. Are you my partner or not?"

As much as I wanted to demand he come with me, the words caught in my throat and tears stung my eyes. That last question was more personal than I'd intended, and the reality of it cut through me like a hot knife. My feelings for Harmon were deeper than that of partner, and I know he felt it through my words; I was in dangerous territory on too many levels. I let his hand slide from mine, and felt an emptiness well inside. I stood from the bed and left him there in the dark, ignoring his plea for me to come back.

Deafening silence enveloped the front room of the house. Moonlight blended with slow burning embers, casting an otherworldly glow over the surfaces. Deep shadows reached behind furniture like inky fingers. I stumbled once, catching myself on a low table. Something under my hand gave way, and I came up with a handful of chain. Harmon's grandmother's locket glinted in the moonlight, dangling between my fingers. Beneath it sat the book. I took both and left the house.

Chapter 21

As I stepped through the door and out into the night, cold wind bit into my wet skin. The second my feet touched bare earth I felt a small trickle of warm energy travel up my leg and into my core. It was no more than a thin stream, but it was more than I'd had before. Tossing the embers under the cauldron had shifted the balance. The energy touching my aura comforted me; I knew I'd been disconnected, but having it back brought a surge of relief. I felt powerful, and more capable, even with this tiny hint of Earth magic at my command.

Glancing around the meadow, I saw nothing moving, so I chanced an experiment. I reached for my core as I had earlier, bypassing the call of the Earth stone. Tiny green sparks crackled at my fingertips like a shorting wire. Resting a hand on my tender rib, I asked silently for the pain to subside. A thin stream of warmth trickled through my hand and into my abdomen. The faintest greenish-white light pulsed dully around my fingers and palm. Within seconds, my ribs felt whole. I took a tentative breath and then inhaled deeper. The pain was nearly gone, and I exhaled with relief.

I locked the results of my experiment away in my mind for further scrutiny. Half-way healing a cracked rib certainly wasn't on the same level as smashing through a wall, but the power at my hand was mine alone. The stone at my neck hung heavy, and I wondered at its real purpose. I knew I could call up some dangerous power with the stone, but maybe Harmon was right; it really was me, and not the trinkets. Maybe I just needed to learn.

The tree line loomed in the distance, carrying the promise of conflict. The closer I edged, the more I heard muffled movement and voices from within the forest. There were eight pack members out there, plus Lawrence. And then there was Schild and his forces. They could easily mistake me for one of the bad guys in the dark. I was certain they were terrified and confused at this point, and they'd probably already phoned in mine and Harmon's potential deaths. Again.

The question of the hour was, where was Martina? She apparently hadn't followed me into the grove, since Lawrence was still looking for her. I let that reality roll over me, and earmarked it as a potential betrayal of trust. You don't let your partners go into danger without some sort of backup. Harmon's suspicions didn't help, and above all else, I realized I did trust him. That stung, too. Another betrayal, but this one at my own hands.

"It's not like you haven't been alone before," I said to myself. Most of my career had been spent alone. Such is the life of a female agent. If men weren't intimidated by me, they usually attempted to control me. That went for partners and dating prospects alike. Harmon was the first one who had purely treated me as an equal and believed in me from the start.

I moved to the tree line as quickly and quietly as possible, listening to the distant sounds of the pack members as they moved through the forest. The thrum of energy just inside the ring of trees stopped me before I touched it. Reaching out, I felt the warmth of the barrier erected around the grove. Lawrence had said Martina could unbind it. I wondered if I could do the same. The trickle of power within me had grown to a steady flow, and I reached for it again, feeling very much like a teenager behind the wheel of a car for the first time. I knew there was limitless potential and freedom there if I could only figure out the controls.

I placed my hands against the barrier and felt the opposing force. The energy that constructed the field repelled the vibration from my own fingertips like two magnets being shoved together. That had to be the key. I closed my eyes and concentrated on the power within me, asking it to unbind what was before it. I felt a shift in the energy flowing through me, and my head spun like I had just climbed off those teacups at Disneyland. The world turned and turned, and energy pulsed from my hands in waves, opening a vortex before me. My feet moved of their own accord, pulling my body along for the ride, and I was sucked into the barrier. Fel energy washed over me as the control over my power collapsed. I hunched on the ground, frozen in place, and wretched up the minuscule contents of my stomach. Rolling over on my side, I reached for the other side of the barrier in vain.

I had the book tucked under my arm when I fell, and it flopped out onto the ground, its pages flicking as if an invisible hand skimmed its contents. The amulet I'd tucked into my pants pocket felt like it was burning through my skin, and I yelped and pawed at my slacks, trying to pry it loose. Convulsions wracked my body, and I reached for the power within in vain, hoping to dull the agony of the barrier's assault.

I found my own source again and pushed hard against the field that dug into my skin, coursed through my nerves. I felt my heartbeat race in my chest and pushed a flow of green and white to counteract the attack. The Fel energy sparred with my own, making my muscles writhe. I couldn't tell if the screams I heard were from me or from someone else.

Hands grasped and pulled at me, yanking me to my feet and shoving me hard through what was left of the faltering barrier. The pain subsided somewhat, but my limbs were paralyzed. I had to force my eyes open with sheer willpower. I tried to prop myself up on an elbow, failed and fell back to the ground. Looking up, I saw the one person I hadn't expected.

"Harmon?" My voice was sandpaper and wax.

"I thought you were dead." I felt his palpable relief.

"I feel dead. What happened?"

"The barrier is weak. I think it's going down, but we have to run. Can you stand up?"

I pushed myself up again, feeling the pins-and-needles sensation of limbs coming back to life. "It hurts, but I'll manage."

Harmon helped me to my feet, and he half-carried me through the trees. My feet caught on every twig, but he kept me upright; he seemed to move effortlessly through the dark.

"How can you see out here?" I asked, after tripping over a fallen branch.

"Not sure, but I can. It's like dusk. It's kind of cool."

"That means it's still inside you," I said. "You still haven't chosen."

He stopped and turned to face me. "What if I choose not to choose?"

"What do you mean?"

"I'm stronger. I'm faster. I can see in the dark. I can hear everything, and I can even sense emotions! Well, yours, anyway. I don't have to change into a wolf; I don't think I even can. I'm still me, as long as I keep the anger in check. I've been doing that my whole life. What's a little more?" He brushed a single finger across my cheek. "And I can choose my own alliances."

I shivered at the wave of emotion that rolled off of him and attempted to convince myself it was just the cold night. We stood together for a moment until he broke the gaze. "I grabbed this," he said, handing me the book.

I flipped through it with forced purpose. Its peculiar text glowed and pulsed, but it no longer felt repelling.

Harmon cleared his throat. "So, what did you do, anyway?" he asked, leading us through the forest at a slower pace so I wouldn't trip.

"I brought down the barrier, I guess."

"Well, that's obvious. But how?"

"I overheard Lawrence say something about Martina being able to dismantle it, so I figured if she could, so could I." He bristled at the mention of her name, so I kept talking. "I can harness this power and use it. I've figured out how, but I really don't know what I'm capable of, or what the effects might be. I healed my own cracked rib."

Harmon stopped again to face me. "See, Kess? You don't need Martina." He spat her name like it was poison.

"I did have the book," I said, waving it at him.

"I don't think you need it. You conjured up your own little ball of energy right there in my bathroom with no help at all."

"The Earth Stone was on my neck," I reminded him. Something in my mind clicked at his words. "Harmon, do you know something you're not telling me?"

His eyes narrowed, and his mouth formed a thin line. "Ask me again later," he said after a long pause.

He held up one hand and put his fingers to his lips with the other. I listened, but heard nothing, and shook my head *no*. He held up two fingers and pointed over my left shoulder, then held up five fingers, and then a closed fist. Two people, 50 yards back.

I listened harder, but still nothing. Harmon leaned in close to me, placing his lips against my ear. His hot breath against my neck sent an exhilarating tension down my spine. I could almost feel his lopsided grin. Awesome.

"Reach for your magic," he whispered. "Let it flow to your ears. Enhance your hearing."

He pulled away, and I felt colder, missing the intensity of having him so close. Trying more magic would be good. I needed to get my mind off this ridiculous crush, especially since I could see his amusement with me even through the darkness of night.

The magic flowed freely and did my bidding. Voices rang in my ears like they were directly behind me. I whirled around, but there was nothing in the trees at my heels.

I recognized Cinder's voice. "You see any more cops?"

"Just one," Another voice replied, this one with a hint of an accent. "I turned, and he nearly shit himself and ran." He and the other shared in a solid laugh.

"Lawrence says don't kill 'em," Cinder warned once they'd composed themselves.

"Nah, just gave him a good scare."

"Unless we find that Ancestral demon bitch. Take her out if you can. Keep scouting west to the road. Come back and report anything you see. I'm going to find Lawrence and inform him the barrier is down."

"Got it."

Footsteps replaced words, some fading with distance, and another set headed directly for us. I flashed a glance at Harmon.

"Shit," he mouthed, looking around for an escape route.

The Asian-reporter-turned-afflicted came into view before we could react. He was a sight, wearing the pack's uniform of just a cut-off pair of elastic-waist sweatpants. His lean, hairless body glinted white against the dark night sky. His eyes seemed lost in the darkness, but the twisted smile on his face revealed the nature of his intent. He wasn't going to play nice.

Harmon grabbed my hand and yanked me behind him, placing himself in the path between the man and me. A guttural rumble emanated from deep within Harmon's chest.

"Whoa, it's all good, Pup." The man said. "Not gonna hurt you or your girlfriend."

"Partner," Harmon corrected. "And save your lies. But you're right. You're going to leave us alone. What was your name?"

The man laughed, smooth as silk. "My name's Jack. And I'm going to take you back to the house now. The Alpha said to try and bring you in unharmed, but since he's going to kill her anyway, I figure I'll just save him time."

"You're about to fail your Alpha," Harmon said, cracking his neck.

Jack's face spread into an even wider grin, showing sharp teeth that no longer looked fit inside a human mouth.

"Kessa, run," Harmon said. I pulled at his arm, but he shoved at me. "Run!" He repeated.

I stood in wide-eyed, unmoving terror as sickening, wet pops erupted from Jack's arms and legs. His torso convulsed, and his extremities bent, contorted, and disfigured. His nose elongated and hair erupted from his chest, legs and arms.

Within moments, where once stood a man who would be considered small and lithe, now stood a being that was no taller, but infinitely more intimidating. The rock-hard, muscled creature of half-man, half-wolf radiated ferocity. Saliva glinted off of razor teeth; his hands ended in dagger claws; his chest heaved with every breath, and steam rose from his wolfish snout. His eyes, previously drawn and tight, were now round mirrors reflecting the night sky.

Before I could stop him, Harmon attacked Jack, landing a surprise jab across his left jowl. The force of Harmon's blow caught the beast off-guard, and his head snapped back in response. But regardless of the surprise attack, Jack wasted no time in retaliation, and it was clear that Jack was stronger and faster than Harmon. He raked a clawed hand across Harmon's chest, shredding shirt and flesh alike. Snarls arose from both men as they exchanged blows, but for all of Harmon's focused concentration, Jack kept his eyes trained on me. It was almost as if he was bored with Harmon's assault.

After several long seconds, Jack must have grown wary of toying with his prey, because he delivered an open-handed cuff across Harmon's temple that sent him sprawling like a rag doll tossed aside for something more interesting.

Me.

Jack dropped to all fours and circled me, edging me into a copse of trees and thick undergrowth. My escape route was cut off entirely as the Jack-beast paced back and forth, never taking his eyes from me.

The book lay on the ground several feet away, but the sight of it stirred the magic within me. I felt the power surge deep inside, but it seemed out of reach again. Jack lowered himself on his haunches and sprang across the clearing with all of the grace of a ballet dancer. He hit, however, with the force of an oncoming truck. I tried to dodge in vain, and wound up pinned beneath his body, with his clawed hands digging into each of my shoulders.

Jack reared his head back and let loose a long howl before lunging his jaws toward my face. The time he took to sound his kill was all I needed. As he moved, so did I. With every force of will, I pulled the energy within, clamping my hands to Jack's flanks, grabbing for anything I could reach. Hot, sharp teeth brushed my cheek but then pulled away. He yelped and spun, snapping at his own haunches. My eyes grew wide when I realized his flesh burned like lava. He dropped to the ground and rolled around, crying out as the smoldering of flesh and fur spread up his body and down his limbs.

His agonized wails gave way to whimpering sobs, and his form shifted back to human. The black, bestial form of a baowal dragged itself from the crippled, charred body like it was pulling itself from out of a pool. It let loose a low howl that brought bile to the back of my throat. I braced myself for a fight, but the spectral beast faded into the darkness of night.

I rushed to Jack's side, feeling in vain for vitals. The man he'd been was nearly unrecognizable through the still-spreading burning flesh. I closed his eyes and sat beside him, hugging my knees to my chest. Hot tears etched down my cheeks.

Harmon's hand on my shoulder nearly brought me out of my skin. "It's not your fault," he said, sitting beside me and wrapping an arm around my shoulders.

"I know. He would have killed me, and probably you, too."

I allowed myself to sink into Harmon's embrace, though, at the moment, I wasn't sure who was comforting whom. We sat in silence for several minutes, watching the corpse of Jack the News Anchor smolder to ashes and disappear to dust.

"Well," Harmon said, pulling me tighter and resting his chin on top of my head, "you never did like reporters all that much anyway."

I shoved him back and smacked him in the shoulder. "That's horrible!"

"Kess, you did what you had to," he said with complete seriousness, "I was useless, laying there, half-unconscious and watching you kick ass."

I bit back tears that threatened to overtake me entirely. I waited until I was certain my voice wouldn't crack before speaking. "I have no idea what I'm doing. Maybe I could have released the baowal without burning the man alive. I reacted in fear. I..."

"Saved both our lives," Harmon said, completing my sentence before I could continue with the self-flagellation. "And now we have to move. The pack is responding to Jack's loss. They can feel it. Hell, I can feel it. They know the barrier is down, they know you've escaped and that I've left. And they are headed this way."

Chapter 22

Harmon led us through the forest as quickly as I could move. I'd tried enhancing my eyesight the same as I had my hearing, but the effect was more comical than useful. I wound up overcompensating and stumbled day-blind directly into a tree. Fortunately, I had been able to reverse the effects, and relegated myself to standard night vision, which, for me, meant stumbling half-blind and probably running into trees.

I'd also tried to convince Harmon to let me heal the rake wound across his chest, but he waved me off with a dismissive flourish.

As we emerged onto the road, a cop car sped off.

"Probably the poor guy Jack terrified," Harmon said.

I nodded in agreement and pointed toward the one remaining cruiser parked next to Martina's truck. "Someone is still out there," I said.

"A couple someones," Harmon replied. "Martina stuck around. Not that she's been any help."

Darkness flashed across his face, and his jaw clenched and loosened. He shook himself like a dog after a bath.

"Anger," I stated with a sidelong glance though it was more for the sake of distraction than discussion. I felt hatred rolling off him. I was positive he sensed my fear in even speaking to him in that state.

"Not at you." He shook himself again. "But yes." His breathing had deepened, and each inhale caused a pronounced rise and fall of his chest and shoulders. "She's not what you think."

"She's most likely not what Lawrence told you either," I countered, trying to keep my voice even and metered and my emotions in check. I didn't want it to sound like a challenge.

His eyes flashed amber for a hair of a second and subsided to normal just as quickly. The ferocity of it made me flinch, and I busied myself by peering into the police cruiser. I tried the door and found it unlocked. Dispatch called in vain over the radio, "Detective Schild, report. Schild, come in."

"Schild's cruiser," I said, stating the obvious. "He's out there somewhere."

"We have to go find him. The pack might just try to scare him off, but I'm really not confident of that."

"Not to mention, dispatch is going to be sending in backup at any moment. Can you use some sort of wolf sense to find him?" I felt stupid the second the words came out of my mouth, but Harmon just laughed.

"Do you have a pair of his underwear I can sniff, maybe? Put me on the trail?" He laughed harder. "Lemme at 'em!"

I giggled in spite of the tension and shook my head. "Sorry. I'm completely out of my element here. Give me a badge and a gun and a warrant and I'm good."

"That's not our reality anymore, Kess. Like it or not, you are what you are. There's no going back."

"For you there is," I said, feeling envy creep through me like a plague.

"Not really," he shook his head and started walking toward the woods. I followed just behind, careful to place my feet directly in his steps so that I didn't trip over the local flora. "I can choose to release this thing inside me. Or I can let it take me over entirely. Or I can just decide to leave it how it is. But I can never choose to believe that it doesn't exist. Or that you don't have these abilities. I can never take away the knowledge that my grandfather has been alive for the last fifteen years right under my nose, and that I—Mr. Investigator Profiler—had no idea it was him." We walked in silence for a time, and he very faintly added, "I can never go back to a time when my grandmother is still alive."

I chose to let the last statement slide and held onto it for later. I was certain he wasn't done grieving. He'd never gotten the chance, but I couldn't exactly walk him through the grief stages in the middle of the woods while looking for a missing cop. Instead, I redirected the focus. "When I got here, you were already convinced we were dealing with the supernatural. I didn't want to believe you, but I should have. Eventually, I had to. You already knew what we were walking into."

He stopped and faced me. "I had no idea. I was still the same wide-eyed kid that you met years ago. I didn't know it would be like this. I figured we had one strange creature to deal with. Maybe even something of the natural world, and we'd take it out with a huntsman's rifle and be done with it." He clamped his hands to his head and closed his eyes tight, shook himself, and turned to continued walking. "This is so much more complex than I'd ever imagined."

"We did approach it rather conventionally," I said. "I guess the whole 'questioning witnesses' thing really didn't pan out for us."

He held up a hand as we breached the threshold of the forest, and I stopped. "The barrier is back up," he whispered, "and I hear something. It's bad. Real bad."

Harmon took off at a sprint through the undergrowth, and I silently cursed his agility as I tried to keep up. Fortunately, he hadn't gone far, and I managed to catch up to him with only a couple minor stumbles.

Schild lay in a pool of blood on the forest floor with a sucking chest wound. Harmon ripped his already torn shirt over his head and pressed it into wound, using his body weight to hold it tight. "He's unconscious, but he's breathing. We need to seal this up properly."

"I'll call for medics," I said, reaching for Schild's radio.

"And then what?" Harmon said. "We bring a bunch of EMTs out here so they can get punctured, too? You said you healed your own cracked ribs. Can you fix this?"

Panic rose up my spine, and I wanted to turn and run. "I'm not a medic, Harmon! I didn't go into medicine for a reason."

Harmon grabbed my wrist with his blood-covered hand. "If anyone can save him, you can. I know you can, because you've already done it once. You saved me; you can save Rick. This is all you, Kess."

I nodded and crouched next to Schild. The power was already welling inside me before my knees touched the ground like it sensed a need before I'd even asked. The feeling introduced a whole new level of fear, but I squelched it and focused on Schild. The wound in his chest seeped around the bloody t-shirt, and his shallow breath began to falter.

"It's now or never, Kess," Harmon urged.

I closed my eyes and placed my hands on either side of the wound. When I called up the power, I felt the same warmth as before, but stronger, and familiar, like wrapping up in my favorite blanket on a cold evening. It responded in sympathy to the need I had, but it stood firmly behind a dam in my core. I pictured Schild as he was when I first met him. I willed the wound to close, and for him to become his former self again. I begged the energy forward. Nothing happened.

Words erupted from my lips through tears. "I will learn what I've become," I directly addressed the power within. I saw in my mind's eye the Grandfather Tree. Wide, green eyes opened and turned their full attention upon me. I felt whole in his gaze as I added my vow, "I promise to accept this gift and rise to my purpose."

The familiar voice that had sung to me in my sleep for the past few nights sounded in my mind. *You are ready.*

Green and white energy shot from my hands, and my head whipped back. Every cell in my body vibrated with the intensity of the effort required to bring Schild back from the cusp of death. When the flow subsided, I lay slumped over Schild, sobbing against his healed chest.

Schild sat up and shook himself, his eyes wide and astonished. "What the fuck?"

Harmon fell over laughing. I held back my tears and helped Schild to his feet.

"You were almost gone," Harmon said, composing himself. "Kessa saved you, though. You're going to be just fine." He looked at me, positively beaming. "We all will."

"Would someone please explain to me what's going on here? Last thing I remember was some—thing—standing over me with an awl."

Harmon and I exchanged confused glances. "Was it a wolf-like thing?" I asked.

"Not in the slightest," Schild said, shaking his head. "It was tall. Thin. Wiry. And—glowing purple? And it was holding an awl. I thought it got me. I remember getting hit and then the pain. It did get me. How the hell am I sitting here?"

Harmon shot me a glance that said, *you shquld know what this means.* I shrugged, and he shook his head, clearly frustrated with me.

Instead of arguing the finer points of my cluelessness, he said, "We need to get back to the cruiser and get the hell out of here. I think they know where we are."

Schild didn't ask who *they* were. He merely agreed and led the run back to the cruiser.

We never got there. Martina stood before us on the road as we breached the tree line. Her eyes grew wide at the sight of us, flicking from Harmon, Schild, me and back to Schild. The slightest hint of confusion had peppered her features before she turned back to me, her mouth spread in a wide, relieved smile. "Kessa! Oh, thank the Ancients you're safe!"

"Drop the act, Martina." Harmon stepped between us and planted himself firmly, with feet slightly apart and shoulders back. Dawn crept through the tree line, and in the faint light, I caught a glimpse of a lavender hue emanating from Martina's aura. She kept her focus on me, ignoring the wall of Harmon between us.

"Quick, get in the truck, let's get out of here," she said. "We need to regroup." Her eyes shifted colors. I realized her gaze tugged at me like a psychic drawstring. I shook the sensation away and reached for my own power. It obeyed my command, and I put up a mental block against whatever magic might be coming my way.

The moment my own magical defenses took its place I saw Martina's natural form. She looked like a Gumby doll if it was stretched thin and colored like foxgloves. Wild, white hair spiked out in all directions, and her elongated nose punctuated almond-shaped eyes that shifted colors wildly, like a prism being spun on its top in the sunlight. The lavender glow of her skin set all the puzzle pieces in place.

"What are you really, Martina? What are you getting out of this? And why me?" I challenged, stepping up beside Harmon and matching his stance.

"You stand beside a Fel adherent and question *my* intentions?"

"I stand beside my partner, and I ask questions. It's what I do." I saw Harmon's sideways smile out of the corner of my eye.

"And I stand beside *my* partner," he said, "and together, we kick ass and take names." He cleared his throat. "Well, mostly, she kicks ass, and I keep score."

Mockery and malice dripped through Martina's laugh. Energy from her being overtook my senses and radiated outward, amplified by her otherworldly appearance. Fear took root deep in my belly, and my eyes grew wide. The desire to run nearly claimed me. I let the magical sight drop and saw her again in her human form. The panic subsided enough for me to hold my ground.

She directed her attention at Harmon. "I can feel that you've chosen." She edged on the word *chosen* like it was filthy. After looking him up and down, she shrugged and returned her attention to me. "You can't trust his word; he's chosen the Fel beast inside. It will forever dominate his every decision. He can not—will not—ever love, unless for selfish gains. He will be consumed by anger and power and greed. He will follow his pack without question. And I wouldn't get too close to him, magically speaking. You might just fan that torch you carry a little too much."

Her lip curled into a self-satisfied snarl at the shock of understanding that flashed across my face. I shifted my weight uncomfortably, seeing in my mind the image of Jack disintegrating to dust and remembering Harmon's offhanded dismissal of my offer to help heal his wounds. I lost my words at the thought of what might have happened.

Harmon rescued me by interjecting, "And how do we trust you, Martina? What have you given us to go on? I think you're using us for something. You nearly killed Schild. You killed the senator, and my grandmother, too. Didn't you?" He was using an assumptive interrogation tactic, letting her believe that he'd figured her out completely; I knew he was winging most of it. But she looked uncomfortable. He was getting somewhere. "You set it up to look like a baowal had done the deed, but it was you with a regular awl. The murder weapon is conveniently hidden away in the Fade so we'll never find it? Is this sounding familiar?"

I suddenly found my voice as a puzzle piece clicked into place. "This land holds some key to that power you've lost, doesn't it Martina? Maybe the power was stripped from you? The senator was going to buy the grove from Virginia Harmon, and he'd probably turn it into his own personal vacation condo. You would be permanently shut out. You wanted me to get Lawrence out of the way, because he was keeping you out, too. You didn't expect that I was truly Adept, did you?"

Martina regarded me with a look of cool indifference. "You're no Adept. You draw magic off of a trinket that I supplied to you. Remember, never accept a gift of the Fae. Your partner even tried to warn you. And yes, once I reclaim this link to the Fade, I'll couple it with our portal to the Ancestral Land. It will reopen the old paths, and we shall reclaim what is ours by rights.

"Regardless, Kessa, you're nothing without my help. You may have a weak link to the Ancestral magic, but like all other Adepts before you, you are, at your core, just a human. You're weak and insignificant."

I yanked the Earth Stone from around my neck, breaking the chain. I held it up with Ginny's journal, twisting both in my hand in demonstration before tossing them to the ground. The book flipped open, and it briefly caught my eye. The words seemed to make sense. I shook it off and held my hand up, calling to my well of power that I felt within. It responded without hesitation and glowed brightly, snaking through my fingers, and pooling over my upturned palm. "I don't need those," I said, "and I don't need you."

The second I renounced my link to Martina and called purely upon my Ancestral gift, I felt a surge of both peace and strength. I knew the truth of my words, and by the perfect O that Martina's mouth had formed, she knew it, too. "I am Adept, with or without your help. I have the might of the Ancients behind me."

I took aim for Martina and prepared to loose a blast of energy, but movement caught my eye.

Schild had taken the opportunity of our conversation to slip silently into his squad car, where he reached for the microphone on his dispatch radio.

"Schild, no!" Harmon and I shouted out in unison.

The moment of distraction was all she needed. Martina closed the distance between us faster than human sight could track and she pulled us into the Fade.

Chapter 23

The world spun as my vision cleared. Harmon lay next to me, propping himself uneasily on one elbow. His head hung limp on his neck. We both fought the sickening and painful effects of plane transition in our own way. Mine mostly involved biting back the desire to vomit. I rolled up to sitting and looked around for Martina, but she was conspicuously absent. We sat in the Fade, on the path we'd traveled before. Together, but alone.

"Now what?" he asked.

"Good question. But I know we can't stay here. We'll be faery food in a matter of minutes."

"I'm fairly confident that was the point." Harmon rubbed the back of his head. "I think I landed on a rock. If you can call this ground *rock*." He ran his hand over the trail beneath us.

The path below us was the consistency of loam and the color of lichen. Occasional bumps rose from the surface, but for the most part, it lay flat and lifeless. The silver-barked trees looming upward on either side of us reflected the same inertness. Branches hung devoid of needles. No birds sat in the boughs. No creatures roamed the forest floor. Even the stagnant air was neither warm nor cold.

"This place is apathy incarnate," I said. "Seems like it's somewhere between life and death. I don't think we're on the same trail as before."

"It's definitely something different," Harmon agreed.

I yawned and stretched. The stillness of the surroundings began to lull my subconscious, and I felt the urge to lay down and sleep. *It would be so nice just to close my eyes. It will all be over soon.*

Harmon slapped my face.

"Ow! What the hell was that for?"

"You were laying down like you were going to sleep. Why?"

"Tired," I admitted, and then I corrected myself. "No. It was like I just wanted to give up."

"Ok, whatever it is, it's not affecting me. Get up."

Harmon pulled me to my feet and dragged me forward, heading in what we assumed was toward the Grove of the Ancient. To be honest, we had no idea if the path we walked even led to the grove. But as we left our landing area, my mind began to clear.

I shook my head. "Why do you think you weren't affected?"

"Probably the magic that's coursing through me. I can feel it, and I know it's different from what's in you. I'm thinking like, the polar opposite."

I shivered involuntarily.

"You okay?"

"Yeah, just thinking," I replied, "if you'd let me try to heal you, I might have watched you burn to ashes."

Harmon nodded. "I had a really bad feeling about it. Honestly, I'd love it if you'd be able to fix me up. And maybe find me a shirt."

I took stock of our appearance and was glad we were away from the general population. My clothes were still damp from the earlier bathtub escape, and my blouse was ripped to hell. The underbrush had not been kind to either of our slacks. Harmon's bare chest oozed from open wounds. Mud and grime covered our faces, arms, and hands, and I was sure my hair contained clumps of wet clay.

"At least we're still alive," I said, forcing a smile. We walked in silence for a while; I had something on my mind, but was having the hardest time determining how to start. I finally decided that direct was best. "Harmon, you said to ask you later what you know. Is this sufficiently *later*? I mean, we may never get out of here alive, so could you tell me now?"

He nodded but said nothing for several minutes as we walked. I felt him struggle with his anger. He finally said, "Think it through. Martina showed up right when we needed her the most on too many occasions. She gave you the stone. She showed you the Fade and the Grove of the Ancients. She led you on this path believing that she was your guide and friend. But there were two things that never sat right with me though I'm ashamed to admit, I didn't see it until the Fel energy started coursing through my veins."

"Not sure I'm following," I admitted.

He held up one finger, "First: she showed up when it was convenient, led us around, helped just enough to keep us alive and running down her track, but she never instructed you. Not really. She gave us one directive the whole time—determine how to pronounce the name of one specific demon. Now, why would she want that?"

He let the question simmer between us for a moment before holding up a second finger. "Second: she wasn't there the first time you opened the book. You felt your ties to the energy of the Ancients before she even got involved. I think she singled you out because you're Adept, but at the same time, you're pragmatic. You wouldn't have readily believed in your abilities. That probably made you easier for her to control with the Earth Stone."

"Surprised the hell out of her, didn't I?" I laughed.

"So, you believe me now?" he asked.

"You're joking, right?" Realization crept over me. "Harmon, the book. When I threw it down at Martina's feet, it flipped open. I could swear I was able to read it."

Harmon ran a hand through his hair, "Too bad we don't have it with us. You probably *can* understand it now. And I'd wager it has some instructions on how to cross the planes."

"And if I can read it, then I might be able to find some clues as to what Martina really is, and how your grandfather fits into all of this. Something is going on between the two of them. Something big. Of course, we kind of have to get back to Earth first."

"Right, first: Earth," Harmon said, continuing to walk down the path. "But it does make me wonder; what could Martina do if she controlled the demon that afflicts my grandfather? And by the way, can we use a word other than *afflict*? Makes us sound diseased."

"I guess 'possessed' is off the table."

He frowned.

"Touched?" I offered.

"Sounds like fun."

I felt my cheeks flush realizing I'd gone from a stupid crush to outright flirting. He grinned, and I sighed. "This is fun for you, isn't it? You can practically hear my thoughts."

"Not your thoughts, but for as serious and stoic as you were when we first met, you throw emotion like a major league pitcher."

"Great. And for the record, you are a closed book unless you're pissed off."

"Your secrets are safe with me."

"Not that I'm desperate to change the subject or anything," I said, "but do you notice something? Or rather, a distinct lack of something?" He gave me a quizzical glance, his brows drawing together. "We haven't come across a single creature since we entered the Fade. Last time we were here we ran for our lives."

"We already decided we're in a different spot. Maybe this is a danger-free zone?" He shrugged. "I have to admit that this isn't my specialty."

"Mine either, but I think I may have a way out of here."

"Well, that's good, because I honestly have no clue, and I'm not convinced we're even walking in the right direction." He stopped again, and I had to turn to face him. His turned-down mouth and hard-set eyes caught me off guard, and his uncertainty flooded over me.

"What's wrong?"

"I haven't really chosen, Kess. Martina was wrong. I'm not fully... touched." His sarcastic smile edged the last word but then faded almost immediately. "I can still let go of this thing if I want to. I'm just not sure. It's all I have left..."

His words caught in his throat, and instead of finishing the sentence, he took my hands between his and pierced my soul with ice blue eyes. Sadness crept around the edges of his features. I didn't need to read the emotion to know where his mind had traveled.

"I'm here for you if you want to talk about what happened," I offered, lightly brushing my thumb over his.

He looked away. "Not yet. But I know you are. And that makes me want to tell this thing inside me to take a hike. But I can't. I need the power and the speed. I need to track down Martina, avenge my grandmother, and maybe even help Lawrence in his very ambitious plan."

I cocked my head to one side. He tried to pull from my hand, but I held him there. "Tell me what Lawrence told you."

He shook his head, "I can't. Not now, anyway." He glanced around at our lifeless surroundings. "Not here. Not if there's a possibility *she* can hear us. I'm fairly certain she's hearing everything we're saying. In fact, I know she is."

Harmon dropped my hands and turned on his heel. Martina, still in her faery form, glided out of the trees with fluid grace. Her purple impish face twisted up in a smile and she laughed, deep and hollow. "I figured you could smell me there, *Pup.* It would be too much to ask for you just to divulge all of Lawrence's secrets, but I was hopeful."

"So what now, Martina?" I crossed my arms and stood erect; challenging; confident; like I'd been taught for so many years. "You're going to kill us here in the Fade? You still don't have what you need, do you?"

"I figured I'd just leave you to the path, and let whatever comes along claim you, yes. And I've waited more than a thousand years; what's a little more time?"

"And if we get back to the Grove of the Ancient, what then? How did you break in there? I'm thinking you're not actually welcome."

"I'm not." In a flash of light, Martina shifted back to her human form. "But I am." She then shifted just as rapidly to the slight variation of her Martina self that I met in the grove. "And so am I."

"So you're impersonating an actual guardian," I said.

"You're a bright one!"

"So what's your real name?" Harmon asked.

Martina's smile curled up at the edges, "Nothing you will ever know."

"A demon," I said, feeling like someone had knocked the wind out of me. Lawrence called her as much, but I hadn't believed him.

"But you're not Fel," Harmon said.

I looked from Harmon to Martina and back again.

"What?" he asked. "I can tell. Can't you?"

I reached out for my magic and asked it to query Martina. The answer came clearly. She was of the Ancients.

"So, there are demons in the realm of the Ancients?" I asked.

"Child," Martina replied, "so sweet and innocent. Are there not those who walk among your civilized society whom others accuse of being unfit or otherwise problematic?"

"Great, she's a thug," Harmon said, "we're crime fighting in an alternate dimension now. I'm not sure we have jurisdiction here, do we? Do we get hazard pay for this?"

"I tire of this," Martina said, waving off his jokes. "It's time for you to die. I'll accomplish what I need without your help."

She spread her hands apart, and her mouth opened in a gaping roar. Green and black energy crackled between her fingertips. She aimed the first blast directly at Harmon.

In one swift motion, I reached into my pocket and pulled out Ginny Harmon's locket, clicking it open and holding it at arm's length. A field of shimmering silver appeared around us like a bubble. The blast of demon breath wrapped around the sphere, leaving us unharmed. Martina cried out in frustration and charged at us in long strides. I turned to Harmon, clutching him in a full embrace, wrapping one arm tightly around his waist.

"Don't let go of me," I whispered in his ear.

"I won't." His voice shook along with his body, and mine. Fear coursed through both of us like acid.

"Ginny, I hope you knew what you were doing when you put this together!" I pressed the locket against the force field that enveloped us and pulled down like opening a zipper.

The rip in the fabric of reality dumped us onto the road in front of Schild's cruiser. He stood, clutching the microphone for dispatch in his hand, staring at us with wide eyes. I turned to see what had become of the rift, but it appeared to be gone.

In its place was something far worse.

Harmon saw it the same time I did. "What the hell?" was all he managed to say.

Along the road, from the direction we'd reappeared, small ripples and crackles of energy pulsed and pulled at the soil, tearing tiny pinpoint holes in the fabric of reality, and sealing them back up again.

"Oh, this can't be good," I said.

"Dammit, Pup!" Lawrence emerged from the wood line, stalking toward us, "What the hell did you do?"

"It was me," I admitted

"You've destroyed everything!" Lawrence shouted.

"Bullshit!" Harmon said, pushing himself between his grandfather and me. "She saved our lives!"

Lawrence stood eye to eye with his grandson, his lower jaw jutting out in challenge. He spoke slowly. Deliberately. "You may think so. But in the act of saving your own asses, you've killed the rest of us."

Schild finally broke his silence. "Would someone like to explain to me what the fuck is going on?"

Chapter 24

"So you're telling me," I said, setting such a pace that Schild had to jog to keep up, "There are *good* and *bad* demons?" I glanced at Lawrence through narrowed eyes. He offered a curt nod in response. "And of course, the one raging inside you is good. That's why you tried to kill me when I was fifteen. That's why you killed the senator and Ginny Harmon."

"I didn't want to kill you. I was trying to chase you off. It worked. Would have been better if Pup here hadn't thought to shoot me with a silver-tipped arrow." He grinned like he was remembering his grandson winning his first trophy. "Have to give him credit for bravery. At least he had terrible aim." He shook himself from his reminiscence and said, "And I already made it clear to Daniel that I didn't kill your senator or my wife."

"And we're just supposed to believe you? How did you get Ginny's locket?"

Lawrence moved way faster than anyone his age should be able to move. He stood in front of me, forcing me to come to stop walking. Schild nearly ran me over. "You have to listen to me, and stop making assumptions. I was too late, child. I couldn't stop your beloved Martina in time. I knew the only way to save the rest of us was to take the portal and use it. You know what it means to call for backup. That's all I did. I used Ginny's locket to call in reinforcements."

We stood, staring each other down for what felt like an eternity before his features softened and he asked, "Is the darkness evil, my dear? Or is it simply an answer to daylight?"

"What the hell is that supposed to mean?" Harmon asked.

"Think about it. There are things that go bump in the night. But nighttime is a necessity. Darkness allows for rest and recovery. It quiets the heart and stills the mind. There is evil that walks at night, but there is such that acts in broad daylight, too. The realms of Fae aren't divided into light and dark, or good and evil. They match the states of the natural world. My kind are the protectors of the Fel." Lawrence waggled a finger in my face, and I took a reflexive step back. "Martina and her faction want domination, and they will use a young Adept such as yourself in any way they can, right up to the point of your own demise. Their power is limited here for a reason. Though your little stunt in the Fade could cost us critically in that regard."

"So your plan," I said, pushing past him and ignoring his accusation, "is to rifle through Ginny's research in hopes that we can turn up a name, or some other identifying something that will lead us to Martina."

"Yes, she means to take full control of this region for the Ancestral demons."

"And that's... bad?" Schild asked through huffed breaths.

"Yes," Lawrence said. "Why are you still here?"

"Curiosity?" Schild said with a grin.

Lawrence shrugged his shoulders and turned to follow me down the road. "I just hope whatever we find we can actually read."

"Read!" I shouted, making Lawrence jump. "Where's the book?"

Lawrence fished it out of his coat pocket. "It's right here."

I took it from him and flipped it open. The text shimmered like green glass floating above a sea of silver. The words came to me slowly, like they were being conveyed through an interpreter. "I can read this," I whispered. A grin stretched across my face, and my pulse quickened. "Harmon, I can read it!" I shouted.

"What's it say?" He leaned over my shoulder.

"This page is an incantation that wards against sprites," I said with a laugh. I flipped to another random page. "Huh. Did you know that gnomes are the protectors of the Earth's fertility? Belladonna, nightshade... mushrooms of one night? Some of this is familiar, and others are completely foreign. These pages I thought were blank are filled with sketches of cities, maps of whole continents. Lists of royal families. It's like there's a whole other world there!"

"That's all very fascinating," Lawrence said, his tone dry, "but is there anything useful?"

"There has to be something useful. I used it to fight you off once already."

"What are you talking about, child?" he asked.

"On the road? When we wrecked the car? Ring any bells?" I shut the book and stared him down.

"I think you have me confused with someone else."

Harmon stood beside me, facing his grandfather, "You're saying that wasn't you?"

"You do realize what your *friend* Martina is, right?"

"Well," I said, "I know now that she's a demon."

"Correct. But more specifically, she's a doppelgänger."

"Um, *gesundheit?*"

"That makes perfect sense!" Harmon said.

"Wait, doppelgängers are real?" Schild asked.

"Am I the only one who is completely lost here?" I asked. "What the hell is a doppel-whatever?"

"A doppelgänger," Harmon said, over-enunciating the word, "is a kind of shapeshifter. But it doesn't just mimic the form of another. It takes on every bit of the other person's being. All the way down to the DNA."

"And you know this because?" I asked, crossing my arms.

"Maybe your cousin was on to something. We played a lot of *Dungeons & Dragons* I read his books." Harmon grinned.

"You can't be serious," I said, crossing my arms.

"He's right," Lawrence said. "And Ginny always warned nothing good would come from playing those games. Good thing you never listened to her, kid."

"Oh my god," I said, realization dawning. "So that's how Lawrence's DNA ended up at both crime scenes."

"See," Lawrence said, "I'm not the big bad wolf you want to believe I am."

I ignored his comment, but his grin told me he saw me twitch.

"But then how did Martina show up at the same time as *you* on the road?" I asked. "Or, what we thought was you."

"Kessa," Harmon said, resting a hand on my shoulder. "Remember the innkeeper? Shari? You said yourself you don't think Martina is acting alone. And she did a number on us."

Lawrence whistled. "Two doppelgängers? That's rough, even for my pack. They're still young."

My stomach churned. "Lawrence, your grove—you say it's a place of power. You keep it sealed off from certain types of energy so that the Ancestral demons can't pass there. But there are others, aren't there. Other places. Other groves."

"Anchors, they're called. And yes," he said, "you were staying on one."

"So that wasn't you the night you broke down my door and chased us into the Puget Sound?" I asked.

"Of course that was me. Scared you, did I? Really, I just wanted the book. I needed it to call forth the pack. But I figured I might be able to scare you guys off at the same time."

"Wait," Harmon said, "I thought you couldn't read it."

"I can't," he tapped the side of his head, "but my buddy in here can read some of it. I'm willing to bet our young Adept here can't read some of those pages so readily."

He took the book from my hand, flipped through it and handed it back.

I squinted and willed myself to read the words, but they took no form. I shook my head. "It's gibberish."

"Ginny was an incredible woman," Lawrence said. I felt a wave of anger emanate from Harmon, which he immediately squelched. "She was gifted in so many ways. She was adherent to neither the Fel nor the Ancients. She was of the Fade. As such, she could straddle all the planes. She was the dawn and the sunset combined."

"And that's why you think..."

Lawrence finished my thought. "She'll have what we need nestled somewhere in her research. We just need to find it."

Chapter 25

Schild agreed to keep watch while we searched for Ginny's notes. We crossed the threshold of Ginny's house, and Lawrence came to an abrupt halt halfway down the hall.

"You forget something in the car?" Harmon asked.

"Can you invite me in, Daniel? This isn't my wife's house anymore. Looks like she intended for you to take ownership. I guess my welcome is worn out."

"But you were able to come in this far," I said.

"I can enter just fine." Lawrence's glanced around as if he was searching for the right words in the yellow flowered wallpaper.

"I think he's trying to say that he's weakened in here and he doesn't like it," Harmon said.

"A renewed invitation will fix the problem."

Harmon shook his head. "I think I prefer you powerless, old man."

The two men stared at each other unblinking. Harmon maintained his calm coolness. Lawrence ground his jaw. After a long moment of palpable silence, the elder Harmon relented with a curt nod, but the scowl on his face said that didn't appreciate being challenged.

Harmon turned and stalked down the hall to where the attic opening was set into the ceiling. He grabbed a pull rod from the coat closet and yanked open the drop ladder.

"I always loved coming up here," Harmon said, climbing up first. He flipped on the light, and the room illuminated as he disappeared into the attic. His voice carried down the ladder. "Tried to sneak up more than once. Those were always bad days for me."

"Your grandmother wasn't the person you thought she was. I'm sure she kept a lot of secrets from you," Lawrence said, ascending after Harmon had cleared the lip of the attic floor.

I climbed up the ladder and poked my head through the opening just as Harmon's hands met Lawrence's chest. He lifted his grandfather off his feet and shoved him up against the sloped ceiling.

"Don't talk about her. You have no right even to mention her name." Harmon's shoulders heaved with each breath.

Lawrence pushed against Harmon, but his lack of strength betrayed him.

I raced the rest of the way up the ladder and put a hand on Harmon's shoulder, which he greeted with a snarl. His eyes had gone savage.

"Harmon! Focus!" I shouted, shaking him by the shoulder.

Lawrence took advantage of the distraction and shifted his weight. Harmon stumbled forward; inertia carried him head-first into the wall. He spun and crouched, poised to strike. Lawrence stood firm, ready for the challenge.

I stepped between them and grabbed Harmon again, forcing him to make eye contact. "Harmon. Knock it off. Breathe. You're being overtaken. Shut it off!"

I could feel the rise of hate within him; it fed off my fear. The link between us served to spin him up, rather than calm him down. He pushed forward, and I struggled to maintain my footing.

I forced myself to take a long, meditative breath. A vision of the grandfather tree stood out in my mind. Peaceful. Serene. Powerful. I let the feelings flood through me, and wash into the link I shared with my partner. It did nothing to calm him. My mind raced for a solution; the one I came up with was uncomfortable, but I had to try.

I recalled the moment in Harmon's apartment that he had wrapped me in his arms, acknowledging the comfort he'd provided and the confidence he'd instilled in me. I let my feelings of kindled interest mingle with appreciation and trust. I felt vulnerable and exposed, but I let my feelings envelop him like a warm blanket.

He sucked in a sharp breath and exhaled slowly, glancing over my shoulder to keep one eye on Lawrence. After several moments of holding him back, I felt his shoulders slack under my grasp. He leaned back into a crouch and rubbed his temples.

"You back with us?" I asked, hearing the hesitation in my own voice.

"Yeah." He stood and pushed past me to cross the attic.

The room felt cramped, partially because of the peaked roof, but mostly due to the number of boxes stacked against the walls. The finished floor was decorated with faded and tattered department-store rugs. And old armchair sat next to a skylight window with a small, round table beside it. On top of the table sat a book; the bookmark was near the end. I picked it up and turned it over in my hands. The cover bore the image of a voluptuous woman dressed in a sheer, flowing gown clutched in the arms of a muscular, naked man—with all the right parts hidden. I smirked and set it down.

"So, what's up here that's so important?" Harmon asked.

"Ginny's research will be here somewhere. I'm only hoping she knew more about this 'Martina' than you two do."

I watched Harmon, searching for signs of the anger that had overtaken him, but he directed his irritation toward a stack of boxes in the far corner of the room. I chose another stack and busied myself.

"What exactly are we looking for?" I asked, after opening a fourth box of scarves, knitting supplies, old paperback romances and random financial papers. I glanced around the room to see Harmon pulling photo albums out of a plastic milk crate. Lawrence was having similar luck, seeming to find old and broken kitchen gadgets.

"Leather-bound journals," Lawrence said, "or papers with notes. She liked to use loose parchment."

"We could check her closet," I offered.

"She wouldn't have been so foolish as to keep this information so readily available." Lawrence rubbed his chin and looked around the room.

"Well, there's nothing here," Harmon stalked back to the ladder. "I say we just make ourselves some nice silver bullets and take her out the old fashioned way."

"That's not going to get us much," Lawrence said. "You would hurt her that way, but only on the mortal plane. We need something that helps us take her out on her level."

"What about my magic?" I asked.

Lawrence scoffed. "You have a thing or two to learn about what you are."

I tried not to feel the sting of insult, but could only shrug in agreement. He had a point.

"Let me guess," Harmon offered, "what would really help would be to have her true name?"

"That would help," Lawrence said.

Harmon turned to me, idly flipping a winter hat in his hand. "I feel like we've walked into a turf war."

"And demon names are the gang signs?" I asked.

"Precisely."

"You were right. We *are* fighting interdimensional crime now. And these creeps are goin' down!" I laughed at my own joke.

Harmon's mouth dropped open. "Down," he said. "Yes!" He raced across the attic and bolted down the ladder. I scrambled to keep up, with Lawrence on my heels.

"The root cellar," Harmon said through as he left the house and rounded the corner to the side yard, "was off limits to me as a kid. So was the attic. But something about the way she told me 'never go down there,' I knew it was more than just a warning." We stopped, and he flipped the lock on the cellar doors.

"Any idea where the key is?"

Lawrence shouldered past us, gripped the lock and yanked it from the door, pulling off a good chunk of the wood with it. He shrugged at my agape expressions and shoved the door open.

"Now you see why I didn't invite him in," Harmon said.

"After you." Lawrence stood aside.

After some groping in the dark, my fingers found a pull chain that turned on a single bulb hanging from the ceiling. The cellar smelled of mildew and rat poison. Rusty nails protruded from the water-stained cement wall, serving as hangers for gardening tools, mud-encrusted gloves, and buckets. Harmon spun in a circle in the center of the room, taking in its extreme ordinariness.

"There has to be something here!" he said. I felt his frustration, and it mingled with my own.

"Doesn't seem like anything but Ginny's gardening stuff." Lawrence flipped one of the trowels hanging from the wall. "Same tools she had years ago, from the looks of them."

I walked across the room, studying each item. There were no boxes or crates. The buckets hung empty, save for condensed water pooled in the bottom.

"Back to the attic, I guess," Harmon said.

Lawrence pushed past us and jogged up the stairs, disappearing into the night. Harmon raced up the stairs behind him.

I reached for the light chain and froze in place, cocking my head to the side. A tendril of energy snaked down my arm and tickled my breast. I pulled the tallest bucket I could find from the wall, flipped it over and climbed on top. Pushing on a little section of the ceiling to the side of the light fixture caused the board to give way, revealing the smallest of openings.

I reached in with one hand and pulled out a small leather journal, the front of which bore an aspen tree etched into the leather. Emeralds adorned each corner. I flipped open the book and watched the text swirl into decipherable words.

I tucked the journal into my waistband at the small of my back.

Next to a rough-drawn picture of Martina in her true form had been a single word.

A name.

I just had to figure out how to pronounce it.

Chapter 26

"You're the master of public relations," Harmon said, picking bits of gravel out of the gashes on his chest. "Rick is freaking out. You deal with him."

I closed my eyes and gathered my thoughts. Schild watched me with all the expectancy of a parent waiting for some lame excuse concocted by his drunken teenager. "Things aren't exactly what you'd expect," I said, feeling hopelessly inadequate. This wasn't like your average press conference; we needed Schild on our side.

"How about I take you both down to County and let the boys down there have a go at you?" He leaned against the door frame of Ginny's house.

"I assure you, that won't be necessary," Harmon said.

"There are forces at work here beyond your imagining," I said, pulling at the caked dirt in my hair. "We came here expecting to bring in the perpetrator of a murder just like you. What we got instead is something that none of us expected."

"You're right. None of this makes sense. Demons? Doppelgängers?" He waved his hands up in the air and paced the front porch. "And now I just watched who I thought was our prime suspect lead you two around by the nose and then stalk off without so much as a word. I want to call for backup if anyone will come back. Actually, I just want to know what the hell is going on." He sized me up out of the corner of his eye, "Tell me, when do we arrest this *Lawrence* person on suspicion of the murder of a US senator?"

"We don't," Harmon said with matter-of-fact resolution.

"Then I'm taking you two in for obstruction." He nodded like the deal was done and final, and nothing could change his mind.

Harmon put a hand on Schild's shoulder. "Rick, we've known each other a long time. Played together as kids; chased the same girls in high school; ran track together. You know you can trust me, right?"

"Where's your shirt, Agent?"

"In all honesty, ripped to shreds, and then pulled off, balled up and applied right there," Harmon thumped Schild in the chest, "to hold back the sucking chest wound that was killing you until my partner here could heal you properly."

I nodded once when Schild looked at me, and I held out my hand, willing a ball of green and white energy to dance through my fingertips. "There's more here than meets the eye. We need you just to go with this one. Lawrence, while I'm not entirely convinced his motives are pure, isn't our suspect."

Schild's saucer eyes took in the magical energy before him. He reached out a tentative finger, and I nodded approval. "You're fine," I said. "It's just raw Ancestral energy."

He brushed one fingertip through the energy and pulled back just as quickly, forcing stoicism onto his features. "I'm not sure what game you're playing at, but something isn't right here. I'm calling it in."

"No, you won't." Lawrence's rasp of a voice came from behind Schild, who turned, reaching for his revolver. Harmon caught Schild's hand before he could reach the gun, and twisted it up behind him.

"I'm really sorry, Rick," Harmon said, "but you're going to have to trust us on this one whether you like it or not."

"I went to check on the rift you two opened coming back from the Fade," Lawrence said. "We have a problem. That sucker is going to keep on opening until anything and everything that lives in the Fade can wander right through."

"And that's bad?" Schild asked.

"It certainly isn't ideal," Lawrence said. He turned to Harmon. "What the hell did you do, Danny?"

"Wasn't me!"

I rolled my eyes. "Very mature, Harmon. Yeah, that was my doing. Not sure how, though."

"You used Ginny's locket from inside the Fade, didn't you?"

I smiled sheepishly, pulling the pendant from my pocket. "We were stuck. I had a hunch it would get us back."

"Well, now we're screwed." He paced along the front of the house. "It's all pinholes now, but when they grow and connect, it will open a passage to the Fade allowing passage for anything that wants to come through, except maybe the largest of creatures."

"In other words, we're safe from dragons, but not much more?" Harmon joked.

"Right," Lawrence said, deadly serious.

Harmon sobered immediately. "There are dragons? Real ones?"

"Where do you think the stories come from, Pup? Your average human isn't all that creative. There are plenty of beings in the Fae realms that want to cross over. Some find ways. They enter through our dreams, or they force their way through with magic. The one inhabiting me came through because Ginny called him here, and I spent a good number of years learning how to live with him. I used to do his bidding, but now we work in consort."

Schild struggled against Harmon's hold. "This still doesn't make sense!"

"We need to do something with him until we can figure this out," Lawrence said.

"Yeah, like convince him none of us are the bad guy," I said. "This is his beat. He protects these people. He needs the tools to do so; not a roll of duct tape and a running bathtub."

Lawrence looked down at his feet, and then back up with just his eyes. He almost looked apologetic. "I thought you were on the side of that Ancestral demon. I did what I thought had to be done. Turns out, I might have been wrong." He straightened himself and his tone went stern, "You're still a threat to the pack; you've already roasted one of us."

"He was trying to chew my face off!"

"How did you know to use the amulet?" Lawrence asked, changing the subject.

"I guessed," I admitted. "I watched you use it to open a portal in the civic center, and figured the door most likely swung both ways."

"I figured as much," Lawrence circled around Harmon, placing himself between the two of us. Harmon turned Schild around, who had given up his squirming protest for the moment.

Lawrence leaned in close, chewing at his cheek while he inspected me deeply. "At least you're starting to figure out what you are. Too bad we didn't find anything useful in that attic. I think we might have a way out of this. But we're going to have to work together. And you can't go guessing anymore. Your lack of knowledge may have just killed us all."

Lawrence's white eyebrows drew into a furrow that mirrored the one I'd seen on Harmon's face when he was frustrated. It was the first moment where I saw a distinct family resemblance. "We are in the uncomfortable position of requiring one another. Even still, I'm not sure we can close this rift."

"What do we need to do?"

The elder Harmon leveled graying eyes at me. "It will require sacrifice, both of this realm and the other."

"Sacrifice, as in..."

"Giving oneself to the possibility of death, yes. The rift has brought forth life of an unnatural sort. In order to close it, a being from either side must either sacrifice himself or be offered in order to seal the doorway. I'm not entirely sure what the nature of the death would entail."

"Doesn't death usually entail—dying?" I asked. Lawrence's cackling laugh in response made me feel like a child.

"Normally, yes. But in this, I can't say where the soul would go or how it might transform. The rift in the Fade is unnatural. Thus the transformation between the worlds would also be beyond the natural order."

"I volunteer Martina," Harmon said. I laughed, and he shrugged. "What? She's no saint; I wouldn't mind if she unnaturally transformed into a pile of dust."

"And who from this side is going to go?" Lawrence asked.

We all exchanged nervous glances, including Schild. I noticed that Harmon had let go of his arm, and he was taking stock of the discussion. I assumed he was still trying to figure out if we were all on drugs, but he wasn't racing for his radio any longer.

"It should be me," I said, lacking resolution. "I opened the doorway; I should close it."

"No, Kess. I'll do it." Harmon took my hand.

"No, you won't," I said, finding the conviction my previous assertion had lacked. He ground his jaw but said nothing.

"I still don't quite know what's going on here," Schild said, rubbing a hand over his bald head, "but it sounds like you're on the right side of whatever it is you're talking about. I'll do whatever you need me to. Do you need backup?"

"What we really need is for your people to stay clear," Lawrence said. "Too much chance of something slipping through and overtaking some hapless human.

I damned near killed my grandson and Kessa here when they were younger," he flicked his head in our direction. "Let's just say it was good that Ginny locked me up until I set this demon in me to rights. Still have bouts and issues. It's a constant struggle."

"So how do we lure in Martina?" Harmon asked.

"We widen this rift," Lawrence said.

"Widen it?" I asked, my voice louder than intended. "You just said we have to close it! What happened to the whole 'risking humanity' thing?"

"This is what she wants. Why do you think Ginny wanted the property in the clearing? Why do you think Martina and her friend appear where they do?"

"The grove," I said. "And the area around the bed and breakfast. Martina said she wanted to link them to reopen the old passages. They're some sort of freeway between the worlds."

"You're catching on." Lawrence sounded amused. "This whole area, up to the power lines here, and down to the road, is a vortex site. That site down by the water is another."

"Like they advertise in the mountains of Arizona?" Schild asked.

"Exactly that kind," Lawrence said. "Those fools don't know the untapped potential of those hills. A full rupture on a site like this, and they'll all open up. Arizona, the caldera under Yellowstone, the faery mounds in Ohio and Ireland, Giza, Las Vegas..."

"Ok, we get it," Harmon snapped. "Opening the rift is bad."

"Bad for us, but great for the faery. Their magic on Earth would be restored, and we would have loads of fun trying to contain them, right up until we were all possessed or dead. It's taken me nearly thirty years to lock down the one beast inside me, and I knew what it was when it got me. Your typical, unsuspecting human," he eyed Schild, "would be hopelessly ill-equipped to handle demonic possession or even faery influence."

"Well, what are we waiting for?" I asked.

Lawrence cocked one eyebrow, "So eager to die, young Adept?"

"Eager to set this right," I said. "Hoping not to die in the process, but if it's me or the world..." I left the thought hanging and avoided Harmon. "Schild, call in the all-clear. Tell them you haven't found us, and that Lawrence fled. Call San Francisco Field and talk to Crase. Tell him the same."

"Wait, are you telling me," Schild leveled a finger at Lawrence, "that this is Lawrence Harmon? Your grandfather, Danny?"

"The one and only," Lawrence said.

"But you're dead!"

"Not the last time I checked, though many times over the last thirty years, I wished for it." Somber reflection shadowed his face.

"What about the civic center? All those missing reporters?"

"They're all here. Slightly changed, but very much alive. Well, except one." The look he gave me was full of anger but only lasted a brief second.

"Jack Wu from Channel Ten perished in a fight," Harmon said.

"I killed him in self-defense," I said, "and in defense of my partner. And he wasn't exactly human when I killed him."

Schild opened his mouth and then shut it again without saying anything. He shook his head. "I'm letting that one go for the moment. I still don't have a clue what you people are saying. It's like a foreign language."

We followed Lawrence back down the power line road until we reached Schild's cruiser, where he picked up the mic and phoned in an all-clear.

"Dispatch thinks my officers were drinking on duty," Schild said after a heavy sigh. "I told them I'd look into it."

"You should probably head home, Rick," Harmon said.

"Not a chance. If this goes wrong, I need to know what my town is up against."

"If this goes wrong, you'll end up possessed or dead," Lawrence said.

"Just as long as the rest of your police force won't be coming back," I said, ignoring Lawrence's doomsday message. "You can figure out what to tell them later if you have to. Lawrence, what about the rest of your pack?"

"They're on patrol. I'll call them in when we're ready. I want them surrounding the rift. If Martina tries to make a break for it, we'll stop her."

I realized how naïve my next question would make me sound, but I had to ask. "What is my part in this, and how do we tear open the rift."

Lawrence held out his hand, "Give me Ginny's locket, and I'll take care of the rift. You just do what I say when I tell you, and everything will work out right."

Chapter 27

Harmon's constant pacing rattled my nerves. I finally placed myself in his path, forcing him to stop.

"Will you just talk to me?" I asked.

"Not until you come to your senses. You're not going in there." His words resonated with strength, but a sense of despondence and gripping fear churned within him.

I caught his chin in my hand and forced him to look at me. The amber glow in his eyes pulsed, and the muscles of his throat flexed in response. I felt his internal struggle with the anger that threatened to overtake him again. He looked at me for a long, silent moment, ripped himself from my grasp and continued stalking the tree line.

"What am I supposed to do?" My fists clenched, and my fingernails pinch into my palms. "Should I throw Schild into the Fade? Maybe grab one of the afflicted reporters? Toss them to the unknown? Or you? Should I sacrifice my own partner?"

He rounded on me, his lip curling back in a snarl. "That is precisely what you should do."

"It's not going to happen, Harmon. You have to trust me. I've got this."

He stopped, faced me and his expression took on a facsimile of the lopsided smile, heavily laced with exasperated disbelief. "For the love of fucking god, Kessa, will you call me Danny at least once before you go kill yourself?"

My heart caught in my throat, and tears welled in my eyes. "Danny, I'm so sorry."

His sudden embrace startled me, but I relaxed into his arms. His chest heaved against my cheek with every breath.

"I need you here, Kess," He spoke so quietly that I felt his words more than I heard them. "I'm not sure I can hold a grip on reality without you. I was ready to give in back there in the cabin until I saw your face. Knowing you were alive was all I needed to hang on. When you walked out that door, it was too much."

The warmth of his body filled my senses. He ran his fingers through my hair and pressed his cheek into the top of my head. I had to force myself to push away from him. "Release the baowal. You'll be better off."

"Without it, I'll have nothing. Just an empty shell of a man who has lost every scrap of family he's ever had. And now I'm about to lose you, too."

My voice turned small and timid. "I'm just your partner."

"That's bullshit, and you know it." He glared at me and then resumed his pacing.

Down the road, Lawrence had built a small fire and placed a cauldron over the top. His pack members brought him an assortment of herbs, iron ore, and wood. Everything went into the pot. A pile of foxglove stems was set next to the fire, close enough that he could reach them, but far enough away so as not to wilt from the heat. As he added each component, he chanted from the book, holding the locket on its length of chain over the mixture. Part of me wanted to know what he was doing, but most of me just wanted to stick close to Harmon. I was sure he'd try something stupid if I left his side.

If anything happened to him, I'd never forgive myself. I dreaded the potential loss of Harmon more than the loss of myself. As the emotion of that realization crested in my mind and cascaded through my soul, his head snapped up, and he looked me in the eye. A whisper of a smile touched his lips but never reached his eyes. My silent admission of the depth of my feelings for him rode in on the coattails of intractable sadness surrounding our inevitable loss. He sat on the ground and picked at the rocks at his feet.

I reassured myself that he knew how I felt. I was never good at expressing such feelings aloud, and I'd avoided even admitting to the growing connection between us. But at that moment, he understood my appreciation for him—his belief in me, his ability to make me believe in myself, and a kindled love for the man himself—he knew it all without the need for words. For that, I was thankful.

"It's time," Lawrence called from down the road.

My feet were lead bricks, stuck in place. Harmon didn't move. Only Schild seemed to spring to action, trotting over to peer into the cauldron. The way he'd been fidgeting by his cruiser, I could tell he was painfully curious to see what was happening inside that pot.

Placing one foot deliberately in front of the other, I forced myself to close the distance between Harmon and my fate. I bit back tears. It would do no good to dwell on fear or sadness now. I had a job to do. I had always been a soldier at heart, and I knew that my sacrifice had the potential of saving billions of lives. That should be enough. It had to be enough.

But at the moment of truth, even the strongest have doubts. I grieved for the love I'd never experience. I longed for the children I'd never wanted. Hell, I'd never even had a dog. I thought of the trips I'd planned but had never taken. The parts of the world I'd always wanted to see, but had only read about in books. I would never have the chance to wake up next to someone and realize we'd grown old together.

A surge of sympathy for Lawrence Harmon washed over me.. He'd suffered the same type of loss that I mourned for myself, but had been around to participate in his own inability to live out his life. In a way, this was better.

I risked a backward glance and saw Agent Danny Harmon standing in position. He'd said he had a game face, and I recognized it well. He was a soldier, too. His training had taken over; he scanned the area, watching for potential problems before they had a chance to become risks to the mission's success. Schild had a spare t-shirt in the back of his cruiser that Harmon had put on; with the claw marks hidden, he looked strong and stout. I felt a pang of regret for my initial doubts. How had I not seen his strength of character fifteen years ago? A new flood of regret hit me. I could have known him for so many years, had I not sworn off this region as a frightened teenager.

As I glanced around the roadway and watched the pack members move into place. They formed a complete circle, evenly spaced. A perfect perimeter. If I'd had more time, I'd have asked how they communicated. It obviously wasn't verbal.

"When I open the locket," Lawrence said, his voice ringing with authority, "the rift will open. The summoning brew will attract Ancestral demons up until the point I add the Foxglove. At that point, it will act as a repellant and will weaken them. Pack, be on guard. Those that come through may not be—most likely *will not* be—the one we seek. These Fae beings *will* try to kill you. Hold them off as best you can until we call forth the demon that calls herself Martina. Only then can I turn the tide.

"Schild, this is your cue to leave. I want you clear of this area before we begin. I cannot guarantee your safety."

Rick Schild climbed into his cruiser and drove down the road to the point that Lawrence had deemed a "safe perimeter." It was far enough away that we couldn't see him; I knew it was still too close.

Lawrence turned to Danny, who nodded. I wasn't sure if they'd communicated nonverbally, or if there was some unspoken agreement. Whatever it was, I had been left out, and I didn't appreciate it.

"What's going on?" I asked.

They ignored me, and Lawrence continued speaking. "Officer Schild will sit by the main road and keep civilians from wandering into danger."

We all held our breath for the span of a silent moment. Lawrence pulled on a glove and extracted the locket. He turned it over in his hand and dangling it on its length of chain between his fingers.

"Here goes nothing," He said, cracking open the locket.

I held my breath, eyes wide, as a dark blue glow emanated from the pendant, snaking out to touch the closest point of the rift. It jumped along the pinpoints of energy that pulsed, opening a widening hole in the fabric between worlds. The tendril touched one tear to the next, like a dot-to-dot, completing a picture of oncoming terror.

With the connection of the final point, the chasm opened like the maw of a great beast, black as coal with a glowing, red center. It wasn't the Fade, nor was it the Ancestral Lands that I saw on the other side, but something else entirely. I opened my eyes to the magical spectrum and realized we weren't even looking at the Fel region. This was something beyond my knowledge.

Steps of dark stone rose and fell at odd angles, falling into deep canyons and jutting up into a blood-red sky. Black storm clouds shot ferocious balls of crackling energy back and forth in a celestial lightning storm. I looked from Lawrence to Harmon, but both maintained their stoic posture. The pack members stood steadfast before the sight like it was something from their everyday lives.

"What is this place?" I asked. "Why didn't it open to the Fade?"

"This is the Fade," Lawrence shouted over the roar and crackle of the rift. "It's the ungoverned space between the Ancestral paths."

A flash of inky darkness rocketed across the opening but didn't emerge. Another edged up to the portal and tentatively stuck out something like an arm, but came no further.

The cauldron belched a cloud of amber that wafted toward the opening. It hovered there, like an invitation. Several of the inky creatures accepted, and slipped along the ground, one by one.

"Now!" Lawrence shouted.

All around me, I heard the pack members shapeshift. A lone howl erupted from behind me, and I turned to see Cinder leading his brothers and sisters into battle. The pack picked up the call, one by one.

Lawrence flicked a single finger, and they sprang in unison. Cinder darted past me to engage with three of the shadowy creatures as they slithered through the rift. Other pack members likewise engaged in the fight.

I felt helpless, waiting for a signal that it was my time to act. I'd been instructed by Lawrence not to use my magic; we didn't want to alert the other side to my presence.

"Where is she?" I asked over the sound of snapping teeth, howls, and snarls. The shadow creatures moved in absolute silence and did battle with the same deadly quiet.

"She'll come," Lawrence called back.

"Kessa!" Harmon's voice rang out over the sounds of the pack. I turned back to the portal to see a shadow creature headed for me. I sprinted for Harmon, who pushed me behind him. His own growl, more baowal than man, escaped him, and I feared he'd made a choice.

But he didn't change; instead, he produced another silver dagger like the one he'd had days before. He slashed at the creature, landing a blow to what could only be described as its torso. It really didn't have a head, exactly. More like a misshapen glob of darkness sitting atop a slightly wider darkness. It moved like a mollusk, but much faster. The small, nubby appendages that protruded from its body elongated on attack and then retracted back into its inky body.

Harmon dodged a blow from the creature and swung wildly with his knife. The blade slashed into its retracting arm, and it pulled back, opting instead to attack one of the pack members who had stumbled within range.

"I can't hold it open much longer," Lawrence shouted. "We'll be overtaken. The pack is weakening to the influence of these Adherents."

"What are these?" I asked.

"Minor demons of the Fade," he replied. "Too many more, and we won't be able to resist."

As if on cue, one of the demons reared itself up and plunged headlong into a female pack member. She let loose a howl of haunted nightmares as she succumbed to the beast. Her body blackened and her skin boiled. The beast engulfed her from the inside out. Her screams outlasted her body and drifted on the wind long after she'd been incorporated into the demon's soul.

With a member of the pack assimilated, the demons moved with greater speed and purpose. Swells of agonized wails rose and fell in the air as the demons swarmed. A second pack member reared up on his hind legs, swiping furiously at an attacking demon, but he fell to the ground just as his sister had, writhing and screaming as the demon overtook him.

"Danny!" Lawrence yelled, but Harmon was already on it. He sprinted across the circle to the form of the fallen wolf and stabbed him straight through the heart with the silver knife.

A second shriek erupted from the dying pack member, but this was deeper, and filled with rage. Red and black fire spread across the man's body, and within seconds he was reduced to smoldering ash.

Another wolf succumbed, and Harmon was on the move again.

"Close the portal!" I shouted.

Lawrence stood, watching his pack fall with terror etched on his face. I ran for him, in hopes of grabbing the locket from his hands, but stopped short. The open rift provided passage for more and more demons. Nyads crossed over and dove into the bushes. Tiny green sprites zipped past me, sounding like overgrown mosquitos. Everything but our doppelgänger seemed to take advantage of the opportunity for escape.

Even if I grabbed the locket, the damage was done.

"Lawrence! We need to close it! How can we close the rift? She's not coming!"

As I yelled, the familiar lavender imp-like form of Martina emerged from the rift. She looked around the road, appearing confused by the activity around her. Zeroing in on the locket in Lawrence's hand, her face twisted into a malicious grin. She lunged forward in loping strides.

"She's here!" I yelled.

Lawrence grabbed the foxglove to the side of the cauldron and tossed it inside. His chanting changed. Martina's mouth opened in an affronted scowl, and she rushed at him with all the speed and agility of a cheetah.

Piercing wails erupted from the Fade demons as their power waned with the desecration of the foxglove. I felt a change in my own energy, but somehow it amplified. Whatever Lawrence had done it was different than the barrier magic he'd used to surround the grove. I held onto the feeling of Ancestral energy that coursed through my veins. I would not forget to reach for that power during this fight.

I raced across the road and dove for Martina, intent on landing her directly in front of the rift. She had been so focused on Lawrence that she hadn't seen me coming. I hit her square and knocked her back. She let loose a raging scream and heaved me up into the air like I was nothing more than a balloon. I fell back to the Earth. My head, ribs and hip hit all at once, and white-hot pain erupted through my body.

I reached for my magic. *Heal*, I thought, directing it first to my cracked skull and rattled brain. It was all I could do to keep that thought alive.

I saw Harmon leap over the top of me, aiming for Martina as she circled and stalked Lawrence, who was rapidly changing into wolf form.

"No!" I said though I had no idea if it came out of my mouth. I forced the magic into my limbs and pushed myself to my feet. I shouldered into Harmon and knocked him into Lawrence. The two went down in a heap, and the locket skittered across the gravel road.

Ancestral energy flowed down my arms to my hands, and I grasped the handle of the boiling cauldron. Searing heat cut into my flesh as I heaved the pot upward in an awkward arc. It sloshed and slammed into Martina's side, erupting into blue-white flame. She screeched in pain, ripping at the welts raised by the boiling liquid across her skin. I snatched the locket from the ground and flung myself around Martina, wrapping her in a firm embrace and shoving us both through the rift. Her mouth opened wide as I tossed the locket into the depths of the chasm below us. The rift sealed behind us with a crack of lightning.

My last thoughts before we fell into oblivion were of Danny Harmon, and of the life we'd never share.

Chapter 28

I closed my eyes and felt dry, hot air rush upward as I fell. Martina's wild scream registered only slightly over the whoosh of falling. It took several seconds to realize that the previous sounds had changed to a cackle. I opened my eyes, surprised that I had ceased falling, and instead sat on hot, sandy ground.

Ginny's locket dangled from Martina's fingertips.

"Stupid girl," Martina said, her voice ringing with satisfaction, "you thought you could just push me over the edge? You thought if you sacrificed yourself along with me then we'd both die?" She twisted at the chain in her hand and watched the locket spin. "This is my domain. It would be like me pushing you into a swimming pool and expecting you to drown."

I rolled over on my back and felt Ginny's journal push into my skin. A wicked smile of my own met her mocking grin. "I have a few tricks, too, Martina."

She moved like an accident victim; slow and deliberate, and lacking her usual grace. Her face contorted, betraying a struggle to hide the damage done to her by the fall.

I stood up, attempting to look tough and whole as well, and was certain I'd failed just as hard.

"After I get through dealing with you, I'll open that rift back up. You've accomplished nothing. You've given me exactly what I needed; access to the space between the Ancestral byways. From here, I can reopen all the paths between the worlds." Martina let loose a cackling laugh.

I rolled my eyes. "Really, cackling? Could you be any more stereotypical?"

"You should show some respect." She moved faster than my eyes could track, and before I knew what hit me, I was pinned against an earthen pillar. Boiling pools in the sand steamed to my left and right. She eyed one keenly and tossed me like a newspaper. I felt my feet leave the ground as I soared through the air to the bubbling pool.

My skin reacted to the shallow water, bubbling and blistering as an involuntary scream erupted from my lungs. Martina grabbed me from the pool and shoved me again, this time back onto the solid ground.

I laid in fetal position, clutching at my arm and abdomen as the skin continued to burn. Martina stood over me, now in her earthly form of the girl in the angora sweater and Ugg boots. "We could have done so much. Think of what we could have accomplished. Wasted. And now you're going to have to die because you choose sides so poorly." She kicked me in the gut, sending a new wave of agony up and down my spine.

I gritted my teeth and turned to face her. "You lost, Martina. I accepted my death the moment I dove through the rift. Whatever happens to me, the Earth is safe. You won't get back."

I willed the magic within and pushed it through the palm of my hand, spraying a blast of energy that caught Martina in the chest. She stumbled backward, and I used the moment to flood my body with healing waves. It took the edge off enough that I was able to get to my feet.

I ran for Martina like a linebacker, catching her chest with my shoulder and knocking her toward one of the steaming pools. Her foot splashed in, and she howled out in agony.

A small trail led up through the rock stacks, and I took off at a sprint. She tackled me from behind, and I felt the wind exit my lungs in one, forceful blow. She turned me onto my back and pinned me at the shoulders.

Martina pushed her slender fingers into her own chest, piercing the skin. She pulled slowly, extracting an awl.

"You may truly be an Adept of the Ancients, but you are still human. And this can still kill you." Her grin widened as she rocked the weapon back for a full-force plunge.

"Aramethena!" I shouted. Her hand froze and her face contorted in wild rage.

She broke the hold my word carried and laughed, but I realized there was doubt behind her eyes, "Not even close."

"Ar-ah-methena!" I tried again.

She faltered backward but then regained composure. She came for me again with the awl, driving it toward my heart. I rolled to the side, but not fast enough. The metal cut deep into my shoulder, and my cry caught in my throat. When she ripped the weapon back, it made a sick, sucking noise, and my stomach heaved from the torturous pain.

"Ar-ah-meth-EE-na," I said.

"You can keep trying this all day; it won't work." Her sadistic demon face twisted into hatred, and she plunged the awl down at my heart.

"Ar-aye-meth-EE-na."

She stopped. The weapon fell from her hand and clanged on the rocky ground at my side.

"I control you, and you will stop this assault on me." I muttered, shoving her aside. I clasped my hand over my shoulder and stopped the blood flow with a trickle of magic, mending muscle, and closing flesh. The demon stood before me, immobile, frowning at the awl on the ground, unable to make herself reach for it.

"What's wrong, Martina?" I asked.

"I don't understand! Where did you find it? How did you know my name?"

"Sit down and I'll explain."

She complied though she didn't look pleased. I pulled the aspen journal from my waistline and propped it open in front of her unmoving face. She glared at the image of herself on the page, and her name written beside it.

"This is the real reason you killed Ginny Harmon, isn't it, Aramethena?" She recoiled at my perfect pronunciation of her name. "You knew she had this, but you didn't know where."

Martina looked away.

"Tell me why, and about Senator Mansfield, too," I said.

"Yes," she growled. "I killed Mansfield to stop him from buying the grove. I killed Ginny because she'd come close to controlling me. Where did you find that book?"

I put a finger to my lips. "My little secret," I said. Martina tried to raise her arms to attack me, but my control over her held her in place.

"So what happens now?" she asked. "You think you're just going to control me forever down here? You can't live here."

"No, I can't. But you can live just fine out there." I tossed my head upward, from the direction we fell. "You are also perfectly capable of transporting us back to Earth. I'm not entirely sure how this demon control thing works, but I'm going to give it a shot. Aramethena, I command you to remain in the human form of Martina."

She let loose a screeching howl in defiance as her body contorted and glowed.

I pulled my shirt over my head and wrapped it around the awl. "Beautiful. And now, you're going to open a portal to the grove, and we're going to go have a little chat with our good friend Detective Schild. He's going to be so glad to solve his first murder case."

Harmon paced the road, occasionally grabbing logs and rocks and chucking them with such force that they shattered against the trees, sending splinters and shards in every direction. Schild stood by his cruiser, wringing his coat in his hands. Lawrence sat on a nearby fallen tree, talking with his three remaining pack members. None of them saw us emerge from the Fade.

"Guess none of you want to solve a murder today?" I shouted across the road.

Harmon jumped at the sound of my voice. His surge of relief nearly knocked me backward. He rushed across the road and grasped me in his arms, lifting me off my feet and spinning me in a circle.

"What the hell, Kess?" He pulled the t-shirt he'd borrowed from Schild over his head and handed it to me. I slipped it on, feeling grateful for small favors. He looked from me to Martina. I handed him the awl, still wrapped in my shirt.

"Schild, come on over. We have your murderer right here, and we found the murder weapon. She'll even confess."

Martina's heated glare rivaled the steaming pools of the Fade.

"How?" Lawrence asked, approaching. He scratched his head. "You obviously figured out her name, but how?"

I smiled and Lawrence and slipped into my practiced FBI persona. "That's need-to-know information, sir. Sorry."

"I guess I'll have to wait for the official debrief?" Harmon asked.

Schild clamped handcuffs on Martina's wrists. He led her to the cruiser and ducked her into the back seat.

"I'll give you the full run-down on our way in," I said to Harmon.

He slipped an arm around my waist, and I leaned into him and closed my eyes.

EPILOGUE

It was easy enough to convict Martina of her crimes. She freely confessed everything while I was there in the interrogation room with Schild. I found I only needed to whisper her name occasionally to keep her on the right track.

However, too many reporters remembered her as the girl who whisked us away after the civic center attack.

"Did you know that she was the murderer when you left with her?" That was the easiest question. We had our suspicions but needed more information. By sticking close, we were able to catch her up in her own lies.

"Can you explain these shadows we saw on film, and do you know the whereabouts of the eight reporters they seem to be attacking?" That one was harder, but I managed to stumble through an answer that involved the time of day and lens flare.

"How do you explain your partner's DNA being found on the victims?" That was the one that made me turn from the podium and walk away, wondering if I'd ever made a right decision with my life.

When the plane touched down in San Francisco, I felt a disconnected loneliness. The Ancestral energy didn't flow past a mere trickle. It barely dripped in some sections of the city. Inside my office, it was entirely nonexistent. Life echoed the grey walls of the cubicles. My beloved city lost its charm, and every breath reminded me that I was cut off. The Ancients heard me, but they couldn't get through the thrum of civilization to answer my call. Maybe they got stuck in traffic.

My final report to Crase read as contrived and hollow as my answers had been to the press. When he called me into his office, I broke down. Told him the whole story, beginning to end. He ordered the psych review before I reached my desk.

Harmon and I kept in constant contact. He grieved his losses to me over text message as we both went through the motions of our days. Pending a full investigation, neither of us was deemed fit for field duty. Pushing paperwork made for long, tedious hours. We were glad they hadn't taken our phones along with our service weapons.

The only thing that kept me going was the knowledge that I could leave the city and find a vortex within an hour's drive, but my soul ached for the connectedness I felt in the Pacific Northwest.

It had been several weeks since I'd left Gig Harbor. I sat atop a windswept cliff overlooking the ocean and called to the Ancients. The energy swirled blue next to the sea. It felt different, and I couldn't wield it like I could the earth energy. I still felt comforted being in the presence of the Fae planes.

I was lying on my back, warming myself from the December chill with waves of ocean energy when the call came.

I flew to Seattle against direct orders. I didn't even bother to pack.

Harmon chose to hold Ginny's funeral on December 21st at precisely 2:18 p.m. The Winter Solstice. The main hall of the Key Peninsula civic center was filled with townspeople to the point of standing room only. He'd asked me to be there next to him through the ceremony and I'd agreed. Standing on that stage was like revisiting a nightmare, starting at the beginning of the dream and knowing what horrors could happen next. They'd fixed the hole that I'd blown in the wall, but I still couldn't help feeling a twinge of guilt whenever I looked past that spot.

Rick Schild stood in the front row, flanked by his wife, Miranda, and their daughter, Kylie. The Rushing family occupied the front row opposite the Schilds. Justin had escaped the drug charge on a technicality, and watching their son sitting between them, holding each of his parent's hands, I was thankful. Sometimes, justice is served best without a sentence.

Lawrence and his three remaining pack members stood sentinel at either side of the back of the room like a row of chess pieces. Harmon worried that Lawrence might try to reconstruct a new device for opening the veil so he could replenish his numbers. Fortunately, neither of us thought he had it in him, and we'd hoped he wouldn't desecrate his late wife's funeral.

But I knew what I had in me. Standing there on the Key Peninsula, I heard the Ancestors welcome me home. My vortex by the ocean helped fill the void, but in the Pacific Northwest, I felt my connection strong and clear.

The room quieted as the music died down. Harmon bowed his head, let out a slow exhale and put on his *game face.*

"I want to thank you all for coming. I've known most of you for my entire life. I went to school with many of you; we ran through the forest; we had dances and parties together in this very room. I grew up to protect this area from harm, first in the local police force, and now with the Federal Bureau of Investigation. It is a devotion that I inherited, soul-deep, from Ginny Harmon, my Grams.

"Grams often said that people celebrate in all the wrong ways for all the wrong reasons. History gives us dates for remembrances that are wholly based on ego-centric or nationalistic principles, and we follow the customs like automatons, never truly grasping any meaning behind the traditions beyond self-satisfaction and the occasional day off work. She never celebrated Christmas, or Easter or the Fourth of July. *Why celebrate these human constructs,* she would ask, *when the cosmos gives us every reason to celebrate, and conveniently repeats the cycles so that we might mark time while giving reverence to the very nature of our existence? The problem is, we fail to look outside ourselves long enough to grasp the important aspects of life as they fly by.*"

Harmon paused and inhaled sharply. I felt a trickle of anger roll off of him, and I gently squeezed his hand behind the lectern. He pulled away, and placed his hand on the smooth surface, bracing himself before continuing.

"Virginia Harmon died defending all of you; none of you realize that. Let me repeat—she was attempting to negate the ability of forces unimaginable to loose themselves among us. She knew more about the world and its inherent dangers than all of our scientists and sages combined. Without her actions, you all would have already been swallowed up by your own childhood nightmares. Even despite her efforts, it nearly happened anyway. And now, if some in this very room get their way, it could still happen."

Lawrence flashed a cut sign at Harmon; his forehead wrinkled into avenues of irritation. Harmon grinned, wide and toothy. Fake. His face fell back to deadly serious. "There are those who think they are doing the right thing. They hide under your noses and pretend to protect you, but really, their desires are as selfish as those whom Grams' efforts stopped.

"Grams was a good woman, and she put up with me. She encouraged me. And at the end, she left us exactly what we needed."

Lawrence shifted from one foot to the other, posturing and challenging. He was alpha, and he didn't appreciate being called out, no matter how anonymously. Harmon appeared not to care. My breathing sped as I felt the anger mounting inside Harmon. "I *will* find truths none of you know exist, and I *will* right the wrongs you didn't know need corrected. You will be safe, or I'll have failed my grandmother and I'll have tarnished her memory. You will be protected, in her name, and for her sake. You have my word."

Harmon stalked off the podium and pushed through the heavy double doors. The organist filled the uneasy silence, and people murmured to one another. I wove through the crowd and ran through the doors in time to see Harmon's car speeding off.

I stood in the freezing rain outside Harmon's house, holding my fist up, trying to figure out whether or not to knock when the door opened.

"You do realize I can still sense your emotions, right?" Harmon said, holding the door wide in invitation.

"Right," I said, crossing the threshold to stand on the edge of the entryway.

"You come to tell me how you knew Martina's true name?" he asked.

I smiled weakly and shook my head. "Sorry, Harmon. I just can't. I can't risk Lawrence finding out."

He nodded in agreement. "We've been over this, and I know. I understand."

"I know you think it's not over, Harmon. And I agree with you. A lot of Fae crossed over when the rift was open. Who knows where they are, or what they're doing now that they're trapped here. And then there's Martina."

"You think she'll escape?"

"Yes, and I think she wasn't working alone." I chewed my lip. "I just have a feeling that this isn't the end. And you're right. Lawrence is a loose cannon."

"So does that mean you're coming back?" His lopsided grin made my stomach flip.

"Possibly."

An uncomfortable silence stretched between us, punctuated by conflicting emotions that each of us felt from the other. Harmon met my eyes and a hint of a smile played on his face. "I've missed you, Kess."

I barely found my voice, so I responded with a nod and a weak "mm-hmm."

He cleared his throat. "Don't you have a plane to catch tonight?"

"Later tonight, yeah," I said, studying the tile by the door. "But," I looked him in the eye, and challenged myself to boldness, "I was thinking maybe I'd skip it."

"Really?"

He moved closer to me, and I took his hand. His desire hit me full-force, and I knew he felt mine in return.

"This is kind of like cheating," I said. "We both know exactly how each other feels."

"That just makes it easier."

He pulled me close, sliding his hand up my back and entwining his fingers in my hair. His mouth met mine, and we kissed deeply, feeling our passion for each other release in unison. We pulled away, breathless and both craving more.

"You realize this violates just about every known rule in the Bureau, right?" he asked.

"I really couldn't care less,"

"How very un-agently of you, St. James." He planted tiny kisses across my brow. "But yeah, me neither. We're both out on psych anyway. What's one more infraction? May as well make it a good one."

He pushed me up against the door and kissed down my neck.

We had a demon in custody, only I could control her, and I wasn't allowed near her. Fae creatures could start raising hell all over the Key Peninsula at any moment. Our respective directors would have our asses if they knew the extent of our involvement with each other.

But at that moment, all that mattered was Danny Harmon.

We spent that night wrapped up in one another. When it came time to leave, I knew I was already planning my way back.

About the Author

Shanan Winters is a freelance writer, editor, and novelist. She has avid interests in geek topics and fandoms, parenting, and technology. She loves archery, cats, aviation, and board games, and has performed in a variety of Irish folk bands over the years playing flute and hammered dulcimer. She also plays fiddle—poorly. She lives with her husband, girl-child, boy-child and two cats in the Phoenix metropolitan sea-of-beige. When not working on projects, Shanan can be found writing about writing at ShananWinters.wordpress.com.

More from Ravensong Digital Publishing

The Magician: Book one of the Rogue Portal Series

by

Courtney Herz

Get the first two chapters here. Then, if you dare, enter the Void and follow the rest of the series. For more information visit http://www.courtneyherz.com, and follow The Rogue Portal on Facebook.

To see more books from Ravensong Digital Publishing authors visit

http://www.ravensongdigitalpublishing.com.

ONE

Connor lay in bed, staring at the ceiling, unable to make out anything beyond a faint outline of the woodwork. The mingled smell of cedar and pine comforted him in the darkness. A single car hummed by his house, and after a brief, dashing glint of light from its headlights threatened to break the stillness, it disappeared, and he was, as he had always been, alone. The only light that entered the room was the dim glow of a streetlamp outside his window, and while its presence did much for his mood, it did little to improve the physical conditions. Despite the streetlamp's sincere attempts the room remained dark. Lonely. Cold.

Home had always been a quiet and desolate place. Connor's mother had withdrawn from him. From life. From reality. His early memories sat framed in his mind, remnants of a time in which his mother had at least attempted to mask the war within. They sat in stark contrast to the portrait of deranged detachment he'd grown accustomed to since midway through primary school. The portrait had become even more grotesque since his sophomore year in high school. Since his mother's single willing moment in which she'd granted him the only conversation they would ever have concerning his father's death. It had been a brief conversation, and concluded in no uncertain terms.

"He was a coward, Connor. Took the easy way out. That's the truth, and you'll just have to find a way to deal with it," she'd said, pausing for a moment before adding, "You're better off without him."

After that she'd shut down.

His theories regarding his mother's anger had evolved over the years. Perhaps she thought it would protect him. Maybe she was incapable of distinguishing anger from mourning. The theories worked for awhile, but at long last they ran out, lost their placebo effect, and he could no longer deny the genuine nature of her hatred for his father. In the most technical of terms his father's actions had amounted to abandonment. But Connor wasn't willing to believe he'd been motivated by cowardice.

His search for information had led him to everything from his neighbors to newspapers, all without his mother's knowledge - and certainly without her approval. He pored over library records. Found articles in which reporters spoke in brutal, authoritative detail about the incident. He could see it all. His mother returning home from the hospital, him in her arms. A rare condition he'd contracted without much explanation, gone, overnight, without reason. Julia searching the house to tell his father the good news. That their son would live. Would thrive.

But, the articles said, his father, overwhelmed by his son's diagnosis, had decided that enough was enough. Had tied a rope to the upper banister. Put it around his neck. Hung himself from the railing, where Julia had found him.

There wasn't a particular revelation that served as the catalyst for his retreat into the uncomfortable mental corner he'd resided in since his quest for the truth began. No single piece of evidence he could point to that proved he was right. That his dad didn't chicken out on life. That the motivation behind his suicide was far more complex than depression, or sadness, or an inability to cope. Couldn't produce a competing theory that had any basis in fact. Just a feeling. But that feeling spoke to him louder than anything or anyone else, and he trusted it.

The memories played against the darkness like a projection of an old horror flick that just happened to be true. Just happened to be his life. By now he'd become an expert at finding ways to distract himself. Ways to keep his father's death off his mind. To silence, if for a moment, the demands for truth that rang through his soul like a battle cry. But in the quiet, distractionless void of the early morning hours, the street lamp and smell of pine-tainted cedar his only companions, he could think of nothing else.

Clenching his jaw, he picked up the blanket nestled around him and threw it back, greeting the cold of the morning with a shudder, and made his way across the floor of his sparse bedroom. If ever he had time to search the attic, it was now. Ever since he could remember the attic had stood a forbidden realm, guarded by his mother and her hate-fueled wrath. But tomorrow he would head off to college, and his mother had agreed to grant him a visit. To take some things with him if he "felt the need to remember the man that abandoned you", in her words. While her tone grated on him, he'd thought it unwise to start an argument, fearing that she would rescind her offer. So he'd inwardly grimaced, shook an invisible fist toward her, and swallowed his pride.

His hand met the coarse granulation of unfinished wood as he steadied himself in the dark hallway, an abrasive reminder of everything beautiful that time and bitterness had long since abandoned. In pictures from his earlier years - those that come into existence because the taker is aware that the infant subject of the photograph won't remember any of the surrounding events - the walls of the home had boasted vivid, beautiful colors. Word had it that his mother, Julia, had taken great pride in her role as homemaker. But after his father's suicide, everything fell apart, the slow and steady decay of a once-grand cathedral, an unholy descent. The perfection of their life - of life within the walls of the home they'd built together - had succumbed to a consistent and painstaking erosion that began with Julia.

A sudden jolt of pain derailed his train of thought, and he clasped his free hand over his mouth, trapping a cry of pain that threatened to escape his lips. Sharp pain seared from his toe through his ankle and gave up the fight in a dull ache beneath his kneecap. He always forgot about the doorstop.

It was a pointless home improvement. Julia had installed it because the door had developed a habit of swinging open. Not just coming ajar, or settling in a way that resulted in a crack, but opening as far as it could go. The situation unnerved him, as well, because once the door latch was in place, nobody could open it without intentionally unlatching it. And it was always latched. Connor had long thought that his mother's installation of the doorstop had been motivated by fear rather than aggravation, but she'd never admit such a thing, and he didn't need her to.

He reached for the door latch and froze. Once again the door had opened, and stood wide, inviting him to explore. With timid steps, he entered the attic stairwell, reaching up and groping in the darkness at nothing until, at long last, the beaded string of the light touched his hand like a ghost. He grabbed it, and tugged. Two clicks. A dim buzzing. Muted light flooded the stairway, and he shut the door behind him.

He ascended the staircase, his heart pounding harder with every step. Breathing transformed from a natural act into a small battle with an evasive foe - oxygen. He wasn't afraid of the attic. Wasn't afraid of anything - at least nothing he knew of on a conscious level. But he was apprehensive about what he might find in the Forbidden Attic. Nervous about what his dad might have left behind - or hadn't. Had his mother thrown everything of importance away? Would he be left with naught but a lint-filled dress sock or discarded tissue to choose from?

Looking down at his watch he took note of the time. The glowing numerals declared it to be four in the morning. In another hour his mother would be awake, and although she'd given him permission to be in the attic he harbored a sneaking suspicion that were she to accompany him on his journey through its contents he would be forced to undertake it to the tune of a berating, angry lecture about every piece he touched - and perhaps the things he thought about touching. Julia had purged his father from the house - every piece of him, every photo - and buried him in the attic. As though the ground was too close to her feet, and the attic was above her thoughts.

Regardless of her feelings or her reasons for having them, he wanted to go through these things on his own terms. Alone. And so, with sleep playing a runaway and his restless mind nagging him out of bed, he'd found four in the morning to be the perfect time to search. For what? He didn't know. Something to take with him. Something to keep. A tangible memory. Or perhaps a piece of evidence that confirmed his father had ever existed at all.

He arrived at the top step and cast an initial glance across the attic space. The light from the bulb downstairs, which had taken to sleeping on the job some months ago, fell short of reaching the top step, let alone the expansive attic. He made a mental note to change it before he left.

The rectangular room boasted an angular, geometric ceiling of Dutch design, its half-trapezoidal shape mimicked by the window on the far wall. The window did little good at this hour, but he found it easy to imagine a sunny afternoon in the attic, its contents drenched in light, the only place of warmth left in the house.

This is almost livable, he thought, and smiled at the irony; in her attempt to eliminate his father, to shut him out, to destroy him, she had inadvertently built him a shrine. She couldn't see it, of course. Her hatred wouldn't let her. And he wasn't about to make her aware of it.

Running a hand through his hair, Connor granted his eyes a few more moments to adjust to the darkness. Shapes of boxes became visible. A bookcase over on the right. A guitar in the corner. And something in front of the window he couldn't quite make out.

He began searching, one by one, through boxes. Getting down on his knees, he looked through the first one. Pictures. High school memorabilia belonging to his parents. Photographs of his parents happy. His mother almost unrecognizable without the boiling anger that now resided beneath the surface. No hatred. Just joy and life. A surge of resentment over the fact that he'd never known that woman threatened to overcome him, and he swallowed it, keeping it at bay.

Slowly he made his way through the rubble. Boxes of old clothing, jackets and boots, two lamps that someone had unceremoniously tossed to one side, boxes filled with his father's books. Pieces of a life. Shards of shattered memories that threatened to break the skin, to cut the heart of the person who came too close. He moved on. Ran his hand over an object he couldn't make out using only his sight. And swallowed the wave of nausea that washed over him.

Rope.

Looped and discarded. Wedged between two boxes in an attempt to remove it from sight - from memory. A secret too painful to reveal, but too personal to do away with. He forced trembling hands to explore its length. Reached a frayed end. Caught himself as a portion of the attic descended into darkness. Closed his eyes, took a deep breath of stifled, musty air, and moved on.

He made his way over to the window, still perplexed by the odd shape he'd seen from the stairwell. The dim moonlight illuminated its features just enough to give its identity away - a large hourglass with ornate carvings. It sat, propped against the edge of the box, threatening to crush the contents below it. The sand had long since run out, piled at the bottom like a child's futile attempts at sand castle construction. A bitter metaphor that summarized the attic's contents - indeed, its purpose - in a single, heartbreaking image.

Connor ran his hand across the top of the hourglass and watched as a century of dust formed a figure at the edge. He let it linger there for a moment, then brushed it to the floor. Dust bunny sacrifice.

A collection of antiques sat, unassuming, beneath the hourglass. A couple of vases. Some old books. Maybe a gravy boat? He couldn't tell given the pitiful light. Try as it might, the moon was just not bright enough to aid him in any meaningful way. He sighed. Maybe he should give up. Go back to bed. Resolve himself to the fact that he'd never have anything of his father's - not the truth, not even a trinket. Nothing to hold onto. Perhaps the father he'd never known had wanted to be forgotten.

And then, a dim but pointed beam of moonlight guided his gaze to an illuminated pocket watch at the bottom of the box. He reached in. Pulled it out. Its intricate, ornate design evoked images of ancient lands and long-forgotten magic. It felt like a lead building in his hand, but he found it easy to carry just the same. As he gazed at the exterior of the pocket watch it began to...glow? But no - no, the moonlight had given up the fight and allowed itself to be consumed by the misty morning sunrise. The shifting light had played tricks on his eyes.

That was all.

As the sunlight grew brighter, Connor collected the pocket watch, conquered the maze of boxes with quick, careless steps, and retraced his steps to his bedroom. Stowing the trinket in his book bag, he climbed back into bed as though he'd never left it. If she found him awake, his mother would wonder why he'd been up. Would start to ask questions. Inquire about what he'd taken. Would steal from him the only secret thing he and his father had ever shared - his trip to the attic, and his selection of a token.

No, he would pretend to have lost interest. If she bothered to remind him of her promise to let him look in the attic, he'd say it wasn't a big deal. That he had his wonderful mother, and what more did he need, after all? Watch her smile. And feel no guilt in his deceit.

Just as he closed his eyes he heard the belabored groan of his door's hinges as his mother walked in.

TWO

"Connor, are you awake?"

Julia peeked her head in the room, and Connor did his best to feign a just-waking-up-Mom yawn, though he'd been awake for two hours.

"Yup," he replied.

"Good. Would hate for you to sleep through moving day."

"It wouldn't be ideal, I'll give you that."

Julia smiled, but Connor knew better than to believe her. Her smiles always lied.

"Took a trip to the attic this morning?"

His stomach did a back flip, but he took pains to make sure his guilt didn't register on his face. Propping himself up on one arm he gave his mother a chiding look.

"Yeah, I walked up there in my sleep."

"I'm serious, Connor. I know how you are with your sick affection for the coward. You want to explain to me how the door got open if you didn't open it?"

"You mean the door that opens on its own all the time? Last time I checked, that's why you put the doorstop there. Not that it does any good."

He comforted himself with the thought that he hadn't actually lied. The door had been standing open upon his arrival.

"Watch your tone! You're just like him, you know that? A lying coward!

What did you do, Connor, search the filthy attic for some stupid trinket? Something to cling to like a child?"

Carrying this conversation further couldn't possibly end well. New tactic.

"I'm mostly packed. When do we need to leave?"

She let out a sigh, crossing her arms and drawing her mouth into a straight line of pure disgust. The bitterness made its way to her voice.

"In half an hour. Be ready. I'll be downstairs."

"Sure, Mom."

The smile of lies, the turn of her face, the smirk of derision she thought he couldn't see but that he always did. And then she left, the click of the door offering him a reprieve from the verbal assault.

He fell back on his bed, heaving a sigh of relief, and stared at the now decently lit ceiling, closing his eyes for a brief moment, trying to swallow the feeling of anticipation and nauseating anxiety that washed over him. He didn't fear leaving home. In fact, he looked forward to it. But his life, which had been a predictable, if not miserable, sort of consistent, had started to offer up drastic changes in a short period of time. And then, of course, he knew his mother would be alone in the house, and he feared that she would succumb to the same fate as his father. Too many times he'd been plagued with frightening images of coming home on a break from college to discover her in the same position as his father. Screaming at her that she was a hypocrite. It was like a flashback to an event that never happened.

And then he would see the psychological masquerade for what it was - his fear getting the best of him. Life had been too disturbing, the atmosphere too negatively charged. For years he had felt that his house was not a home but a beast, welling with anger, ready at any moment to consume its occupants. His father had been taken, and now his mother was fading away into the clutches of the darkness that surrounded the house. He had no intentions of going with them.

Heaving a sigh he allowed resigned steps to carry him across the room to his backpack. He unzipped the front pouch. Reached in. Picked up the pocket watch and felt the cold metal as he turned it over in his palm. It had once been gold, but time had eroded its previous splendor to a rustic bronze that held a charm of its own.

He carried it back to his bed, allowing gravity to do its work. Felt the comfort of the pillow beneath his head. Stared once more at the wooden boards of the ceiling, knowing it was likely the last time he ever would. Flipped the pocket watch open, then shut. Open, then shut. Open...

His stomach dropped without warning, and a sense of being an article of clothing in a washing machine overwhelmed him. The spinning sensation gave way to one of falling. Voices broke through the silence around him. Children, women, tribal songs. A faint humming of a melody he'd never heard before, but that something within him recognized on a primal level.

Scenes of lives he'd never lived covered the wooden ceiling. Flashes of memories that weren't his own. A swampy marsh against stark mountains. Flowers unlike any he'd ever seen. Darkness. Light. A universe of color stitched into the silken tapestry of human consciousness. A violently beautiful blue light that drowned all of it in a sea of mystic neon.

And then nothing.

As he looked at the pocket watch in his hand, he snapped it shut. The world returned, unassuming, to the way it had been moments earlier. Only not quite. The room expanded, shrunk, distorting everything around him, transforming them into images seen in a cosmic funhouse mirror. And then, with no more warning than he'd had when it shifted, the world snapped back into place.

He needed sleep. That had to be it. He cast a hopeful glance to the clock on the far wall. Heaved a thankful sigh that the time of his departure had arrived. Giving the pocket watch a suspicious gaze, he rose from the bed and stowed it away in his backpack.

After packing what few things he hadn't packed the night before - toiletries, mainly - Connor left his bedroom, pausing for a moment at the banister at the top of the stairs, running his hand across the cracked center. Who in their right mind goes twenty-two years without fixing that? he thought.

The darkness grinned.

Taking a final look, he allowed himself to absorb the place he'd called home, a melancholy snapshot stored in his mind. The banister, the wooden hallway, the door to the attic, all absorbed in a single image like a portrait, once colorful, now a time-worn remnant found in the attic of a man long since dead.

Blinking back the tears that threatened his mask of composure, he ran down the remaining steps to find his mother waiting, as promised, at the door, his final suitcase in hand.

"Connor."

He looked up at her.

"What?"

"What do you mean what?" she said in a gruff manner.

He frowned.

"You just said my name."

"No, I didn't. Did you sleep okay? Or did the attic get to you?"

She snapped the word attic, making it more of an accusation than word. As though she had any right to ask him about such a thing. Being the resident expert on insanity, he should have been asking her that question. But this was not the time to start a battle. It was too late for that anyway. If you can't beat 'em, join 'em.

"You know I did toss and turn. Must just be hearing things. I'll get more sleep tonight after I'm settled in at school."

"Alright then."

She exited the house, and he followed. Pausing at the doorway, he turned around and addressed the swelling emptiness of the place. The nothingness that breathed, as though the boards of the structure composed its ribcage, sucking the sanity out of its occupants as air. The darkness that watched, never abandoning its post.

"Whatever you are, leave my mother alone," he murmured through gritted teeth.

As he turned to leave, he extended his middle finger to the home, a farewell salute, knowing that something saw it, almost able to hear the disembodied laughter, a return farewell from the evil that would now have his mother all to itself. Stiffening his jaw, he showed his back to the door and put a foot on the front step.

"So long for now, Dearie."

He spun back around to face the source of the voice, but an empty front stoop greeted him. Shaking his head, he jogged down the front steps...and froze. A crimson top hat sat on the porch bench.

"Hey, Mom, what's this thing doing here?"

He looked toward his mother, her severe silhouette a stark contrast to the colorful garden beside her. He gestured with a jerk of his head toward the hat.

"What thing?"

"The…"

He turned, and it was gone. Casting nervous eyes across the porch, he found no evidence to indicate that the wind had blown it away. Or that it had ever existed at all. He blinked, willing his sanity back in its place, refusing to get so close to freedom only to allow the beast to steal his mind. The darkness screeched with laughter.

"Just um…there was a rat. It's gone. Thought it was something else."

"Oh. Well, let's go, then."

"Yeah," he said, not sure he heard her.

Turning his back for a final time toward the house, he felt pressure on his back. A shove. Stumbled, thankful that his mother hadn't seen it. The house was as happy to get rid of him as he was to leave it. He didn't stop to turn around. Never looked back as he threw his last bags into the van and shut the door. Never saw the man in the crimson and gold suit wave at him with gloved hands, or the old woman who had taken the hat's place on the porch bench beside him.